GARDEN
OF
SALT AND STONE

A. L. BURGESS JR.

Garden of Salt and Stone.
Copyright © 2017 by A. L. Burgess Jr.

The right of A. L. Burgess Jr. to be identified as the author of this work has been asserted by him in accordance with the Copyright, Designs and Patents Act, 1988.

ISBN: 978-0-9915621-6-9 (trade p,bk)
ISBN: 978-0-9915621-7-6 (ebook)

Library of Congress Control Number: 2017912510

Publisher's Cataloging-in-Publication Data

Names: Burgess, A.L., Jr., author.
Title: Garden of salt and stone / A. L. Burgess Jr.
Description: Desert Hills, AZ : A. L. Burgess Jr., 2017.
Identifiers: LCCN 2017912510 | ISBN 978-0-9915621-6-9 (pbk.) | ISBN 978-0-9915621-7-6 (ebook)
Subjects: LCSH: Eden--Fiction. | Tree of Life--Fiction. | Lilith (Semitic mythology)--Fiction. | Uriel (Archangel)--Fiction. | Good and evil--Fiction. | Fantasy fiction. | BISAC: FICTION / Fantasy / General. | GSAFD: Fantasy fiction.
Classification: LCC PS3602.U743 G34 2017 (print) | LCC PS3602.U743 (ebook) | DDC 813/.6--dc23

First Edition, 2017

For Lillian—

Cherish every piece of clay you add to your sculpture of life.

GARDEN
OF
SALT AND STONE

Prologue

Weathered hands finished smoothing over the mud-like lime mortar that coated the home's demure walls. Nicholas, a man of small stature and aged beyond his true years, knelt near the freshly repaired area and placed an open palm on the hardening mixture. He mumbled incoherently while his brown eyes feverishly scanned the new surface looking for the slightest of imperfections. After a long moment, Nicholas nodded his head of unkempt black hair and rose to inspect the totality of his work. Satisfied that his effort would go unnoticed, he carefully maneuvered a well-worn table back into its former position to obscure the reconstruction.

Nicholas's vocal pronouncements grew louder and more frenetic. Without warning, a sudden and intense bolt of anger coursed through his body causing him to spin around and face the home's sparsely furnished interior. He thrust a trembling finger toward an imaginary antagonist. "Never speak of it!" he screamed into the unoccupied, medieval dwelling. "Demons covet that which I would give freely, and they watch it still!"

The sharp sound of Nicholas's own voice startled the monk back to awareness. He stood, staring into the small confines of the darkened room trying to comprehend the nature of the specters that had long haunted him.

A grinding metallic noise alerted Nicholas to the presence of someone at the front door. He surveyed the room for any telltale signs of his recent activity and wiped his hands clean on his tattered robes.

A young woman wearing a heavy, drab-colored dress entered the home. Startled by the monk, the woman shrieked and dropped her basket, spilling its meager goods across the wooden floor. "Get out! My husband told you to never come back!"

Nicholas gazed absently at the young lady. "Forgive me. They beseeched me to come."

The woman sneered at the bewildering statement and pointed to the open door. "Leave!"

Nicholas nodded and made for the door. "May God protect you," he said, moving meekly past the woman and onto the porch.

The door slammed shut behind Nicholas, and he heard a wooden lock sliding into place to bar his return. He lingered on the porch, quelling the voices in his head and listening to the owner's footfalls as she retreated into the home. He took a heavy breath and bent down to retrieve a small earthenware jar from behind a stack of firewood near the front door. A clear viscous liquid spilled over the jug's open brim as he hoisted it to his hip. With his free hand, Nicholas pulled an old rosary from his pocket and wrapped it around the small pot. He held the two carefully together and set off down a dirt road to the nearby village of San Cielo.

It was nearly midmorning and the small town was abuzz with the day's activities. Early spring brought an influx of travelers from all classes of society. Pilgrims from Western Europe headed to the Middle East and points beyond, stopping at the strategically-situated hamlet to rest and replenish their supplies. As was the custom during the first few days of spring, a large bonfire burned at the center of the village to welcome the visitors and to ward off evil spirits that otherwise would lay waste to a healthy new growing season.

Carefully carrying his burden, Nicholas navigated the crowded streets. His haggard appearance allowed him to keep a low profile and to blend in with the weary travelers. He set his eyes on the column of smoke rising from the spring bonfire and pushed forward.

The first townsfolk to see Nicholas wading through the sea of pilgrims were the blacksmith and the men of the livery. The monk ambled past the smithy, catching the attention of the tradesmen during their afternoon libations. They stopped drinking in order to get a good look at the aloof clergyman.

"Get out of here!" the blacksmith spat. "You're not welcome!"

Laughing drunkenly at the sight of the slovenly monk, one of the livery men spewed, "You bring the devil with you!"

Nicholas cast a wary glance at the jeering men. "I forgive you— God forgives you all."

The blacksmith took exception. "God? What do you know of the Almighty?"

Stung by the words, Nicholas ignored the carousers and pressed on.

"You've been defrocked, you crazy old monk!" the blacksmith bellowed after him. When the reclusive hermit failed to stop, the blacksmith furrowed his brow and hefted his forging hammer. "I won't allow him to do this again."

The intoxicated men of the livery paused to gauge the seriousness of their friend's outburst, and then laughed him off.

"He invites Lucifer," the blacksmith said. "Who would stop him?"

The liverymen held their friend's stern gaze for a brief moment and looked away.

"I thought so," the blacksmith grumbled and strode off after the monk.

The deeper Nicholas pushed into San Cielo, the more its residents took notice. The villagers were terrified the fallen monk would cast a wicked spell on their omen of good fortune and doom them to wallow in the clutches of starvation for the entire year.

The people of the town formed a loose mob around the old clergyman, following Nicholas closely and forcing unwary pilgrims to the side. A group of children threw rocks at the wayward monk while the adults hurled a barrage of taunts and insults. The few brave enough to have physical contact with Nicholas tried to halt his advance, but the monk broke free of the forceful attempts and continued.

Nicholas approached the town's bonfire and raised an arm skyward.

Frightened, a man from the village threw a large stone, striking the monk squarely in the chest. "You will curse us all!"

One of the women stepped out of the crowd and hurled another stone that found its mark. "Satan is your master now!"

The blacksmith stood in the rear of the group and dropped his hammer. He picked up a large rock and held it aloft. "Stone him!" he yelled, eliciting cheers from the crowd.

"Hold!" a mounted nobleman commanded, pointing his broadsword at the blacksmith and then back to the gathered crowd. "Why do you treat this monk so?"

The crowd erupted into a litany of off-handed remarks, but the blacksmith's voice rose above them. "He is possessed by demons— he will bring the plague upon us once again!"

The nobleman nodded and maneuvered his horse to face Nicholas. "Does this man speak the truth, monk?"

Nicholas heard the nobleman's words but showed no sign of understanding their meaning. He shook his head forcefully. "They cannot have it; I will not let them!"

The nobleman eased his horse closer. "What do *they* want?"

A shudder ran the length of Nicholas's body as he locked eyes with the nobleman. "All of creation will be doomed," he responded, raising the earthenware jar aloft as if to strike the rider.

Fearing for his safety and those around him, the nobleman pointed his sword at the monk. "Withdraw!"

"Do you not see?" Nicholas asked. "This is the only way." The monk upended the clay jug and poured the viscous liquid over his frayed robes. When the vessel dripped out the last of its contents, he threw it to the ground.

"Lamp oil," the nobleman muttered. "Certainly, there must be another way?"

"No," Nicholas replied. "God requires it."

The blacksmith pushed his way through the crowd and approached the monk. He drew a burning branch from the bonfire and pointed it at the clergyman.

Nicholas moved forward and placed a hand on the smoldering bough to stop the blacksmith. "That would be a sin, my son."

Seeing only sincerity on the monk's face, the blacksmith lost his nerve and let go of the branch.

Nicholas held the tinder and stared solemnly at those assembled around him. "I forgive you all," he said and set fire to his body. The monk fell to his knees and writhed in pain, but made no sound as he burned to death.

Chapter 1

Lucifer stood on the rim of a steep incline overlooking a sprawling valley of exceptional beauty. His piercing white eyes scanned the lush trees and fruit-bearing plants below. As was the case with all angels, his sight was keen and the vast distances were of no concern. The angel concentrated his attention near the center of the valley and furrowed his brow in contempt at the sight of two humans cavorting in the warm sunshine.

At nearly ten-feet tall, Lucifer stood head and shoulders above most of the other angels. His broad shoulders and slim physique gave Lucifer an air of confidence, while his platinum-blond hair and olive skin spoke to his refined elegance and grace. His brilliant white robes were indistinguishable in color from his folded wings stored neatly behind him. Every aspect of Lucifer's being exuded his status as a respected leader among his divine brethren.

The sound of beating wings announced two angels who flew in from the crystal-blue sky and landed on the precipice near Lucifer.

Both wore similar off-white robes, but each brought a bearing as distinct as their personalities.

The smaller of the two was slim and frail, almost to the point of being feminine. He had a pale complexion and sported curly tufts of dark brown hair. His eyes bordered on emerald green and stood out amongst his rather plain facial features. The other angel was brutish in form. His muscular build and stern gaze gave the angel an unwelcoming appearance. His striking red eyes peered out from under his rust-colored hair and punctuated his ill-tempered demeanor.

"Sitri, Asmodeus," Lucifer said, acknowledging the two angels. "I trust you bring good news?"

Asmodeus cast his crimson gaze to the ground. "Scarcely a third will join in your efforts."

"Many trust the Creator's judgment," added Sitri.

Lucifer frowned. "In other words, they believe I'm exceeding my authority and being rebellious."

Asmodeus raised his broad hand in a tempering gesture. "None have said as much."

"Do they not see what is happening?" Lucifer asked absently, shaking his head in disgust and pointing at the humans in the valley. "They will supplant us and we will be deemed unworthy—all for the trust in *him*?"

"My lord—"

"Do not call me that!" Lucifer spat. "I need no homage from my brothers and sisters."

"Forgive me," Asmodeus said, bowing his head.

"I have no power to forgive either," Lucifer said dryly, casting a mournful glance at both angels. "For that, you must beg our Creator."

Asmodeus and Sitri stepped back and respectfully waited for the moment to pass.

"A third," Lucifer mulled, pacing back and forth. "Hard to fathom that only a minority feel as maligned as we do."

"Perhaps we could postpone the endeavor until more favor our position?" Sitri asked.

"No," Lucifer replied. "We will not receive more support than has already been gained. I had hoped for a diplomatic solution, but the longer we wait, the more our brothers and sisters will turn against us. We cannot linger and must proceed forward if we are to stem the coming tide."

"Will not the Almighty be more powerful?" Sitri asked. "Surely, the others will come to his defense."

Asmodeus shook his head. "Lucifer, we are not ready. We cannot hold off twice our number as well as the Creator's wrath. I fear failure will be upon us."

"I do not know which is more troubling: your cowardice or your lack of faith," Lucifer scolded both angels. "Did both of you not choose to follow me willingly?"

A solemn chorus of agreement echoed hollowly from the two angels.

"Then both of you must choose to have faith."

Asmodeus and Sitri acknowledged their acceptance with a curt bow.

"This will be his undoing," Lucifer said, stretching out his arm to sweep across the expansive view of the valley below.

"The Garden of Eden?" Asmodeus asked.

"It is more than a simple garden," Lucifer corrected. "The Almighty created it for the humans and filled it with wonders. There are secrets within that I believe will ultimately bring about his downfall and that of the humans as well."

"In what way could you use the Garden against them?" Asmodeus asked. "I see no way forward."

"Of course you do not," Lucifer replied. "I have studied the humans and their habitat since both were brought into existence. In my anger—" he paused and composed himself. "In my research, I found that both the Garden and the humans were connected. Those trees at the center," Lucifer said, pointing to a pair of young fig trees that grew near a natural spring whose copious runoff supplied all of the creeks and rivers of the Garden. "They are tied to Creation itself and must be integral in some way to the fate of the humans."

Sitri rubbed his jaw as he studied the far-off trees while Asmodeus nodded knowingly as if following the logic, but in truth, neither was closer to understanding the import of the facts presented to them.

Lucifer sighed heavily at the ignorance of his two subordinates. "The Almighty dotes on them like spoiled children. He is blinded by his love for them. They were given free will, yet they use it poorly. If we can influence their behavior slightly, we can catch the Almighty off-guard and exploit the situation to our advantage."

Lucifer's plan intrigued the two angels, but their interest soon faded once they scrutinized the extenuating circumstances surrounding Adam and Eve.

"They cannot leave the Garden, and we cannot enter," Sitri said. "How could we possibly influence them?"

"Two angels may enter," Asmodeus corrected. "The Guardian will be of no use to us and Adam's teacher—" Realization washed across his face. "You intend to ask Lilith for help?"

"She loved Adam," Lucifer acknowledged with heartfelt sorrow, "and he turned his back on her to fawn over a contrived, frail woman conceived as a muse because of his own shortcomings."

"Are you certain of this? Lilith is—"

"More powerful than you will ever be," Lucifer snarled.

"Yes," Asmodeus replied, "but what if she loves him still? Why would she betray him for you?"

Pain and anger contorted Lucifer's visage. He had loved Lilith since the day they were forged from the ether of Creation. They traveled the newly-formed cosmos in blissful companionship until that one fateful day when the human known as Adam rose into being. Lilith was so smitten with the abomination that she left Lucifer to be with him. Lucifer was devastated. He had given Lilith everything. He had been her devout companion through an eternity of exploration, and yet Lilith *chose* to be with Adam. Eventually, the human grew tired of Lilith and shunned her for yet another of his own kind: Eve.

To hear now that Lilith may still love Adam was as unbearable for Lucifer as the day she left. He gathered his emotions and let his anger subside until a melancholic acceptance settled over him. "Lilith must help us—our plan is for naught without her."

"And the Creator's wrath?" Asmodeus asked. "What would you do to forestall his might against us?"

Lucifer let a smile escape his otherwise pained façade. "I have been laboring on a solution to that very problem, and I am very close to completing it."

Chapter 2

The faded brown convertible sped along the narrow and twisting country roads of the Italian foothills. Peter Andrews was gleeful behind the wheel of the rented car and kept his hazel eyes glued to the road. His closely cropped auburn hair stirred with the breeze, and the sun glinted off his silver-rimmed eyeglasses as he pushed the car through several high-speed straight stretches and white-knuckle, tire-squealing curves.

Peter's wife, Renée Alcott-Andrews, gripped the passenger door with her right hand and held her summer hat tightly to her head with the other. Uncontained strands of blonde hair fluttered in the vortices created by the open-air car. "Slow down, Peter!" she yelled over the rushing wind. "You're going to kill us!"

"We're not going that fast," Peter replied. "See?" He let go of the steering wheel and held his hands in the air. The car drifted in the lane and ran onto the dirt shoulder with a frightening thud.

Renée screamed as the car neared the outer edge of the roadway and an irrigation ditch with a steep embankment beyond.

Peter seized the wheel and anxiously returned the vehicle back onto the paved surface.

"Yeah—see?" Renée scoffed, narrowing her blue eyes at her husband. "You've always been a bad driver. I don't know why I ever let you talk me into—look out!"

Emerging from a blind corner, the convertible ran a stop sign and continued headlong into an intersection. A single car, slowly making the turn onto the country road, blocked most of the thoroughfare and forced the racing convertible into the oncoming lane of traffic. Peter turned the steering wheel hard, causing the vehicle to lose traction and spin uncontrollably, narrowly avoiding a collision. The convertible screeched to a halt, coming to rest in its original lane of travel, but pointing in the opposite direction.

The driver of the turning vehicle slowed down to gesture and scream out what was undoubtedly an unkind observation of Peter's lack of driving prowess. Satisfied with his retort, the driver rolled up his window and continued past the unmoving convertible.

"You almost killed us!" Renée shrieked. "We won't be able to see much of Italy if we're dead!"

Peter knew all too well that his wife was correct, but he tried to fend off her comments with a semi-assertive, "Give it a rest."

Renée glanced back to the intersection and eyed the connecting road that led to a small town about half-a-mile off the main highway. "Let's go over there for a while and give your poor driving a break."

Chapter 2

Peter quietly accepted his fault. "Maybe we can find something to eat?"

"Whatever, as long as I don't have to sit in this car with you anymore."

Peter chose not to respond. In all their years of marriage, he often found himself on the losing side of arguments. Whether this instance classified as righteous ground was not the issue; Peter did not have the interest, nor the stamina to continue their years-long battle. Making his point, as it were, had lost its luster. He sighed and turned the car around for the short drive into the small town.

San Cielo was a quaint tourist trap nestled in the foothills along the lower Alps region of Italy. Train tracks divided the town into two distinct portions: a much smaller section had the old-world charm of several centuries' worth of buildings interwoven by haphazard and narrow cobblestone streets, while the other gave off a more modern, industrial type of feel with its structured blocks and paved roads reminiscent of the twentieth century. Adventurous inhabitants had long ago appropriated the forested landscape around San Cielo, dotting it with homes and small farms.

Closest to the main highway were three mid-century merchant homes renovated into commercial shops. They had big windows that opened onto the feeder street heading into downtown San Cielo. Two of the shops were empty, but the rightmost of the three was overflowing with goods. Stacks of old magazines and vinyl records sat prominently on the sidewalk near the concrete stairs leading up to the entrance of the building.

"Park right here," Renée said, pointing to an empty parking space in front of the establishment and trying to contain her excitement. "We'll start with this one."

"It's a junk shop," Peter said. "Don't you want to start over there—where's it's nicer?" He motioned to the more populated downtown area.

"These smaller dealers always have better stuff," Renée answered, commandeering the rearview mirror so she could straighten her sunhat and reapply lipstick. "Besides, we'll get over there soon enough."

Peter parked the car and realigned the mirror. "Look, I'd like to be in France before nightfall. We can't be messing around here all day."

"Relax, I'll be quick and you can stuff your face," Renée said, staring back at Peter with a wry smile. "Deal?"

Peter nodded.

Renée giggled with glee and gathered her large purse. She leapt out of the car and made a beeline for the front door of the antiques store, her white and yellow sundress billowing in the slight breeze.

"Remember, we're not staying forever," Peter called after his wife.

In a show of dismissal, Renée merely waved her free hand in the air and continued through the doorway, out of sight.

Peter scowled. Although he was hungry, he did not like the idea of stopping to shop, but as usual, he decided to bite his tongue. The small town was at least pleasant and perhaps he could find something that interested him enough to make it worth his while. He unbuckled his seatbelt and exited the vehicle.

Peter wore an old, white collared golf shirt and a cheap pair of brown pants. His sneakers were new, but sensibly off-brand. He reached into the open convertible, grabbed his small gray daypack from the rear seat, and slung it over his shoulders.

Peter's stomach growled. He scanned the area looking for a restaurant or something to sate his hunger, but the upper end of San Cielo catered to small shops and was devoid of eateries or street vendors. He found himself with a choice to make. He could wander off and enjoy a few hours alone, marveling in the town's history, or he could follow his wife into the junk shop and wait for her to accompany him to a restaurant. Peter's appetite diminished at the thought. However much he wanted to delight in the bliss of solitude, tempering his wife's spending habits, especially on an already over-budget trip, was a more pressing need. Reluctantly, Peter resigned himself to his fate and climbed the steps into the store.

Inside the door, an old greeting foyer found a purpose as the shop's main counter area and exhibit location for the smaller, more valuable items. A hodgepodge of different-sized display cases lined the walls of the room, and sunlight streaming through the plate glass window illuminated the various knickknacks contained therein. A wide doorway at the back of the vestibule granted access to a larger, poorly lit portion of the antique store where a crushing amount of merchandise was stacked and shoved so tightly into every inch of available floor space that navigation through the disorder was nearly impossible.

Peter was aghast at the ill-managed mess. "*Look* at this place."

"Yeah, isn't it great?" Renée quipped, eyeing the sparkling merchandise in the display cases.

Peter rolled his eyes.

"Welcome, welcome!" a soothing, female voice called out from the back room. "Welcome to San Cielo," said the grandmotherly woman, gingerly making her way through the aisles of junk.

She was a large lady, tall and big-boned. The woman looked to be in her sixties and wore a faded flower-print dress rubbed practically see-through near the pockets. A soiled, full-length apron around her waist did its job of distracting the casual observer from the woman's threadbare attire, while scuffed white loafers, with neatly tied laces, adorned her feet. Peter thought she was wearing her own stock of mid-century clothing, but after a long look, he concluded the outfit was probably her regular, daily garb. She seemed friendly enough. Her short, graying, curly hair and pleasant smile was enough to disarm the surliest of patrons. Peter respectfully acknowledged the purveyor with a nod.

"Please call me Edda," the woman said. "You like beautiful jewelry, no?" Edda surmised from Renée's interest in the display cases at the front of the store. She walked to the opposite side of the case and fumbled the latches open.

"Oh yes," Renée responded, throwing a sardonic smile back to her husband. "I'm particularly interested in that piece there," she said, pointing through the glass at a rather odd-looking, tarnished bracelet.

"Unbelievable," Peter muttered, shaking his head disapprovingly at the nuances and rituals required in prelude to a sound fleecing.

Renée relished in her husband's misgivings. "I'm Renée," she said to Edda, extending her hand to shake. "That's my husband," she added, gesturing indifferently to Peter.

Peter nodded at the slight, but unwilling to concede his demotion to a mere bystander, replied, "I'm Peter."

"Peter, very nice to meet you," Edda responded warmly, slowly migrating back to her primary mark. She retrieved the desired bracelet from an array of clunky jewelry and presented it to Renée. In an attempt to show her patrons the worldliness of her store, Edda brought out a jeweler's glass and inspected the piece.

Peter scoffed and approached the case to see what exactly piqued his wife's curiosity enough to warrant wasting time in an establishment such as this.

The bracelet appeared to be made of silver and was black from years of tarnish. It was wide, very wide for a women's bracelet. Along its face were three raised fleurs-de-lis with coarsely-set semi-precious stones in between.

Renée slipped the heavy bracelet onto her skinny wrist. "I like it," she said, waving her arm to show Peter. "It looks *very* old," she said as if trying to conjure the spirit of an ancient pharaoh.

"Yes, quite old," Edda assured. "San Cielo was on a crusader route during ancient times," she added in a studious tone. "It could be that old, no?"

Peter took hold of his wife's arm and studied the bracelet.

"Let go," Renée huffed. "This doesn't concern you."

Peter let his wife's arm drop. "It's not that old. Turn of the century—probably Victorian reproduction. It's real silver though."

"Oh," Edda sheepishly said. "You must be a student of history?"

"Professor, actually."

"Actually," Renée interrupted, "he teaches at a junior college, and I always ask forgiveness for his rude behavior—*especially* when he butts into things that don't concern him," she said, glaring at her husband.

Peter knew when he had said too much. He decided to spare the proprietor the ugliness that would surely ensue if he stayed his present course. "Can I look around?" he asked Edda.

"Please, please," Edda replied, gesturing to the back of the store. "Everything is for sale, no?"

Peter stepped quietly into the darkened back room. Behind him, he could hear the store owner and his wife discussing an appropriate price for the gaudy piece of jewelry. He tuned them out and reached for a light switch near the archway. Peter turned the small knob several times back and forth, but to no avail. He studied the high ceiling and the incandescent bulbs hanging by strands of electrical cord. Peter could clearly see bare spots in the exposed wiring where the insulation had rotted away long ago. The lights were so old he thought it likely they were no longer functioning. It was probably for the best.

The long, rectangular room was not much to look at. A small window placed high along the back wall was the only source of illumination save the ambient light spilling in from the front of the building. The merchandise crowded the wood floor and continued in haphazard piles for the entire length and breadth of the space.

Peter waded into the mass of goods and took note of the household furnishings placed against the walls of the room. None of the furniture was very old and most required repair of some sort to be of use. A desk sat nearby, covered in old newspapers, while another was home to several discolored brass lamps. A dresser had a rather ornate and interesting looking mirror on it, but the glass was broken and the frame cracked. Along the back wall were various dresses hung on a rack. The clothes were so worn and the patterns so stale they reminded Peter of the owner's personal wardrobe—no coincidence really. The rest of the store contained the usual odds and ends of people's lives. No real finds. He lifted a price tag from one of the more interesting looking desks—no real bargains either.

In one corner, close to the back of the room, an ornate hand railing peeked out above a few boxes of magazines. Peter would not have given it a second thought, but the railing appeared to be standing on its own and not resting against anything. His curiosity got the best of him and he ambled his way through the merchandise to examine the oddity.

Indeed, the old railing was attached to a staircase that led down to a basement. A faint light from the cellar illuminated the rickety staircase, and a musty smell wafted up to greet Peter. A rope that had barred access to the stairway now hung limp from the nearby newel post. He bent down to get a good view of the basement, but the angle was wrong. Peter could hear the lively conversation coming from the front room and, interested in the architecture of the old building, did not see any harm in having a quick look.

The splintery treads of the staircase creaked as Peter gingerly descended the steep flight. Once he got below the level of the floor, he could only see small portions of the basement in the dim light. It was a crude, unfinished cellar. Stone walls, cobwebs and several areas of rotten wood in the subfloor of the main room above gave the basement a forbidding air. The area was obviously being used as a storeroom. Cardboard boxes and wooden crates were stacked haphazardly along with broken or unsalable items. His curiosity satisfied, Peter turned to trudge back up to the main floor when a sharp noise from the wall of the basement caught his attention. He squinted through the shadows and saw several blocks of the foundation's supporting wall lying on the dirt floor of the cellar.

For the most part, Peter did not care about the establishment's crumbling underpinnings, but as he studied the exact source of the noise, he noted the workmanship and quality of the stone was reminiscent of architecture much older than the structure it supported above. The falling blocks left a hollow within the wall and even if the old building were about to collapse, Peter could no longer contain his interest. He descended the stairs and approached the broken wall.

The cellar proper was only half as big as the floor above. The beams and supporting structures of the main living area receding toward the front of the store where the ground level rose to nearly the same height in that area. It appeared that a newer building with a bigger footprint had been erected over the smaller existing basement many years ago.

Peter neared the broken wall and examined the edges of the hole. He tested the ancient lime mortar by breaking it between his fingers. The hollow itself was several feet deep, and he had a difficult time seeing the bottom of it in the dim light. As he adjusted his glasses for a better view, a lens flare temporarily shone on something trapped within the confines of the wall. He reached down into the hole and pulled out an old, leather-bound manuscript.

The book was about the size of a modern hardback, with a crude, leather cover that contained no discerning title or marks of any kind. Peter hefted the manuscript and thumbed through its pages. He was immediately intrigued. The book contained handwritten Latin text on a very early form of parchment. The paper was of a thick and heavy, hand-beaten stock. There were about fifty pages in all with evenly-spaced lettering written on every page. The lines of text were perfectly spaced from page to page as well as letter to letter from top to bottom. It was a magnificent piece of work produced by what must have been a well-trained scribe.

The sound of rustling cloth and shifting footsteps startled Peter. He turned to find the source of the noise and struggled to see in the tenebrous basement. The area nearest the stairway was sufficiently illuminated to see the floor, but further away, the cellar was obscured by darkness. Peter concentrated his search in the direction of the front of the building. He tried to discern the odd shapes of storage items from the more regular form of the building's architecture and then gasped at the sight of two eyes peering back at him.

Standing in the dark on the far side of the basement was the silhouette of an individual. At first, Peter thought it was a mannequin, but upon closer inspection, it appeared to be a middle-aged man. The short-statured individual stood quietly behind a broken display counter. He wore a dusty brown overcoat with a dark gray undershirt that was barely visible at the collar and sported a full head of unruly graying hair that gave him the look of a beleaguered mad scientist. He nodded curtly, acknowledging Peter's less-than-forthright entry into the cellar.

Embarrassed at being caught rummaging in the walls of the basement, Peter returned a guilty smile and said, "Sorry, I didn't know anyone was down here." He started to leave and then remembered the manuscript. Peter presented it in the dim light and set it down on the derelict display case in front of the man. "Here, this is yours," he said, pointing to the wall. "I found it over there."

Peter turned to leave, but the man motioned for him to come closer. His first instinct was to withdraw, to go back to the more comfortable surroundings of his berating wife and her narcissistic habits, but some primal curiosity in the book propelled him forward to stand across from the man.

"I'm sorry," Peter started, shaking his head, "I don't speak much Italian so I'm not—"

The man held up a hand and laid it on the leather-bound manuscript that rested on the glass case between them. He gestured for Peter to pick up the book.

Peter accommodated the request. He flipped the manuscript over in his hands several times and thumbed through a few pages, trying to make a good show of it for his audience. "It's well put together, probably late medieval period." A few of Peter's academic interests were old languages and dead cultures. He studied the ink of the Latin text and made a serious attempt to read it. After a few lines, he stopped. "It doesn't make sense; it could be some kind of practice book or something."

The man nodded as if he understood the issue at hand.

Peter flipped the manuscript over and studied its binding and page attachment. "It could be an early puzzle book, I guess."

The man shrugged.

"The style is definitely consistent with the 12th or early 13th centuries." Peter began to set the book back down on the table, but the man stopped him and motioned for Peter to take it. "What?" he said. "You want me to buy it?" As had been his experience, anything was for sale in these junk shops, even something recently found. He shook his head. "I can't afford this. Even as a simple curiosity, you can get much more from a book dealer."

Peter tried to set the manuscript back down on the display case, but the man stopped him, pushing the book back into Peter's hands. He pursed his lips and asked, "How much?"

The man shook his head, pointed at the book and then back to Peter.

"Free? You want me to have it for free?"

The man nodded affirmatively and smiled.

"You don't speak English and I don't speak Italian—I don't think you know what you're saying."

Again, the man pointed to the book and then to Peter. He was unequivocally signaling for Peter to keep the old manuscript.

Peter cast a wary glance to the strange man. "Do you own this store with Edda? Are you her husband or son or something?"

The man pointed to the upstairs, in the general direction of the front room and nodded.

Peter thought about it for a moment and turned the manuscript over in his hands a few times. It was a great find and would make a wonderful souvenir. After all, his wife was treating herself to things that were not nearly as interesting as this book. "Well," Peter said, "I guess I'll take it then."

The man nodded approvingly.

Peter unslung his daypack and stowed the book safely inside. "I really appreciate this. It's the best thing I've gotten on this whole trip." He motioned to the upstairs. "Should I let Edda know on our way out?"

The man shrugged and shook his head.

Chapter 2

"Thank you very much. I can't wait to share this with my students," Peter said, donning his daypack and turning to climb the staircase. As he was about to disappear above the line of the floor, Peter gazed back at the strange man and saw him smiling contently as if everything would be fine.

From the front room, Peter could hear his wife calling his name. "What is it?" he answered, weaving through the narrow aisles of antiques.

"It's about time," Renée scolded. "Haven't you been listening to me? Where have you been anyway?"

"Well, I was—"

"I don't care," Renée interrupted. "I'm ready to go." She shifted her attention back to Edda. "Thank you for the beautiful bracelet."

"You're welcome, my dear Renée." Edda met Peter with a warm smile. "It was nice to meet you."

"Yes, thank you and your—"

Renée tugged on Peter's arm. "She doesn't need to hear anything from you—we're short on time as it is," she said, guiding her husband through the front door and out of the store.

Peter, no longer able to contain his anger, burst out, "I was trying to thank her!"

"Look, not everyone wants to listen to your history lessons. Everywhere we go it's the same thing—can't you just give it a rest already?"

Peter pointed to the bracelet Renée purchased. "How much did you save us buying that thing?"

"I don't have to tell you," Renée replied, turning her back and walking in the direction of the downtown area.

Peter strode after her. "We're working on our communication, remember?"

"Does it matter?"

"Yes—yes it does."

Renée hesitated, but kept her deliberate pace. "A hundred and twenty-five Euros—and it was a bargain at that price."

"It's probably not worth half that," Peter argued.

"I don't care—I like it and that's all that matters."

"Whatever," Peter grumbled. "I don't feel so bad now."

Renée stopped. "What do you mean? You did something back there, didn't you?"

Peter unslung his daypack and took out the ancient manuscript.

"You stole it!" Renée snapped. "I can't believe you. That's really low—stealing from an old woman."

"It's not like that—her husband—"

"Edda told me she wasn't married."

"Okay—son then—employee, I don't know." Peter held up the book. "He gave this to me. It was just down there with all the broken junk."

"It looks like more than junk to me. Is it worth anything?"

"It could be worth quite a bit—if it's real."

"If it's worth money, why would she give it to you? I mean, it's not like she has a ton of customers in that place."

Peter searched for a flaw in his wife's logic, but found none. The antique store was off the beaten path and did not seem to be very prosperous. His joy faded.

"You see? You *are* a thief," Renée said, storming off down the street.

"It's not like that and you know it."

Renée ignored her husband and maintained her defiant gait.

Peter chased after her. "Do you want me to take it back? Will that make you happy?"

"I don't want to talk about it anymore," Renée said, waving her hand through the air. "We came here to see Europe and work on our problems."

"Yeah, so?" Peter said, keeping pace, stride for stride with his wife.

Renée stopped. "Don't you see?"

Peter cocked his head and scanned the immediate area. "See what?"

"Nothing," Renée said, bristling at her husband's ignorance. "We'll talk about it later." She pivoted away from her husband and continued her walk as if trying to outrun a predator.

Peter returned the book to his daypack and followed his wife from a distance. Confrontation never worked well for him and there was no use in trying to reason with her when she got into one of her moods. His best strategy was to play deaf and dumb.

As Peter and Renée neared the end of the old-town area, the sidewalks and surrounding buildings became more contemporary and utilitarian looking. The cozy cobblestone street came to a halt at a busy, three-way intersection with a modern road. To the left, traffic moved down the hill, curving back underneath old San Cielo toward the newer portion of the city. To the right, the road led out of town to the surrounding rural areas. With the addition of merging lanes to allow traffic to cross in three directions, the intersection was substantially wider than most.

Peter caught up to Renée as her progress was impeded by a small crowd gathered on the corner of the intersection. A group of elderly people, led by a young female tour guide dressed in a navy-blue uniform, pointed and gestured to an old church on the far side of the roads' confluence.

The guide's scripted words droned over the group, "On the other side of the street, you can see the Church of the Monk Nicholas or simply, Nicholas's Church. A knight, Raymondé de Villet, while on his way to the Holy Land, witnessed the monk commit ritual suicide on that very spot. Later, de Villet reported having strange dreams and visitations from angels. He took the visions as a sign from God and commissioned the church in the late twelfth century. It was finished some years later and now bears the suicidal monk's name."

Renée saw her husband's interest in the presentation and rolled her eyes. "Let's turn around. Maybe we can find something to eat on the other side of town, huh?"

"Wait, I want to hear this."

"You said it yourself—we don't have the time."

Chapter 2

Peter did not respond as he was becoming engrossed in the tour guide's lecture.

"The initial cost of the church grew enormously, as the stone required to build the structure had to be quarried from sources not indigenous to this location." The petite young lady made a gesture directing the group to see the detail work on the stone. "As you can see today, the building still harbors some of the original Templar influences, but it is in such poor condition, its grounds remain off limits for safety concerns."

Peter studied the building. What remained of the old place of worship was in an appalling state. Once upon a time, the church had been a tall, single-story building with a grand steeple and a vestibule at the front. The beautiful stained-glass windows that had once adorned its hallowed walls were now only shards of glass jutting from broken sills. Heavy wooden doors hung unhinged and partially ajar from the main entrance of the church. The roof was a web of dilapidated rafters, missing most of its slate tiles and allowing the elements to invade what was left of the old building's interior. Tall grasses and weeds grew wild over the property and modern barricades warned prospective adventurers to steer clear of the dangerous conditions. In ancient times, the old church and its grounds would have commanded a view of the small village as a beacon of beauty to visitors and citizens alike, but now the building was nothing more than a curious ruin.

Peter, sympathetic to the misinformation that tour guides had to endure, noticed a glaring discrepancy in the approved monologue and raised his hand to ask a question.

Standing behind her husband, Renée audibly groaned.

"Yes?" the guide asked.

"You said Templar influence?" Peter inquired politely.

"Yes, I did."

"Well, I don't mean to interrupt, but there appears to be quite a bit of Hospitaller influence in the design as well as the exterior elements."

Visibly annoyed, the tour guide lifted her cue cards to show the group. "I'm sorry, but that's not what our research shows."

"Please," Renée pleaded. "Do you have to do this now?"

"Sorry, but you should check on your—" Peter trailed off, his eyes fixed on the entrance to the old church.

The tour guide smiled wryly and waited impatiently, "Sir?"

Irritated that her husband was making a scene, Renée asked, "What is it?"

"There," Peter said, pointing to the entrance. "Do you see him?"

At the front of the church and behind the modern barricades, a small, dark-haired boy of about ten years old made his way out from the tall grasses and weeds that choked the grounds. He wore torn, knee-high breeches and an old-style linen shirt, but Peter did not notice the boy's clothes as much as he did the child's face. The youngster seemed familiar to him somehow and as soon as the boy emerged from the undergrowth, he locked eyes with Peter and never let go. Entranced by the little boy, he watched as the young man made his way to the edge of the sidewalk in front of the old building.

Renée, along with the assembled group, squinted through the sunlight in the given direction but could not see anything out of the ordinary. "What are you looking at?"

"There," Peter said, pointing and gesturing at the gated entrance to the church grounds. "Right there—the little boy."

Whispers of concern permeated the sightseeing group at the mention of a child. The members searched the indicated area and when no child could be seen, they looked back to Peter to see if he was attempting a cruel hoax.

Concerned, the tour guide asked, "Sir, are you feeling alright?"

"What?" Peter responded incredulously. "He's right there."

Several of the gathered individuals shook their heads and others simply shrugged as they turned their attention away from the annoying stranger.

Peter closed his eyes and took a moment to clear his thoughts. When he reopened them, the little boy was staring back and smiling as if he was being recognized or rewarded for doing a heroic deed. Peter looked for support amongst the tourist group, but no one appeared to notice the child.

Despite the distance, the youngster acknowledged Peter with a nod and tried to speak to him. The boy's mouth moved, but Peter could not hear him over the cars on the road. The lad stepped closer to the street, moving his head back and forth as if he were gauging the speed of the oncoming traffic.

Cars roared along the modern highway into San Cielo. It was a dangerous stretch of road for pedestrians as there were no hardened dividers between the lanes and no crosswalk out to the old church.

Alarmed, Peter waved his hands in the air motioning for the little boy to stop. "The kid's going to run into the street!"

"Peter," Renée cautioned, "You're scaring us—*and* you're making a scene."

"You don't see him—the little boy?"

"Of course no one sees him, because he's not there," Renée replied.

A gap opened in the traffic. The young boy said something inaudible to Peter and darted out between the cars.

Horrified, Peter leapt off the sidewalk and ran toward the child. As he closed the distance, he could see the blissful, almost playful expression on the young boy's face. The child showed no sense of danger or fear. After the first few strides, a light ringing began to rise in Peter's head. He tried to shake off the sensation but could not. The nearer he got to the little boy the more the noise invaded his senses. His head throbbed in harmony with the incessant sound, and each stride forward heightened its intensity until the sensation became cacophonous. Peter's mind blurred. A feeling of lethargy took over his body and his breathing became labored. He tried to focus on the small child but could not. He broke out into a cold sweat and stumbled forward. Peter lunged the last few feet and grabbed at the small boy but came up empty. He fought to stay upright, hazily scanning the street for the child, but the lad was nowhere in sight. A

Chapter 2

car horn startled Peter as it raced past. He knew his life was in danger, but he could not move. He staggered a few steps and then collapsed on the roadway to the fading din of screeching tires and angry shouts.

Chapter 3

Lucifer sat atop a rocky outcrop, gazing across a sea of dunes. Broken only by an occasional crag of stone, the bleak, unrelenting sand of the planet's surface stretched to the horizon in every direction. Above, the sky roiled as if it were a pot of boiling oil stirred by an unseen deity. The contrast between the peaceful sand and the turbid sky made for a striking and surreal landscape.

Lilith sat a few yards away. She was smaller in stature than Lucifer and possessed a striking array of distinctly feminine features that set her firmly apart from her masculine-leaning brethren.

Angels were, by the act of Creation, androgynous. They changed their outer guise at will to take whatever form suited them best for the task at hand. This made them the perfect beings for adapting to the harsh physical environments they may encounter while traversing the wonders of the Universe. As time progressed, some angels diverged from their given state and evolved. They began displaying features that any observer would categorize as distinctly masculine or feminine. These angels acted appropriately for their gender-based gravitations, but unlike their even-tempered brethren, they tended to have intense feelings that permeated their personas.

Lilith's violet eyes focused on the bizarre movement of the heavens above.

"Do you like it?" Lucifer asked.

Lilith kept her attention fixed on the sky as it swirled and twisted like thick and viscous goo. Grays and blacks were the sky's dominant hues, but short-lived splashes of reds, blues, and greens were also present. The varying colors would flare into existence and bleed out into nothingness as if being consumed by the heavens itself. "This world is bewildering."

"I have always thought it was quite beautiful, actually," Lucifer said. "Something else—did you notice?"

Lilith searched the horizon for anything out of the ordinary. Next to the surreal sky, the landscape was barren. The rocks and sand were all too commonplace. "I see nothing."

"No star—yet there is light."

Lilith scanned the heavens and took notice of the hot breeze, wafting through her ginger hair. The clouded, turbid sky would surely block any light from a nearby star, yet this world was near scorching in temperature and aglow as if lit by several suns. Curious as to the solution, Lilith looked to Lucifer for an answer.

With a coy smile, Lucifer responded, "We stand outside of Creation."

Lilith nodded. The muddy sky above was the shadowy reflection of the Universe. Its seemingly random, and varying perturbations were a reverse image of the movement that came from within Creation. Illumination, even without a star, was possible due to the excess and ongoing energy present at the time of Creation's formation. The energy permeated the surrounding area and manifested itself as visible light. Straightforward enough, Lilith thought, but there was still the issue of how this world came to be. If it existed outside of the physical confines of the Universe, that could only mean one thing. "*You* created this world?"

"Yes," Lucifer acknowledged, trying to gauge Lilith's temperament. "Are you surprised?"

"You are a bold one, Lucifer—you know this is forbidden. Do you openly seek the Creator's wrath?"

"He is blind to all that transpires here," Lucifer knowingly answered. "Besides, he looks elsewhere for comfort."

"He could be watching and neither of us would be any wiser."

Lucifer opened his arms wide to the surrounding plain. "As you noted, this world is a clear violation and retribution would be at hand—especially by now."

Apprehensive, Lilith scoured the area as if the Almighty would immediately appear and exact a terrible punishment for what Lucifer had done, but after several moments, she let her unfounded fears subside.

"You see? Our well-being is no longer of interest to him," Lucifer said. "Besides, he has no power here."

"His power is *everywhere*."

"Is that what you believe?"

"Of course I do."

"Transform for me then," Lucifer said, gesturing in the female angel's direction.

"What?"

"Transfigurations are still your specialty—or am I misremembering?"

"They are," Lilith responded, unsure what game Lucifer was playing.

"Anything will do—a bird, an insect, some sort of inanimate object—I care not."

Lilith was adept at all things physical. She prided herself in holding conjured visages longer than any other angel and relished in her ability to hide in plain sight. She was confident that Lucifer's test would be for naught.

Lilith rose to standing and majestically waved her arms through the air. Her facial expression was one of absolute concentration as she looked inwardly to her physical form. After several long moments, her power failed to reveal itself. Uncertainty swept through her. Lilith sneered at Lucifer's attempt to deceive her and fought off her doubt. She took a deep breath and composed herself. Calmly, Lilith tried once more to tap into the vast reserve of energy she knew she possessed, but to her dismay, nothing happened. She could neither use her might nor sense its presence. "What did you do to me?"

"I control this place," Lucifer responded. "I can give you power or take it away—all at my discretion." He raised a finger and made a small gesture toward Lilith. "Do you feel it now?"

In a sudden and overwhelming rush, Lilith felt immense power return to her being. The irrepressible might within her was more than she had ever sensed in the past. Her aura vibrated with energy and seemed held at bay by only the thinnest of veils. It was as if the most inconsequential of gestures would set it free to course through her veins and obey her every command. The only thing that came to mind was the sheer intoxication that it brought. "How is this possible?"

"There is massive energy here," Lucifer replied. "Once I attenuated myself, I blocked the path for all others unless I see fit to bestow it as a gift."

"So, you used it to fashion this world to while away your time—to distract you from your feelings toward the humans?" Lilith asked. "Or was it simple boredom?"

"I was quite lost when I first came here," Lucifer said, quietly poking at the grains of sand trapped within the cracks of the rock. "My mind was a blur of hatred and anger toward the unfortunate turn of events forced upon us. It was during that time that I found a new purpose—a new beginning—one that allowed me to see clearly once again." He outstretched his arms to the plain of sand. "The power that exists here is akin to the same power the Almighty uses to command the Universe—the same that was used to shape our existences and those of the humans. I realized I had a choice, and one not accepted lightly—nothing short of a fight for our own existence using the power of Creation itself to my advantage."

Stunned by the admission, Lilith shook her head. "How could you win such a battle? Do you mean to destroy the Creator—*our father?*"

Lucifer raised a calming hand. "I merely intend to lure him onto this world where his omnipotence can be negated. Perhaps then he will be more reasonable and hear what I have to say."

"You would plead for concessions while keeping the Almighty in confinement? Is your existence worth this issue you have with humanity?"

"He has brought this upon himself by giving life to those creatures!" Lucifer hissed. "I would see nothing less than our rightful place restored and the humans subordinated beneath us!"

Lilith's eyes widened. "So you could be their god—is that what you desire?"

"I seek nothing of the sort," Lucifer replied. "They are animals, nothing more. They are mortal and weak and have no place among beings of light."

"He has given them immortal souls," Lilith rebutted, "and the same freedoms to choose between right and wrong that we possess. Their mortality makes their freewill more pronounced—more damning should they choose poorly. I know this to be true."

"How can you defend them?"

"How could you risk open rebellion over *them*, Lucifer? The Creator loves the humans and would do anything to stop you."

"Love?" Lucifer scoffed. "What do humans know of love? They have not the capacity nor the inclination to grasp the concept of love—let alone reciprocate it. You of all people should know that. Adam's betrayal of you proves it as fact. Surely, you must find yourself seeing things as I do?"

Lilith turned away from Lucifer to hide her anguish. He blindsided her with her own past and it hit her tenfold. The emotions that welled up within Lilith were so raw that it was painful for her to recall them in full. She remembered the days from long ago when the Universe was in its infancy. She had spent her time with Lucifer exploring the vastness of Creation. She had fallen in love with him early on, but his aggressive nature and bold ambitions pushed her away. She had distanced herself from Lucifer and had broken his heart in the process, but that was not the only thing that he sought to lay bare.

After she left Lucifer, Lilith continued on her travels alone, roaming the vastness and searching for something to give her existence meaning. That is when the Almighty came to her with a new opportunity. He had recently created a new sentient being called Adam. The Almighty needed help in teaching Adam the ways of the Universe and sought out Lilith for the task. She accepted the charge and took Adam under her wing, shepherding him through his early and awkward stage of existence. Adam was a charismatic individual who, at the same time, was vulnerable and innocent. It became easy for Lilith to defer from her own endeavors and acquiesce to Adam entirely. She fell in love with him, and for a time, he was her one, all-encompassing passion. She gave him everything and yet, through it all and despite their professed love for one another, Adam turned his back on her and asked the Almighty for a new, *more human*, companion. She had been devastated.

Lucifer saw Lilith's pain and fought back his own emotions. "Your feelings for Adam were strong and I understand that now. I was a fool for not showing you the true love you deserved, and for that I am sorry."

Lilith wiped tears from her eyes. "Why did you ask me here?"

"I need your help."

Lilith saw right through Lucifer. "You would have me betray the Creator?"

"Betray? Did they not both betray you? First Adam and then the Almighty for his role in fashioning the woman that now shares Adam's bed?"

Lucifer was right. The Creator had known Lilith had feelings for Adam and disregarded them completely. She felt jaded, but she was not the only one. Existence for all the angels changed dramatically once the humans arrived. The Creator spent more time occupied with the humans than he ever did with angelic affairs. Every angel felt lessened because of the *human* problem. Lilith shook her head and drew a deep breath. None of the current plight was her problem. Lucifer was obsessed with humanity, and she could not let his thinking affect her. Lilith stiffened her resolve. The Creator's path was unknown to all and her emotional pain, however severe, was not enough to overcome her loyalty to the Almighty. "You ask much."

"I only ask for you to show the Creator what he wrought."

"I cannot help you."

Lucifer bowed. "I understand your decision."

Lilith spread her wings to leave.

"Please wait," Lucifer said. "There is one other thing that I think you should know."

Lilith turned an ear in the direction of Lucifer. "Yes?"

"Eve," Lucifer said. "She is rumored to be with child."

Anger welled inside of Lilith. She railed against it, tried to bury it deep within her, but it rose to the surface spawning a tumultuous and powerful rage. She did not want to believe Lucifer but could not ignore him either. Adam had betrayed her and now she knew the reason why. Angels were incapable of procreation and this fact had created an ever-widening rift in her relationship with Adam. Angels existed to serve for an eternity and carried out their lives with a common focus. Humans were carefree creatures—they came and went, lived and died. To live a mortal life was naught but a fleeting glimpse into the whole of the Universe. To be an angel meant to be a fixed point among all else—there was no need to have offspring. Yet somehow, Adam had chosen a human to be his companion—to bear him children, to heal his wounds, to nurture his wellbeing. They would have offspring and soon their kind would outnumber the population of angels. Lilith and her brethren would be overwhelmed. Scores of angelic beings would become superfluous in the eyes of the Almighty.

Chapter 3

Lilith looked down and sobbed. She did not want to go against the Creator, but this new revelation proved she had no choice. Hurt, fear, loathing, and rage all permeated her voice as she spoke. "I will help you, but I will do so for my own reasons."

Chapter 4

Peter's feet were slightly elevated as he lay unconscious on an examination room table. An intravenous bag hung from a stand nearby and dripped a clear liquid through a taped-down catheter into his arm. A small sensor hung loosely from Peter's finger and relayed his vital signs to a monitor that beeped regularly in the back of the room.

Renée sat in one corner of the exam room watching the elderly Doctor Valente shuffle around Peter. He checked Peter's breathing and took his pulse manually as if not willing to trust the digital readout of the monitor.

"Will this take long, doctor?" Renée asked.

Doctor Valente pulled at his well-worn physicians' coat and shrugged. "Perhaps he needs hospital, no?"

"Hospital?"

"Yes," Doctor Valente replied, shrugging his shoulders and showing a little contempt for Renée's impatience. "He could be seriously injured—brain trauma is not to be taken lightly."

Renée bit her tongue and reined in her intolerance of the situation.

After completing a thorough inspection of his patient, Doctor Valente bent over Peter and asked very loudly, "Can you hear me?" The doctor looked for any signs of recognition and when he saw none, continued, "Can you move your legs for me?"

Peter shifted his legs and moved his arms slightly.

Doctor Valente took a pen from his pocket and prodded his patient in the hands. "Peter, can you feel this?"

Peter opened his eyes and blinked.

"Very good," Doctor Valente said. "Can you see me?"

Disoriented, Peter fumbled around trying to find a handhold to raise himself up from the exam room table.

Doctor Valente put a firm hand on Peter's shoulder. "Please, I will raise the bed." He worked the table's controls and elevated his patient into a sitting position. "Better?"

"Oh man," Peter said, wincing and rubbing his temples. "My head is killing me."

Doctor Valente grabbed a cup from the examination room counter and filled it with water at the sink. He handed it Peter who immediately drank the contents.

"What happened?" Peter asked.

"It seems—"

"It was awful, Peter," Renée blurted out. "You passed out right there in the middle of the road—almost got hit by a car. It was a huge scene in front of all those people."

Doctor Valente raised a hand to quell Renée's emotional outburst and went back to his patient's care. "What were you feeling when you collapsed?"

Peter waded through his memories and resurrected the moment of his ill-fated rescue attempt. "I got dizzy—there was a ringing in my ears—I couldn't move." He stopped when he remembered the purpose of his physical exertion. "There was a boy!" he exclaimed. "The kid ran in front of the car—he must have been hit—" Peter trailed off. "I tried to stop him."

"There was no kid, Peter," Renée said. "No one saw anything."

Doctor Valente listened carefully to his patient's recollections and to the circumstances surrounding them. "Peter," he said, taking the most authoritative tone he could, "have you been drinking, perhaps taking medications—drugs?"

Peter shook his head. "I know what I saw and he was real."

"Doctor?" Renée begged. "Could you please tell him?"

"Tell him?"

"That he's having hallucinations."

"I wasn't hallucinating anything," Peter argued. "He was standing right there—I could even tell you what he was wearing."

Renée sought reinforcement from the doctor. "He's wrong, right?"

Doctor Valente chuckled. "I'm no psychologist, no?" He inspected Peter's medical chart. "The mind is a powerful thing. It can lead you to believe many things."

"But Peter almost killed himself!"

"Yes," Doctor Valente replied. "This is a very serious malady." He took out a small flashlight and tested his patient for pupil dilation. Finding nothing amiss, he took a hesitant breath. "Peter, that church, there's a lot of strange things over there."

Peter scoffed. "Like?"

"Perhaps you saw an old statue or some sort of carving on the side of the building—maybe the plants moving in the wind made you think someone was there?"

"I'm not crazy."

"That church has been there for some time, no?" Doctor Valente stated calmly. "Years ago, people thought they saw the ghost of a woman appearing on the door of the church."

Peter's interest stirred. "A woman?"

"Yes, some thought it was an angel—others a demon."

"What was it?" Peter asked, attempting to fortify his non-psychosis position.

"It was nothing," Doctor Valente chuckled. "The holes in the porch over the door cast a strange apparition in the correct light." The doctor's mood turned serious. "But everyone thought it was real, no?"

Peter knew what he had seen and there was no convincing him otherwise. He appreciated the neutral viewpoint, but the doctor was not there when it happened. No one else saw what was going on because either their view was blocked or the scene unfolded so fast they found it incomprehensible. He could see that Doctor Valente truly cared for his wellbeing, but Peter did not want to be treated like a child. He endured it every day from his wife, and he found it uncomfortable to linger on the matter further. "I think I'm better now. Thank you for helping me."

Doctor Valente put a hand on Peter's shoulder to stop him from rising. "I will need to run some tests."

"Tests—will they take long?" Renée asked impatiently.

"Yes, two, perhaps three days. I need to send them out. You will need to stay here in San Cielo while we wait for results."

"But we're on our way to France," Renée pleaded, hoping for some latitude in the doctor's orders.

Ignoring Renée, Doctor Valente spoke to Peter directly. "This could be very serious. You should wait for the results."

"You're not going to listen to him?" Renée asked Peter.

Peter gave his wife a sour look. "What difference does it make to you?"

"Monaco? We'll have to skip it and go straight to Paris."

"I don't care about Monaco," Peter responded with disgust as he thought about the doctor's proposal. Perhaps there was some merit in delaying their journey for health reasons. He smiled. If the decision displeased his wife, then it was definitely a good idea. "Besides," Peter said, "think of how much money we'll save by staying here locally."

Chapter 4

Renée went flush with anger.

Doctor Valente felt the tension and stepped in between them. "Very good, Peter. There's nothing in France better than Italy, no?"

Chapter 5

Plants and trees of all varieties thrived in the fertile soil of the Garden of Eden. Their verdant hues spread to every corner of the expansive reserve, punctuated only by the colorful flowers and fruits they bore. The lush forest of green wove a tapestry of floral life that spread across the ground like a thick blanket, making passage to some areas impossible.

Animals prospered in the Garden as well. Birds soared through the azure sky, playing in the gentle breezes and hovering in warm thermals. Larger animals strolled along well-worn paths, frolicking in wide meadows and taking repose in the shade of tall trees.

At its center was the lifeblood of the Garden—a spring that welled with such intensity that it overflowed its banks. The water's surface area was no more than a few yards across, but the flow surging from beneath was extraordinary. The crystal-clear water spilled out of its confines and served as the primary headwater to all the rivers and tributaries in the Garden. Life teemed within its waterways, with frogs, fish, and other aquatic animals inhabiting even the smallest of fens and estuaries.

Along the banks of the wellspring grew two trees. Well past the sapling age, both trees had developed strong trunks, covered in hardy, deep-grooved bark. They stood next to each other, and at no more than fifteen feet tall, both were equally stout for their height. The limbs of the trees intertwined within their canopy of thick, lively green foliage. Deep red, fig-like fruits hung at evenly spaced intervals along most of the trees' branches.

A random passerby might not have noticed the trees amongst the varied wonders of the Garden. They looked similar to any other, yet were the individual to stand and attempt comprehension of the trees, they may have seen much more than they originally desired. Although the trees were of the exact same species, each gave off an aura that was markedly different from the other.

Growing closer to the source of the headwaters was the Tree of Life. It swayed gently in the breeze, its branches moving in harmony with the ebb and flow of the wind. Thick roots, some taller than a man's waist, sprang from the tree's base and grew toward the life-giving stream. Light poured from above and bounced off the Tree of Life's leaves, bathing the surrounding area in a warm, pleasant glow. Fruit vied for every inch of space along its branches, yet the heavy burden seemed almost welcome and of no particular consequence to the tree.

The Tree of the Knowledge of Good and Evil projected a darker energy from that of its sibling. The light of the Garden did not radiate from this tree as it did from its sister; instead, the Tree of Knowledge consumed it, allowing only a small fraction of the abundant illumination to escape. The tree's thick roots carved into the shallow earth of the embankment and dredged up a multitude of rocks. It was as if the ground was in collusion with the pure waters of the wellspring to fight against the incursion brought on by the Tree of Knowledge. The fig-like fruit teemed along its branches similar to that of its sister's, but the fruit hung much heavier and made the limbs strain under the added weight. The Tree of Knowledge was the balancing force to the Tree of Life. Both of the trees stood their ground defiantly, each in direct contrast to the other.

Each day, Adam and Eve ventured throughout the Garden. Oftentimes, their individual duties took them in opposite directions. Adam spent the daylight hours hunting the wild animals of the Garden, while Eve gathered a bounty of fruits and vegetables. When night fell, they both returned to the centrally-located wellspring they called home.

On the opposite bank from the Two Trees, Adam and Eve had constructed a small shelter of animal hides stretched over a wooden frame. The only item of consequence within the simple abode was a reed mat covering a thick layer of dried grass that served as their primary bedding. Outside the dwelling, clay pots and other storage wares lay scattered about the clearing. Piles of roughly cut firewood dotted the vicinity and nearby, an animal-hide sack hung limp from a sapling, dripping the last of its contents to the ground. Overall, the area surrounding Adam and Eve's home was unkempt and in disarray.

Lilith flew in silently over the wellspring and over the Two Trees during the early morning hours before sunrise. She landed in a clearing and made her way through the dense undergrowth. The sound of the flowing water masked her entry as she approached the open end of the makeshift shelter.

Lilith quietly watched Adam and Eve sleep. With the exception of the handmade jewelry worn by the female, they were naked. They slept together with Adam's arms draped over his human mate. The angel's heart panged at the sight of Adam lying next to his new wife and forced Lilith to struggle with her storm of emotions. Adam had hurt her so deeply that she could not come to terms with it. She had been willing to be anything or anyone for Adam, but he cast her aside like refuse for the woman who now bore his child.

Lilith stood over the sleeping humans and wept. With one burst of her power, she could end their lives and solve the issue once and for all, but to do so would be in direct violation of the Creator's decree. Lucifer's plan was devious. The only thing required was to utilize the freewill bestowed upon humanity by the Almighty. By showing the Creator exactly what he had wrought, there would be no one else to blame but himself.

Lilith turned her attention to the eastern sky as the sun breached the horizon and signaled the dawn of a new day. Below her, Eve stirred. Quickly, Lilith spread her wings and thrust across the raging water of the wellspring's outlet. She landed on the far bank and navigated around the massive roots of the Tree of Knowledge. Once she had chosen the appropriate branch, the angel transformed herself into a serpent. The bright green snake slithered up the bark of the tree and settled itself onto the low hanging limb.

Lilith's snake was long and lithe. She had taken great care to distance the snake's appearance from anything menacing and dangerous. The bright green color was festive and easy to distinguish from the bark of the tree. The head of the snake was slender and did not have the protruding diamond shape of most poisonous serpents. Lilith made the eyes wide and the pupils big enough to see so they would be comforting to the humans. Every aspect of the snake was non-threatening and pleasing to the eye.

Lilith kept her gaze on Adam and Eve. They woke slowly and spent a needless amount of time lying in bed, engaging in idle chitchat. She waited patiently for nearly an hour while they made no effort to begin, what should have been, their standard routine of the day.

Adam rose first. He was a strapping young man who had not aged a day since Lilith last saw him. He was above average in height with olive skin. His hair was almost black but retained some tamer, lighter-hued undercurrents. His eyes were deep brown with the surrounding white sclera bright like a newly driven snow. Adam rummaged through a pile of handmade belongings to retrieve a coarsely woven basket. He checked it for something to eat but discovered it empty. He made the rounds of the encampment looking for food, but found none.

Chapter 5

Eve got to her feet to help with Adam's search. Her skin was lighter than that of her husband's. Her hair was thicker and richer brown than Lilith had seen on any angel. Her dark blue eyes showed her attentiveness and revealed her confident and precocious sprit. Eve giggled as she watched Adam haplessly scour the area. "Hungry this morning?"

"Yes. I was hoping we still had the fruit we collected yester-day."

Eve yawned and stretched out her arms. "Sorry, it's all gone."

Adam sighed. "I'll go and collect more."

"No need," Eve said. "You rest—I know just where to look."

Adam nodded his appreciation and sat back down on the grassy bed.

Eve made her way around the back end of the spring and to the other side of the rushing water. She came to stand in front of the Two Trees and stared at the fruit hanging high on the branches of the Tree of Life. It had been so tasty that Adam and Eve had stripped the lower branches clean. Unwilling to climb into the tree, Eve turned to find another source of nourishment but stopped when she heard a very pleasant voice coming from the tree itself.

"Is not the fruit of my tree pleasing to your eyes?" the serpent asked.

Eve followed the sound to a green snake resting on a lower branch of the Tree of Knowledge. She was startled at the sight and inspected the snake. "I've never seen a snake such as you in the

Garden before," she said with wonderment. "And one that speaks as well."

"Oh, naïve child," the serpent licked, "I am unique as most things in this garden are. Surely you must know that?"

Eve was not certain what the strange snake was asking and shook her head.

"Well," the serpent said, "this garden has many mysteries, even more than you could possibly imagine."

Eve was captivated by the snake. "Really?"

"Yes, of course. Did you know that the Garden of Eden occupies only the smallest fraction of this world? Or that this earth is only one of a multitude scattered throughout Creation?"

Eve shook her head, in awe of the knowledge the serpent possessed.

"You see? There are many things you do not understand."

Eve nodded. It was true she did not understand all there was about the Garden, let alone about Creation.

"May I ask you a question?"

Eve giggled. "Of course."

"What is it that offends your eyes to the fruit of my tree?"

Eve looked longingly at the tree and then shied away from it. "Eating of its fruit is forbidden."

"Forbidden?" the serpent asked, feigning incredulousness. "Forbidden by whom?"

"The Almighty."

"Did *he* speak these words to you?"

"No."

"Then how do you know this?"

Eve turned to look across the spring at Adam. "Those words were spoken to my husband."

"I see," the snaked hissed. "Did not the Creator say for you to eat fruit from all the trees and plants of the Garden?"

"Yes, but from this tree we shall not eat lest we die."

"You certainly will not die," the serpent snickered. "The fruit of this tree is perhaps more satisfying than that of any other. Why would he create something only to forbid it?"

"I do not know," Eve replied. "I have often wondered this same thing."

"Do you know the name of this tree?" the snake asked.

"It is called the Tree of the Knowledge of Good and Evil."

The snake laughed. "You admit you do not understand Creation, yet you turn your back on the knowledge you seek."

The snake saw the indecision on Eve's face and let the moment fester until it became a paradox of frustration. "Time is your answer."

"Time?"

"Of course," the serpent hissed. "The Almighty did not think you were ready to gain the knowledge you so rightly deserve, so he was saving this tree as a gift."

"A gift?" Eve's eyes widened. "For us?"

"Most certainly," the serpent affirmed. "The Creator understands you have grown and are in need of the knowledge of good and evil—and that is something he wanted to share with you at the right time." The serpent poked its nose at a perfectly ripened fruit only a few inches away.

Eve reached up to the limb and held the fruit without severing it from the branch. She looked to the serpent for approval. "Do you believe this is truly his intention?"

The serpent smiled. "Of course it is, dear."

Eve plucked the fig-like fruit from its branch and took a huge bite. The juices ran down her face and onto her hands. "This *is* the best fruit in the Garden!" Eve exclaimed. "I must show it to Adam!"

"Yes," the serpent said approvingly. "Adam will be pleased."

Chapter 6

The ride to the only available hotel in San Cielo was decidedly quiet. Renée drove the rental car as Peter sat and recovered from his recent medical episode. The hotel was nothing more than a large family home repurposed into bed-and-breakfast style lodging. As the car arrived in front of the inn, Peter took note of its exterior. There was nothing special about the building; it retained its mundane architecture reminiscent of San Cielo in general.

The lobby was small and reminded Peter of Edda's antique store. The decade of the 1950s must have been good to the town of San Cielo to warrant such fanaticism, he thought. Period décor occupied every nook and cranny of the lobby. The haphazardly arranged items were displayed in such a manner as to make them appear more important than they actually were. A few threadbare and heavily trafficked rugs hung on the wall like priceless pieces of art. Trinkets and knickknacks housed in locked display cases gave the impression they were heirloom jewels. A reproduction suit of armor occupied a prominent place along one wall. Peter's Italian was rough, but he surmised the armor was a leftover prop from a movie filmed nearby several decades ago. The collection was unremarkable and only of local interest at best.

Peter and his wife checked in and made their way up a steep staircase to the last room the hotel could muster. To his relief, the room was clean, large, and had its own bathroom. It overlooked San Cielo through a large window that faced the now darkened downtown area. The room's furnishings echoed those of the lobby. An old, tube-style television anchored high in one corner by a metal arm sat above a dated armchair next to the window. The all-tiled bathroom was sparse and the queen-sized bed looked to be sagging under the weight of the numerous layers of bedding cast upon it. Peter could not complain. For a town that did not see an abundance of overnight visitors, the accommodations were a welcome sight. He set his daypack on the bed, removed his shoes, and sat down.

Renée carried her purse into the small bathroom and began reapplying her makeup. "I'm starving—I'm going to find something to eat. Do you want to come?"

Peter narrowed his vision on Renée to see if she was joking. "What?"

"Dinner—you must be hungry?"

It was the first time in a long while that Peter's wife sounded concerned for his wellbeing. He nodded. "I am, but if you could bring something back, I would appreciate it."

Renée finished primping her hair and left the bathroom. "I'll see what I can do," she said, gathering her purse on her way out and closing the door behind her.

Peter shrugged off his wife's odd behavior and turned his attention to his daypack. He reached into the main pocket and gingerly removed the leather-bound manuscript. He studied the nondescript binding and caressed its worn edges. Peter opened the book and carefully examined its coarse parchment pages. He ran his fingers across the symmetrically-spaced lettering and randomly picked a place within the main body of the work to read the Latin conventionally. When that failed, he followed the letters backwards and sideways as if trying to unscramble a puzzle. With no luck, he read every other letter and then tried diagonally—all to no avail. He flipped from page to page looking for any pattern or clue to the manuscript's secrets. With every failure, Peter's curiosity grew until he found himself increasingly obsessed with the ancient book.

Renée roused from her fitful slumber and peeked out from beneath the heavy bedspread. "Could you turn that light off— *please*," she said to her husband who was still engrossed with the old book despite the late hour.

Unwilling to give ground on the issue, Peter simply tilted the nightstand lamp's shade further afield lessening the impact on his wife. "Better?"

Renée scoffed at the futile gesture. "It's still on, isn't it?"

"You do this to me all the time at home."

Renée was well aware of past circumstances, but this was a vacation—a time for sleeping in and relaxing. Besides, she did not want to admit that her husband was right. Instead, she bypassed her admission of guilt and redirected the conversation. "I thought you couldn't read it anyway?"

"Well," Peter responded, happy that his wife was interested in something he was working on. "The text is Latin, but the letters don't form words or sentences. It doesn't make any sense."

"So you're keeping me up late at night because you can't read anything?" Sarcasm permeated Renée's voice. "Okay then, I'm sure when the doctor asked you to rest, he wasn't thinking about you being up all night."

Peter nodded. His wife had a valid point. "Fine, I'll go to bed."

"Thank you," Renée said, pulling the blankets back over her head to block as much light as possible.

Before turning off the table lamp, Peter mulled his observations aloud for the sole purpose of pestering his wife. "You know, at first I thought it was an old puzzle book. Crusader knights would buy them to while away the long hours on their way to the Holy Land, but I'm pretty sure it's not one of those."

From underneath the thick layer of bedding, Renée's muffled voice angrily quipped, "Great, now go to sleep."

Peter ignored his wife and continued his train of thought. "There's no primer—no beginning sequence or code." He thumbed through the last pages of the book. "There's not even an annotation as to the author—that's when I thought that it might be a treasure book."

"Treasure?" Renée perked up and peeked out from under her blanket fortress.

Peter snickered in disgust at one of the few things he knew would still interest his wife. "Highway robbery was such a problem that the Templars set up an organization quite like today's banks. Travelers would give them money at the departure point and receive a coded document that would translate back to cash at their destination."

"But this is an entire book?" Renée asked curiously, questioning her husband's logic.

"Yeah, since it's large, it must be something bigger."

"You said you couldn't read it, so now it's a treasure map? If it's so valuable, why would the antique store just *give* it away?"

"I don't know."

"I think you stole it," Renée said. "Edda told me her husband died a long time ago."

"Maybe it was her son or helper or somebody?" Peter countered. "All I know is the guy gave it to me."

"It's great to think you might have stolen something valuable from that old lady who could really use the money."

Peter sighed. "Fine, if it makes you feel any better, I'll go back in the morning and offer to pay for it."

Renée sealed off her barrier of bedding and managed a muffled and self-righteous, "Good, because if you don't, I might have to report you to the police."

"Good night," Peter said wryly and turned out the light.

Chapter 7

The fruit from the Tree of the Knowledge of Good and Evil was delicious beyond measure. The red juice streamed down Eve's face, dripping onto the fertile ground below. Her eyes opened wide and she found it difficult to contain the overwhelming sense of joy that came from eating the simple fruit.

Eve ran around the headwater to Adam's bedside and showed him the half-eaten fruit. "Take a bite."

Adam took one look at the familiar fruit and rubbed his weary eyes. "I'm tired of those."

"This one is different," Eve insisted. "Take a bite."

"It looks the same as the others."

"I thought so too, but it's not."

Adam took the partially-eaten fruit from Eve and studied it. It was large, about the size of a grapefruit, and looked like a small melon with a hint of a bell shape to it. Juice, the color of blood, leaked from the open bite leading Adam to conclude that perhaps the fruit was overripe. Even so, he raised it to his mouth and took a large mouthful from directly over the top of Eve's previous sampling.

Adam mashed the fleshy pulp between his teeth and savored the richness of the fruit. The flavor was unique. It was sweet, but not so much as to be offensive to his tastes. Undertones of a bold and tangy essence spanned the gamut of anything similar in the Garden, but underneath the fruit's physical traits was something else. Adam lowered the fruit to his lap where Eve took the opportunity to scoop it away for another bite.

Adam withdrew from his wife as he became increasingly aware of his surroundings. He watched Eve's consumption of the fruit from a surreal vantage point he could not explain. All around him, the Garden's animals and plant life took on new personas. Their corporeal forms were intact, but their existence—no, their purpose within the Garden—as food and shelter for the two humans had suddenly changed. Adam blinked and rose to standing. He strained to see into the Garden's depths beyond the edge-water of the welling spring and the Two Trees. In particular, Adam could sense the lions and hear their early morning chuffing in the distance. The realization of the moment was difficult for him to comprehend. He grew frightened and took deep breaths to calm himself.

The lions of the Garden were not the friends Adam had once thought. They were killers. They killed for their food and would continue to do so when presented with an opportunity—*they murdered other creatures*. Adam quickly thought back to his own recent encounters with some of the wildlife in the Garden—he had murdered them for the sole purpose of sating his hunger. Suddenly and without pause, the Garden of Eden grew in complexity in Adam's mind until he could no longer understand it. It inundated his consciousness and made him feel guilty and vulnerable.

Realization dawned across Eve's face as well. She lowered the tantalizing fruit and took new stock of her familiar surroundings. She shivered in the damp cold that was the shore of the spring and waded into the tall grasses in an attempt to heat her rapidly cooling body. Eve spun in different directions as she tried in vain to reconcile her place in the Garden. She felt as if she were a small eddy within a raging river of change. She stared blankly at Adam as if looking for an answer to their predicament or some kind of absolution that would end the misery of her newfound awareness.

Adam recognized the manifestation taking place within Eve as it had done in himself. He pondered the commonality of the simultaneous revelations and could find no other source than the fruit itself. In a hushed, almost secretive tone, he asked, "Where did you get that fruit?"

Trembling with fear, Eve rigidly raised an arm and pointed to the Two Trees on the other side of the stream.

Adam gazed at the trees and let out a deep sigh. "Take me to the exact spot."

Eve led Adam around the headwater and stopped directly beneath the branch where she found the fruit. She pointed to a bare spot on the lowest limb. "There," Eve said penitently.

Adam traced the branch through the thicket of the interwoven canopy of the Two Trees until he reached the trunk of the Tree of Knowledge. He closed his eyes and used his inner strength to quell his anger. "Fruit from this tree was forbidden by the Creator."

"I know," Eve sobbed, "but the serpent said—"

"What serpent?" Adam interrupted, scanning the area. "I don't see anything."

Eve placed her hand on the branch the snake had rested on. "It was here a moment ago," she said, searching frantically around the wellspring. "It couldn't have gone far." Eve sat down on the large roots that protruded from the base of the trees and cried. "I'm sorry."

It was difficult for Adam to find the words to articulate the ramifications of Eve's actions. This was by far the biggest breach in the commandments laid down by the Almighty that he could remember. To make matters worse, he had eaten from the fruit as well.

Before they could speak further about their actions, a strong wind penetrated the undergrowth of the Garden. It was brisk and driven with purpose. The wind flowed around the thick branches and wispy grasses as if the air itself had become an unseen liquid. It seethed in density and pressure as it poured its way to the two humans.

Dread engulfed Adam. "The Creator's here."

Eve wiped away her tears and peered through the vegetation. "I don't see him."

"He is here."

Chapter 7

Eve realized that it was her decision to eat the fruit that had loosed the Creator upon them. For the first time in her life, she experienced the hand of guilt weighing on her soul. Her breathing quickened and she gasped for every swallow of air. She fought to control her emotions, but fear closed in and surrounded her. Eve wanted to run far away, but knew the gesture would be futile. She held the half-eaten fruit in front of her and, wanting to hide the evidence of her disobedience, dropped it quietly between the tall-standing roots at the base of the Two Trees.

Adam looked to Eve and then back to himself. He understood for the first time they were both naked. He took her by the hand and moved closer to the trees. "Quickly, we must cover ourselves."

"Why?"

"He cannot see us like this," Adam replied, pulling the lower branches of the Tree of Life closer to their bodies to conceal their nudity.

A deep, thunderous voice emanated from the thick air surrounding the Two Trees. "Adam?" the voice asked into the stillness of the Garden.

Frightened, Adam and Eve retreated further into the undergrowth.

With a hint of dismay and a noticeable rise in anger, the voice demanded, "Where are you?"

Ashamed, Adam could no longer keep up the ruse of his absence from his god and, fraught with fear, stepped forward. "I am here, my Creator."

The tendrils of dense atmosphere quickly pulled away from the paths and open corridors of the understory. It formed a large pillar of air that floated above the wellspring. The air churned as it gathered itself and became more opaque with each passing moment. As the Almighty spoke, flashes of light danced to each syllable along the column of tumultuous atmosphere. "Why do you conceal yourselves from me?"

"We are naked and feel ashamed."

"Naked?" A black streak like a thunderstorm coursed through the pillar of air. "You have eaten fruit from the forbidden tree!" the Almighty roared. The column of roiling clouds pulsed with streaks of red-hot lightning.

Eve stepped forward, her panic-stricken voice stuttering out, "It—it was my fault, O Creator; it was I who gave Adam the fruit."

"Why did you do such a thing?"

Eve shrunk back from the blistering question.

"I have endowed you with the greatest of all powers—to choose between right and wrong," the Creator fumed. "And yet, you squander your gift!"

The column of roiling clouds shuddered and a powerful blast of air rocked the Garden. Adam and Eve struggled to stay upright and withdrew from the display.

"In your arrogance you would seek to become equals with your Creator?" the Almighty thundered, turning the thickening mass of clouds black with a sickly sheen. Lightning shot out and coursed through the column with blinding effect. "Now and henceforth I forbid you from eating from the Tree of Life!" The mass of clouds and turmoil within grew larger with the Creator's every statement. "I banish you from the Garden of Eden, and cursed be the ground because of you! In toil shall you eat its yield for all the days of your life! Thorns and thistles shall it bring forth, and by the sweat of your brow shall you get bread to eat—" a slight pang of despair crept into the Almighty's rapturous tone, "until you return to the ground from which you were taken."

Dark clouds enveloped Adam and Eve and the soil of the Garden beneath them disappeared. Their vision obscured, the pair felt as if they were flying at great speed through the sky. The journey lasted only a moment and, as the clouds dispersed, Adam and Eve found themselves in a desolate valley flanked by two rivers. They felt the presence of the Almighty diminish and then leave. They were all alone.

Adam and Eve dropped to their knees and surveyed their surroundings. The color of the sky was the same, but the terrain and vegetation adorning the area was sparse. The Almighty had seen fit to deposit Adam and Eve onto the same world, but to an area that was bereft of the wonderment and plenty of the Garden of Eden. Because of their transgressions, they would have to fend for themselves in this strange new place.

Watching from a secluded perch, Lucifer sensed the enormous power emanating from the Garden. It flowed with great force from the Creator's column of black air, sending animals fleeing from its path. As the energy reached the outermost boundaries of Eden, it began to peel the ground away from its bedrock and throw it high into the atmosphere along the Garden's perimeter. The scale of power intensified as the Creator surgically removed the entire area from its native earth and lifted it above the surrounding landscape. The amount of material was massive and equaled many millions-of-tons of soil, plants, and rock. The Garden of Eden hovered several hundred feet over its former position like an earthen island in a sea of blue sky.

Lucifer watched the display in awe. On occasion, he had been lucky enough to bear witness to the Almighty's immense power, but in those few opportunities, Lucifer had never seen anything such as the spectacle he now experienced. It was a symphony of power and balance stained by the feeling of despair and solitude.

Of particular interest to Lucifer was the way in which the Creator was destroying the Garden of Eden. Certainly, the Almighty had the power to obliterate the former human habitat in one swift stroke, but throughout his show of force, he had not attempted to destroy or harm either of the Two Trees or the Garden's immense variety of plant life. The entire area was the most influential factor in the humans' current predicament, yet the Creator chose to spare it from an exacting and absolute destruction. Not only was the Garden and its contents to be spared, but it seemed as if the Almighty meant to secret it away to some other place entirely.

Why would the Creator want to go through the tedious work of relocating the Garden of Eden and the Two Trees instead of simply destroying them? Lucifer did not need to ruminate on the problem as the show of force before him added credence to his theories. The Garden of Eden and the Two Trees must be special to the needs of the humans.

The words of the Creator further aided Lucifer in piecing the puzzle together. One particular phrase rose to the top: *...until you return to the ground from which you were taken.* This statement by the Almighty was strange and out of place for his generally stoic demeanor. The Creator seldom spoke and when he did, his words were significant. Lucifer knew that to cast the Almighty's words as superfluous or unintentional was an exercise in extreme ignorance. Slowly, Lucifer realized what was missing from the puzzle of humanity.

Adam and Eve were *nephesh*. They not only existed as flesh and blood, but also in spirit. They were imbued with a soul that would allow them to live forever—beyond their earthly and mortal demise. Had the two stayed within the decree of the Creator and ate only from the Tree of Life, their earthly bodies would have been spared the fear of death. As their new predicament came to light, the humans and their progeny would forevermore be in perilous dan-ger—stalked by death, until humanity itself was no more.

The Almighty formed the Garden of Eden to house the nephesh and the Two Trees to protect them. With the Creator's covenant broken, there was no place for humanity's souls to go after death. To save them, the Almighty needed to create a realm outside the physical world and sequester the Garden within so the nephesh could find their way home after they died. The Garden of Eden and the Two Trees were the key, and without them, humanity's souls would be lost forever.

The buildup of the Creator's power vibrated the surrounding atmosphere, and streaks of red and orange lightning lashed out from the column of air as it began to envelop the floating island. Dark clouds poured off the hovering mass like waterfalls cascading through a canyon. With every deafening blast, large clumps of earth rained to the ground below.

Lucifer sensed his time running out. The Almighty would be at his weakest soon after the creation of the new realm to house the Garden. Lucifer and his followers would need to act quickly to catch the Almighty off guard, but the Garden's purpose could not be overlooked. By disrupting the Creator's plan and seizing the Garden of Eden, Lucifer may yet add to his position in negotiations over the fate of the unwanted nephesh.

Lucifer called out, "Asmodeus, Sitri."

The two angels manifested from thin air in front of Lucifer and bowed in reverence.

"It has begun," Lucifer said. "His hold has been released. Direct the Garden to the world I created—we must disrupt him at all costs."

Asmodeus and Sitri nodded their acceptance of Lucifer's charge and flew off to the quaking, power-enveloped Garden of Eden.

Lucifer produced a twisted ram's horn from his robes and raised it to his lips. He took a deep breath and blew into the gilded mouth-piece. The horn trumpeted a sweet and longing sound that rose into the air and scattered to the riotous winds. He waited for a response, but none came. Lucifer pressed his mouth against the horn and once again, blew with all his might. The horn produced a high-pitched sound that pierced the turbulence swirling about the Garden.

From all points of the compass, angels began to appear in the sky. They gleamed in every shade of white and formed waves so vast they appeared as a tsunami of clouds backlit by the blue sky. The angels turned their attention to the Creator's storm and flew head-long into it.

The onslaught took the Almighty by surprise. The Creator had no choice but to rush the completion of the Garden's separation and use his power to hurl it through time and space toward its final destination. As the Garden of Eden left the confines of his influence, the Almighty witnessed the entry of two of Lucifer's most trusted lieutenants. His intent to move humanity's last refuge to a realm apart from the corporeal bonds of Creation was in jeopardy. "Uriel," the Creator uttered into his self-derived maelstrom.

Uriel appeared within moments, his breastplate armor gleaming in the daylight. The angel bowed and took a position slightly above the Creator's column of air, the soft beat of his wings keeping him stationary. Uriel assessed the impending attack and his muscular frame tightened in ready defense of the Almighty. He pulled a broadsword from its sheath and the weapon ignited into flame.

"Go!" the Almighty bellowed into the direction of the fading Garden of Eden.

Uriel offered a look of confusion to the Creator.

"Uphold your vow and keep the Garden free of treachery!"

Uriel said nothing. He simply nodded the acknowledgement of his given task and powered his wings forward. He dove through the Almighty's turbulence, chasing after the receding Garden of Eden and vanished with it into the distance.

With the Almighty's attention focused elsewhere, Lucifer pounced on the opportunity and charged into the fray. His first task was organizing his followers to disrupt the Creator at every level. He barked out orders to the angels, and thousands upon thousands of them converged on the swirling mass of black clouds. They struck at the Creator from every conceivable angle and swarmed him like a hive of angry bees. The angels harried him with powerful attacks that forced the Almighty to single out and expend energy defending against each one individually.

The Creator's atmospheric display grew as it lashed out against the rebellious angels. Bright, multicolored lightning and pure spheres of energy pummeled the instigators, causing distortions in the three-dimensional space around them. Angels caught in the surges of power were badly damaged and sought refuge at the rear of their formation. Others used their aerobatic skills to avoid the Creator's counterattacks and continued to press their advance.

Even with a multitude of angels by his side, Lucifer knew they would surely lose the fight. Their only hope was to force the Almighty closer to the planet Lucifer created. Once there, Lucifer could use its vast influence to disrupt the Creator, allowing negotiations to begin on even terms.

Chapter 7

Lucifer took a deep breath and conjured his own power. Brilliant, luminous energy poured forth from his body like a river, filling the sky around him. Lucifer swept his arms through the velvety white aura and wasted little effort in beginning the arduous task of changing the surrounding environment for the dimensional crossing to his world.

Through the clamor, the Almighty sensed an immense force bending the fabric of Creation. He knew right away the only other entity capable of that kind of might was Lucifer. The Almighty searched the skies, but the rabble of angels intensified their attack, blocking his vision. His anger grew exponentially and the Creator's column of thunderous clouds exploded outward with such force that it sent the rebellious angels reeling. During the brief respite, he turned his attention away from the battle and sought out the location of the disturbance. The persistent and regular buildup of energy was coming from below him, but he could not see Lucifer through the mass of angels regrouping for another assault. The Creator had no time to react as the winged aggressors renewed their offensive, forcing him once again to counter their onslaughts.

Lucifer worked as quickly as he dared. He concentrated his power on an infinitesimally small point in the space directly below the Creator. The point grew, stretching and morphing into a two-dimensional disk whose diameter dwarfed that of the ongoing hostilities. A dense black star field emerged within the flat plain and flashed through a sequence of muddy gray hues that eventually swirled into a stable view of the flaxen-stained surface of Lucifer's heat-baked world.

From the depths of his being, Lucifer directed all his energy toward the two-dimensional edges of the spatial rift. The force penetrated and surrounded the circular edges of the disc. He strained under the effort as he turned the two-dimensional portal into a three-dimensional sphere. The displacement of Creation encompassed the Almighty and all the angelic combatants. From inside the sphere, Lucifer folded space and time again until the entire group stood on the edge between known Creation and his world. With the trap set, he raised his horn and blew a long, rolling note.

Lucifer joined the angels as they intensified their destructive firepower upon their Creator. They pushed the Almighty's raging tempest toward the sun-drenched world to a position just shy of the outer boundary of Creation.

The Creator's dark clouds whipped and frothed as he fought back. Lightning, the color of fire, shot out at his attackers, forcing large groups of angels to retreat and regroup. Behind him, the Almighty felt the pull of the strange world. Foreign and maligned to Creation, it drained his power away. His fury rose to dizzying heights, but he refused to let his rage muddle his senses. The Creator knew the source of his betrayal and called out to the leader of the rabble, "You dare challenge me, Lucifer?"

Lucifer held up a hand to quell his followers' assault and advanced gracefully through the crowd. His platinum-blond hair mussed with each beat of his wings as he emerged from the assemblage and positioned himself in front of his minions. Lucifer bowed deeply, showing a sincere reverence toward his Creator. "I do not seek open conflict; rather, I wish only to discuss the ultimate disposition of the humans."

As if on cue, the angels spread out, hovering along the boundary line between Creation and Lucifer's strange world like a wall. They did this to prevent the Almighty from striking an all-powerful final blow.

With a melancholy tone, Lucifer continued, "You gave us life— all of us, to bask in your glory and to wonder at your Creation, and for that we are eternally grateful." He paused and looked squarely at the Almighty's whirling tempest, "But to supplant us with this mortal combination of flesh and blood is intolerable."

"Intolerable?" the Almighty thundered, his column of gases expanding to a greater height than ever before. "I am your maker. I created you and your brethren from the vacuum of nothingness! You defy my will and risk my wrath!"

Lucifer listened to the Almighty's diatribe with a disinterest not dissimilar to an errant schoolboy's lack of concern for an overbearing administrator's monologue. The more time it took the Almighty to admonish them, the better it was for their cause. Lucifer plainly saw the Creator's clouds siphoning away into the influence of his rogue world. He felt the Almighty's awesome power diminish with each and every passing moment. The once great and powerful Creator was dwindling right before Lucifer's eyes, and all because the Almighty felt the need to lecture his subjects.

Stoking the fire further, Lucifer added, "We humbly ask that you subordinate the humans and restore us to the position you so generously gave us at the dawn of Creation."

"What I do, I do for my own purpose, Lucifer, not yours!" the Creator spat. His manifestation transformed from a pitch-black bank of dark and ominous clouds to a column of flames that raged red-hot like the interior of a furnace. It burned with the intensity of a thousand suns causing the air immediately around the event horizon to crepitate as the atoms separated and were consumed by the firestorm.

Lucifer calculated they did not have long. Either the Almighty would destroy him and his followers or the exhibition of power would take its toll and become too much to bear for the Creator. Lucifer watched keenly as the Almighty's inferno grew and then, for a brief moment, subsided ever so slightly. The Creator had reached his peak—he could no longer maintain his power indefinitely. Lucifer took out his horn and signaled his followers to renew the attack.

Energy pummeled the Almighty from all sides. He fought back, striking down the rank and file with swings of huge protuberances of seething potency. The fire was so intense that when it enveloped the angels, it burned their skin, charring it permanently black. The Almighty punished them for their rebellion and the ashen hue would forever mark them as enemies to Creation.

Lucifer retreated and took a position safely behind his line of minions. The angels fell in broad swaths to the sand below, but he did not care about the individual toll it was taking, nor did he linger on the loss of their strategic value. Lucifer simply wanted the Creator to suffer as much damage as possible while using the maximum amount of power defending himself.

The onslaught slowly abated and the multitude of angels that was once airborne now lay smitten on the surface of Lucifer's world. The Almighty's column of raging fire dwindled to no more than a relic of its previous glory. His flames licked out harmlessly, their reach diminished to the point of being benign. The strange planet continued tugging at the Almighty's power until he struggled to keep his manifestation intact.

Lucifer hung in midair and smiled. Out of the horde of angelic attackers, he was the only one left standing. He clapped his hands and bowed before the diminutive bank of wavering conflagration. "Bravo! You have fought well, my glorious Creator!"

"You would patronize me, Lucifer?" the Almighty said, his voice shallow and weak.

"Patronize? No," Lucifer replied, flying closer to the Creator. "I simply wish to discuss the ultimate fate of the humans."

"And if I refuse?"

"That would be most unfortunate," Lucifer answered, gesturing to the planet's surface below. "I would imprison you here for all eternity and grind the helpless nephesh under my merciless heel."

"That *would* be unfortunate," the Almighty repeated hoarsely, "for you." The Creator's column of fire rekindled in intensity and burst forth, nearly trapping Lucifer.

Lucifer righted himself and let loose with an explosive discharge that encircled the Almighty with a white energy field. The barrier sought to consume the Creator, closing in on him with a tightening malice.

The Creator brought his own power to bear, filling the sphere with red-hot flames. He pushed his being to the limit and forced the energy field open. The Almighty escaped, but he fell nearer to Lucifer's world, draining his power and weakening him further. The Creator's control over his visage fluctuated. His form as a whirling tempest changed to a near-representation of a human being. Arms and legs began to appear and the shape of a head was clearly visible.

"I think it has been some ages since I last gazed upon your true image," Lucifer mocked, and without warning, charged straight for the Creator. The angel's form erupted into a sizzling white aura that filled the sky. Energy licked off Lucifer's wings leaving a trailing pattern in his wake. As he converged on the Almighty's location, the angel raised his arms and conjured his full power to strike.

Imperceptible through his unfinished visage, the Creator smiled. Small at first and with a wry tinge, he let it become more apparent as Lucifer closed the distance.

Caught off guard by the show of defiance, Lucifer tried to halt his advance but was too late.

The Almighty rose to the imposing figure he had once been. His flames reached out and engulfed the rogue angel. He held Lucifer firm while flames scorched the angel's flesh.

Lucifer thrashed back and forth in agony. "Please," he begged, "be merciful."

"I gave you every opportunity to be merciful to me," the Creator thundered, "yet you sought only destruction and despair!" He intensified his power, forcing the angel to scream out in withering pain. "Forever will you inhabit this foul domain and never will you see the light of Creation again!" The Almighty cast Lucifer down to join his minions on the planet's surface. "I hereby seal this foreign realm so none of you may ever escape and may anyone who chooses to follow in your footsteps suffer the same fate as you!" The Creator produced a blinding explosion that filled the sky between himself and the strange world. The light glazed over the roiling, oil-stirred sky of the strange world, changing it to a flat, opaque barrier. The Almighty looked mournfully to the scorched world below and let his column of unrelenting fire give way to a bank of darkened clouds that slowly dissipated until nothing remained.

Lilith held her serpent form long after the Almighty cast away the Garden of Eden. She had slithered into the thicket of under-growth and waited for the battle to subside. She heard the deafening reports and felt the low resonance of the conflict's vibrations travel through the earth of the Garden. Lilith sensed the movement through space and time as the Almighty hurled Eden from the zone of conflict. She spied Asmodeus and Sitri as they entered the Garden to do Lucifer's bidding to redirect it to a new location. Lilith heard the Creator call out for Uriel, the guardian of Eden and the Two Trees. She saw Uriel enter and use his flaming sword to battle Asmodeus and Sitri. Yet still, she only watched from afar.

Lilith knew Lucifer would choose the path to confrontation over that of diplomacy. He was a fiery and arrogant spirit, full of hatred for the humans. Although an angel's primary goal was to show love and compassion toward all living creatures, Lucifer's being had been torn, forming a great rift over his loyalty to his duty and to the nephesh.

Lilith could not help but think Lucifer's course of action was a righteous one. The Almighty designed the humans to outshine the angelic brethren. The nephesh had all the tools necessary to do so, but their poor decision-making and penchant for self-destruction railed against all the Almighty had taught.

Lilith had a difficult choice to make. She could side with the Creator and rise up to help Uriel defend the Garden, or she could align with Lucifer and correct the injustice thrust upon them. Either way, she knew there would be no going back to the quiet life she so desperately enjoyed.

In the background, Lilith heard the fighting between Uriel and Lucifer's henchmen intensify. The Garden was being rent asunder by the unbridled energy thrown by both sides. The animals of the Garden were being slaughtered. Their blood soaked into the fertile earth and ran into the small streams, staining the water red. Trees and plants of all varieties were being burnt to ash. Death and devastation followed the fighting like that of the wake from a powerful ship. Neither side was gaining the advantage as Uriel proved to be the strongest among them.

Lilith could not stop thinking about the way Adam had cast her aside in favor of Eve. Just the simple act of trying to reconcile her raw emotions brought Lilith to a palpable rage. She owed her allegiance to the Almighty, but he had made a terrible mistake in creating the humans.

In a flash of light, Lilith transformed back into her angelic being and conjured silver chainmail that covered her wings. With one sweep of her arm, she produced a heavy shield and a long spear that sparkled and glinted in the low light of the Garden's interior.

An ear-splitting explosion rang through the Garden of Eden as Lilith felt the ground's movement cease. Her attention was drawn up and away to the sky overhead where she saw a brilliant flash of crimson stretch from one end of the horizon to the other. The light faded to an impenetrable dark barrier that left only a faint ring of illumination emanating from the far edges of the Garden.

Lilith heard the Almighty's curse reverberate through the atmosphere, and with its dying echo, her form began to change. Her beautiful and graceful angelic figure morphed into that of a burnt and leathery demon. The marvelous and intricate chainmail that once adorned her wings, deteriorated into rusty links held together by plain wire rings. Her shield and spear gave way to wooden versions that provided little protection. Shocked, Lilith fought the transformation. She conjured all her power and changed herself back to her former glory. She held the angelic façade for as long as she could, but the drain was tremendous. Lilith waivered and crumpled to the ground in a sobbing heap as her visage turned back to that of a foul and monstrous demon.

Chapter 8

Peter awoke to the hustle and bustle of Renée's morning routine. She frittered about the room, gathering personal items and primping herself. Normally, she was not an early riser, but that ebbed and flowed depending upon her mood. Mostly it meant that Peter's wife wanted to go shopping. He knew the familiar scent of her chic perfume—she only wore it to impress others. Peter recognized the expensive dress clothes and accessories as an added bonus for her invented pretentiousness. "Where are you going?" he asked out of habit, fully aware of what the response would be.

"I ain't sitting around here all day," Renée replied. "And you?"

Peter still felt slightly out-of-sorts from his fainting episode the day before but wanted to make good on his promise. "I think I'll go back to that antique store," he said, gesturing to the old book on the nightstand next to him. "I'll do some investigating—find out if she knows it's missing."

Renée huffed at her husband's last statement. "She could call the cops, you know and have you arrested. I don't need more embarrassing moments like yesterday's, that's for sure."

Peter shrugged off the insinuation of thievery. "If she wants money, I'll pay her, but her husband—whoever he was—*gave* it to me."

Renée looked steadfastly into the bathroom mirror, puckered to correct her near-perfect application of lipstick. "Uh huh, sure, but if they put you in jail, I'm not bailing you out." She finished her routine and left the bathroom. Renée hurried through the room, picking up her purse and the keys to the rental car from the dresser nearest the front door. "I'm taking the car; I may want to drive to the next town over. I'll see you when I get back." She did not wait for a reply, walking through the door and closing it behind her.

Peter sighed at what his marriage had become. It did not matter what she did, as he was in no shape to do anything strenuous and planned nothing more than a very light day of investigation. He would wander around the close proximity of the old-downtown area and research his antique book as much as he was able. Under no circumstances did he intend to overexert himself.

Peter dressed comfortably for his morning stroll around the city center. He wore a nondescript cream-colored collared shirt with a slightly stretched-out breast pocket. His khaki trousers ran down the full length of his leg and cut off slightly above his sneakers, which allowed his brown dress socks to peek out below the hem of his pants. As usual when he was off on an errand, Peter wore his gray daypack strapped over his shoulders. His auburn hair and silver-rimmed glasses completed the ensemble of the neophyte tourist.

Peter's first stop was Edda's antique store where he had picked up the manuscript the day before. He opened the front door and stood in the main display area of the establishment. He scanned behind the display cases and then into the larger, merchandise-cluttered main room. There were no signs of the proprietor anywhere. Peter cleared his throat noisily and listened for a reply. When he was certain no one had heard, he asked loudly, "Edda, are you here?" He was attentive to any sound, but once again, nothing stirred. Peter carefully eyed the front door. It had been unlocked and, despite its age, appeared to be in perfect working order with no signs of foul play.

With artificially heavy footfalls, Peter made his way through the archway separating the two areas and navigated around the multitude of haphazardly stacked piles of merchandise in the larger room. He stopped when a faint scratching noise of a broom sweeping back and forth across an uneven floor rose to the forefront. The sound came from underneath his current position. Peter realized that no nefarious activity was afoot and let his tense state ease. He headed to the corner stairway that led to the basement and descended.

"Edda?" Peter timidly asked into the dim light.

"*Un momento*," Edda replied.

Peter smiled at the friendly voice and continued to the bottom of the staircase. Edda stood at the far end of the basement with her broom clutched tightly in her hands. She wore a similar dress to what she had on the previous day. The fabric was missing color in the various areas around the pockets. He could not be sure, but it might have been the exact same article of clothing.

"Peter, good to see you again, and so soon! San Cielo is a wonderful village, no? Have you come to buy those other pieces for your beautiful Renée? You are a lucky man, I think."

"You have no idea," Peter muttered. "I actually came about something else—another item."

"Another item?" Edda pondered briefly and then returned to sweeping. "I'm sorry Peter, I must finish to clean down here and then we can talk business, no?"

Peter nodded politely. The basement was extraordinarily tidy in comparison to the mess it was the day before. The broken and disjointed display counter was still present, but the merchandise cluttered around it was gone. The floor was devoid of the miscellaneous items seen previously and the corners were clear of boxes. "Wow, you guys must've worked through the night to get this cleaned up."

Edda gave Peter a puzzled look. "No, I come down every week and sweep," she said, sighing heavily. "The mold grows; it's terrible."

"What about all the stuff that was down here?"

Edda shook her head. "I don't keep anything in the basement. The moisture ruins everything, no?" She leaned on her broom for support. "I'm an old woman—it's very difficult climbing those stairs."

Peter furrowed his brow in incomprehension at the ailing merchant. "You have a helper of some kind. Your son perhaps?"

Edda laughed boisterously. "My son lives in Rome, with my grandchildren. I run the shop by myself." She could see the consternation in the man's face. "What can I do for you, Peter? You wanted to see another item?"

"Not really," Peter replied, taking the ancient book from his daypack and holding it out for Edda. "I came here about this."

Edda took the manuscript and perused its pages like the real antique professional she was. "It's very old. The leather is good. The parchment is coarse—ink is correct."

"Have you seen it before?"

Edda shook her head. "Never."

Peter thought for a moment and tried to piece together the clues. Edda seemed genuine in her response. Either someone broke into Edda's store unbeknownst to her and gave him the book, or he was in the middle of a severe hallucinogenic episode. Which, given the circumstances, was very possible. Peter shrugged off the train of thought. The manuscript was real and there was no getting around that fact. He had no stomach for confrontation, but his need to investigate the origins of the ancient tome superseded his phobias.

He stood as straight as he could and looked Edda in the eyes. "I got this book while I was down here yesterday."

Edda was more than a little surprised at the confession. "What?"

"Yes, a man was down here and gave it to me. I tried to pay for it, but he made me take it."

Edda laughed cautiously. "Peter, you are joking, no?"

"No," Peter replied, shaking his head. "A man gave me this book. I thought he was your son or husband or something."

Edda went pale. She turned to several pages in the book and eyed the Latin text. "*Il mio dio!*" She crossed herself and pushed the manuscript back into Peter's hands. "I'm sorry, but you must go," she said, motioning for him to retreat out of the basement and back up the stairs.

"I don't understand—I'll pay you for the book."

Edda waved him off. "No—please, just go."

Not wanting to make matters worse, Peter complied and moved up the narrow staircase. He stopped on the landing of the main floor and turned around. "Can you at least tell me why?"

Edda looked pensively at Peter. "That book is the work of the monk Nicholas. He was crazy."

"The church, down the street—it honors the same monk?"

"Yes," Edda replied, "but it is foolishness, no? The monk was possessed by Satan. He killed himself to escape the evil of that book."

Peter fought his natural instincts to mock the existence of the devil and the unfathomable possibility of possession, but steered clear by stating, "I'm sorry, it's just an old manuscript, nothing more."

Edda did not want to hear any of it. She resumed herding Peter through the various piles of shabby antiques and toward the front door.

At the door, Peter slowed his forward progress and made a tentative stand. "Isn't there anything else you can tell me?"

Edda shook her head and opened the door. With a firm hand, she pushed Peter over the threshold and closed it behind him. She flipped the store's *aperto* sign over to *chiuso*, which meant closed. Muffled by the glass of the door, she gave her advice, "Destroy it. Burn it, Peter, rid yourself of its evil. Never tell anyone you have it. You're in great danger while you carry that book." Visibly distressed and wringing her hands, Edda turned away and hurried into the bowels of her store.

Peter stood on the stoop for a long moment and contemplated the shopkeeper's words. There was no way he was going to do anything she mentioned. The book was far too old and valuable to throw it away like some common piece of garbage. All that nonsense about the manuscript being evil was just that: *nonsense*. Peter scoffed. There was nothing to be afraid of. The book was a real, factual item created by the hands of humans and not by some imaginary demons.

Peter brushed off the rude and very awkward encounter and stashed the book back into his daypack. At the very least, he had planned his day thinking Edda would be more open to discussing the old manuscript and its origins. He would have been able to get answers and feel confident in its story enough to satisfy his curiosity. However, it seemed the fates conspired against him, leaving Peter grasping at innuendos and misconceptions.

Peter pointed himself toward the center of old San Cielo. It would be cathartic to visit the ruins of the church where he had stumbled the day before, and it was a good place to pick up further clues as to the mysterious book's alleged author.

After weaving through various groups of tourists, Peter found himself standing in the same spot as the day before—directly across from the remains of the ancient house of worship. The dilapidated old ruin had not changed in his mind. The grounds of the church were overgrown, the building's roof sat open to the elements, and the heavy, oaken entry doors were unhinged and rotting away. The crumbling façade, complete with broken stained-glass windows, gave the old church all the hallmarks of being the creepiest place to visit on a late-night dare.

From his vantage, Peter could discern nothing out of the ordinary. The outer walls contained a few chiseled reliefs that appeared interesting, and the wooden doors contained intricate carvings, but nothing really stood out as being definitive enough to cause an illusion.

Unsatisfied, Peter waited for a break in traffic and sprinted across the road. His senses rang as he came near the spot where he had passed out, but Peter fought through the sensation and was otherwise fine. When he reached the sidewalk in front of the old

building, he was stopped from going further by the warning barricades placed to keep tourists and curious onlookers, such as himself,
from entering the dangerous grounds. The ancient ruin looked safe
enough to him, and after doing a thorough scan of the area for police,
Peter stepped past the barricades and entered the property.

The grass and weeds were higher in some places than Peter was
tall. He pushed his way through until he found himself on the stone
steps leading to the unhinged doors. They were chained shut, but the
skewed doors stood enough ajar for Peter to get a partially obstructed
view of the inside of the church. He could see what was left of the
entry vestibule, but nothing else.

Peter backed away from the front of the church and moved
around to the side of the ancient building. The broken stained-glass
windows were set high off the ground, but in one place, a piece of
wall had fallen and provided the perfect step to see into the main
nave area of the house of worship.

Peter peered in. Heavy roof beams and broken slate tiles littered
the floor. The debris was lumped together with the remains of
shattered, wooden pews in the center of the room. He noticed pieces
of broken candlesticks mixed in with the rubble. They must not have
been valuable to looters as the corrosive patina they carried gave
away their cheap bronze metal. No altar or effigies were present
anywhere in the old church. From the look of it, the building was
deconsecrated long ago and picked clean.

Peter was disappointed. The interior offered him no new
insights over that of the exterior. He maneuvered himself to jump

down from his perch but stopped when the distinct sound of breaking glass came from inside the church. He studied the far wall and the small shards of stained glass that remained in the window casings. In one corner of the opening, nearest to where the altar would have stood, was a face. It took Peter a moment for his brain to assimilate the information. It was not an illusion or a trick of light but the face of a little boy—and the child blinked. Peter recognized him as the same young man from the previous day's encounter. Peter's anger flashed. He was nearly killed trying to save the little beggar from passing cars and now the boy was mocking him as if nothing had ever happened.

Peter stumbled off the makeshift perch. "Stay right there—don't move! I want to talk to you!" he yelled, before setting off through the tall grass and weeds to circumnavigate the ruin. The towering flora gave way to smaller weeds as he traversed from the soft soil at the front of the church to the hardpan scrabble that made up the rear grounds. He rounded the corner in time to see the small boy scamper up and over the mud-brick enclosure wall.

Peter did not slow his pursuit. His only chance to catch up to the beggar child was to use his greater stride length to its full advantage. He reached the wall and jumped into the air, planting a sneaker halfway up its six feet of vertical height. He then used his considerable momentum to pull himself over the top. It was then that Peter realized the ground on the other side sloped down steeply. The topography behind the church enclosure was significantly lower in elevation than at the building's front. He fell headlong down the scrubby hill, barely missing the trunk of a large oak tree. Bruised but not badly hurt, Peter fumbled around for his glasses that had come off during the tumble.

San Cielo had been constructed in various stages over the years. The church and kitschy shops of the original village were significantly older than the bulk of the contemporary city. Across the street from where Peter lay was the modern-day San Cielo. Most of the town's influence came from the early- to middle-twentieth century. Familiar, symmetrical street blocks delineated the city's boundaries. Paved roads and the use of manufactured materials in the building process spoke to architecture reminiscent of the 1930s. San Cielo must have seen a revival period during that time as the newer town bore a definite art deco flavor. A few cars were parked along the streets, but it was mostly quiet and devoid of tourists. This portion of San Cielo was the everyday center of working and shopping for the locals.

The little boy stood on the street corner diagonally opposite to where Peter came to rest. The child was grinning ear-to-ear with his eyes fixed on the disheveled man.

Peter rose to his feet, adjusted his glasses, and dusted off his clothes. He gestured to the boy. "Now stay there, okay? I just want to talk—that's all."

The young man cocked his head to the side and smiled as if trying to understand the tourist. He opened his mouth and said something, but the words were too faint for Peter to hear. The little

boy ran up the block and looked back to see if the man was following him.

Peter gave chase. He sprinted across the street and made an
effort to catch the child at mid-block, but the young boy was too fast,
reaching the far corner before Peter could gain the sidewalk.

The little boy stopped and turned to taunt the much older man
with laughs and gestures designed to bring shame to the pursuer's
obvious lack of athletic prowess.

Winded, Peter moved slowly up the sidewalk in an attempt to
close the distance between them covertly. "You run really fast, kid,
you know?" he chided, breathing heavily. Peter inched closer and
held out his hands as if to signify he had no weapons and intended no
harm. "I only want to talk." The nearer he got to the young man, the
more ill Peter felt. A ringing rose to fill his ears and his vision closed
in around him. Peter's head ached and he went flush with a cold
sweat as it pushed its way onto every surface of his body. His
balance waivered and he found it increasingly difficult to move
forward.

The little boy held his ground and watched with interest as the
older man began to feel the full effects of his incapacitation. As Peter
staggered his way closer, the child calmly spoke a few words that
were inaudible and darted around the corner, out of sight.

Fighting his disorientation, Peter pushed himself forward in a
final effort to catch the beggar, but a loud *CRACK* echoing through
the narrow confines of the downtown street stopped him. From
above, a large piece of cornice molding broke free and fell toward

Peter. He lurched out of the way, tumbling into a heap on the concrete sidewalk and narrowly escaping the wrath of the granite façade. He rolled onto his back and waited for his head to clear. After a few moments, the ringing subsided and Peter's vision returned to normal. He raised his head and adjusted his glasses. The side street was empty and the boy was gone. "That little bastard."

Peter examined the fallen cornice. Hewn upon the granite were a number of carved-relief cherubs. Grouped together at what was once the exact corner of the building, the cherubs, with their chubby checks and mischievous smiles, stared lifelessly back at Peter as if mocking him. He smacked the playful cherubs' faces with his hand and used them as an advantage point to get to his feet.

The buildings along the side street were two-story. The lower portion of the structures once contained shops and small businesses that overlooked the road through large windows. Most were empty, and by the looks of it, they had been for some time. Above the shops sat residences. Some of the properties had signs of habitation and appeared to be active homes, but most, like the shops, sat in disrepair. Directly across the street from Peter was one of the few open stores. The proprietor of the business stood in the window and studied Peter as if to confirm the tourist had not been injured.

Peter was immediately taken by the woman gazing back at him. Her burgundy hair was short and angled forward in an a-line bob that further pronounced her sharp facial features. The woman's large violet eyes stood out above her aquiline nose and curt small mouth. She wore a tight, off-white pencil skirt and a deep red blouse that hugged her slim and athletic curves. Jet-black, kitten heel pumps made her appear taller than she actually was and rounded out her serious, business-type look. The woman was quite fetching and oozed confidence.

The woman pointed at Peter and said something through the storefront glass he could not quite make out. She said it again, but all he could do was shake his head. Visibly irritated at the communication difficulties, the woman walked around to the front door and opened it. "Are you okay? Do you need help?"

The first thing Peter noticed was her clean and crystal-clear command of the English language. She had an upward lilt to her voice that made it positively bewitching to listen to. The other thing that stood out to Peter was her sincere and seemingly heartfelt concern for a total stranger. Most individuals would not have given him a second look once they realized he was unharmed. She not only took the time to check on him but was clearly distressed as well.

When there was no response, she queried again, "That old building has been crumbling for years. It's a wonder it hasn't killed anyone." When there was no response, she followed with, "You hit your head pretty hard, I see?"

"Huh?" Peter came to his senses. "I'm—" he started, and then visually checked for injuries, "I'm okay—I think."

The woman smiled. "You don't look so good. Would you like to come in and sit down—have something to drink?"

Peter hesitated, wondering what his wife would think of the offer. A beautiful woman was asking him to share a drink, and he felt

Chapter 8

suddenly guilty, as if accepting the shopkeeper's charity would somehow endanger his relationship with his wife. It was a silly thing to think about. Renée would not find out, nor did she need to know on a voluntary basis. He was simply accepting an offer of kindness. Nonetheless, Peter was apprehensive. "Yes—please."

Peter crossed the street and introduced himself, holding out a friendly, but professional hand to shake. "I'm Peter."

The woman stood in the doorway and shook Peter's hand delicately. "Kea. Very nice to meet you, please come in."

Peter followed Kea into the store, the shopkeeper's bell ringing as the door closed behind them. His anxiety quickly left him when he detected the odor of stale and musty books. Peter scanned the small shop. Shelves, crammed full of books, covered the walls. Freestanding racks overflowing with manuscripts occupied the center floor space with even more books and periodicals stuffed into the corners.

Kea gestured to tables and chairs next to the front windows. "Please sit down. I'll get you something to drink," she said and disappeared up a flight of wooden stairs at the rear of the store.

Peter unslung his daypack and took a seat. His eyes perused the nearby racks for interesting manuscripts. He was struck by how old the books were. Most were centuries old. Some were known collector's items, while others were only rumored to be in existence. Peter grabbed one of the manuscripts off a nearby shelf and thumbed through it.

"I see you appreciate old books," Kea remarked, carrying a silver tray with a tall bottle and two glasses.

"This is incredible," Peter replied, barely able to contain his enthusiasm. "It's a first edition *Don Quixote*."

Kea nodded and set the tray down on the table.

"There," Peter said, pointing to the bookshelf nearest him. "I see a *Filostrato*. And there," he said, gesturing to the top of a nearby pile, "that's a *De remediis*."

"Yes," Kea replied, taking a seat across from Peter. "I've collected many books over the years."

"They're in pristine condition. What do you do with them?"

Kea nodded and poured Peter a glass of mineral water. "I buy them, I sell them—sometimes I'll barter if there's something I want."

"It must be fate or something," Peter said, rummaging through his daypack and producing the old manuscript. "Can you tell me about this book?"

Kea's character changed visibly at the sight of the old tome, but after a few moments, her polite demeanor returned. "I'd love to," she replied and took the book from Peter. She flipped the manuscript over and inspected the binding. Kea caressed the heavy leather covers and examined the coarse stitching. She thumbed through the thick parchment while scrutinizing the handwritten text. Once Kea was confident of her analysis, she said, "The monk Nicholas wrote this book."

"Impressive," Peter replied. "How did you know?"

"It's impossible to escape the story of the monk Nicholas." Kea smiled. "This *is* San Cielo, of course."

Peter nodded at his own ignorance. "Yes—I'm sorry. What can you tell me about him and this book?"

Kea handed the manuscript back to Peter and cocked an eyebrow. "What do you want to know?" She filled her glass with mineral water and took a small sip. "He had a very dark and troubled past."

"I would appreciate anything you could tell me."

Gracefully, Kea rose out of her chair and walked the few feet to a shelf of books. She sifted through several old volumes before pulling out the largest of the group. Kea brought the book back to the table and opened it to an illumination within the text.

Peter scrutinized the illuminated manuscript. The painted picture was that of a stately monk, wearing robes and holding a cross. Above the figure's tonsure-cut hair was the familiar aura-like halo that adorned many religious images of the period. Peter was struck by how similar the image looked to that of the man who had given him the book in the basement of Edda's antique store. For fear of sounding insane, he did not mention it to Kea, but the resemblance was unsettling. Along the bottom of the illumination, hand scrawled and barely visible amongst the border filigree, was some Latin text. Peter read aloud, "Brother Nicholas."

"It's refreshing to see someone appreciate the fine art of Latin as much as I do," Kea praised. "Did you learn in school?"

"I teach history," Peter answered meekly. "Archaeology is my main passion, but I never liked digging very much."

"A professor?" Kea said. "Very interesting, indeed."

Peter was embarrassed, but kept quiet so as not to confirm his lower echelon standing in his vocation as a junior college professor. Though technically speaking, Kea was correct; his current position *was* a faculty professorship.

Kea was calm and spoke evenly, "Nicholas was taken in as a child and lived at the San Pietro monastery for many years." She gestured off to a distant part of the country. "It's on the other side of Rome." She paused and took a small drink from her glass. "Nicholas lived a peaceful life. He studied, worked, and prayed. By all accounts, he had proven himself worthy to the brotherhood." Kea took Peter's manuscript and opened it atop the illuminated book. "One night, he was caught by the other monks chanting and crying— writing in this book."

"Chanting?" Peter asked. "Worshipping the Devil?"

Kea shook her head. "Not according to Nicholas, but the monks jailed him and held an inquisition. Nicholas told a strange tale of visitations by angels who instructed him to write this book. It was nearly finished when he was discovered."

"They would have considered it heresy."

"Yes," Kea replied, "and they ordered him to burn at the stake for his sins." She held up Peter's old manuscript. "His work was to be destroyed with him to purify it from this world."

Peter flipped to the end of the book. The Latin text ended nicely on the last row of the last page. "But the book is complete and he lived—how could that be?"

Chapter 8

"The night before his execution, he was freed by a few of his sympathetic brothers." Kea smiled. "They believed Nicholas was telling the truth and burning him at the stake would go against God's wishes, so they let him go."

"And he came here?"

"He needed to escape and money to live," Kea replied. "San Cielo was on the pilgrim trail to the Holy Land. He wrote prayer books and sold them to passing soldiers."

Peter flipped through the indecipherable text. "This just leaves me with more questions."

"Once Nicholas completed the book, he became obsessed with the idea that demons were after him to possess it. Visions haunted him day and night."

"And so he killed himself."

"After years of enduring the torment, he grew mad and burned himself alive."

"All because of a book that's impossible to read," Peter said, flipping the old manuscript closed.

Kea placed her hand on Peter's and helped him reopen the book. "Look at these individual letters," she said, guiding his hand across the old parchment. "They're here for a reason. Nicholas inscribed them for some purpose—I'm sure he knew exactly what this book was for."

Peter felt enthralled by Kea's touch. The sense of her warm hand on his was intoxicating. He felt like a schoolboy on his first date and could not remember the last time he had felt that way about a woman. He forced himself to quell his enthusiasm and concentrate. "He's dead; we may never find out what the book was about."

"There are rumors—stories really."

"What stories?"

"Some say the book is imbued with God's power."

Peter scoffed at the insinuation. "A magical book?"

Kea noticed the sarcasm in Peter's voice. "You don't believe in God?"

"It's just a fairy tale—a supernatural being created to make us feel more significant, nothing more."

"You're an interesting man," Kea responded. "Faith is such a small thing to ask, yet you choose to ignore it."

"That's not it," Peter countered. "It's just that I prefer to see things in a more scientific light—tangible proof, that's all."

"Nicholas believed he was doing God's will," Kea said, gesturing to Peter's manuscript. "The book is proof of it."

"He was a monk, raised in a monastery—he must've been a believer."

"Of course he was," Kea pressed. "So much so that most scholars assumed the manuscript had burned with him—that Nicholas's self-immolation proved that he intended to bring the book in front of God to read it after his death. That you have come across it now is quite curious, indeed. Something or someone must have intervened."

Peter sat back and pondered Kea's words. He was captivated by her charms, but to suggest that a book could traverse into a fairy tale afterlife was a little off-putting. Death, as Peter thought of it, was the end—lights out, darkness, your life extinguished—nothing more. To believe in a physical realm outside of your Earthly existence was natural, although extremely misguided. He was certain that life beyond the grave was nothing more than a fanciful desire conjured from the deepest part of our psyches meant to assuage our fear of the unknown, or as the case would merit, our deep-seated fear of nothing. Humans had long endured troubled dreams, and in their ignorance, they had invented religion to explain them away. Peter was an educated man and not a fool.

"I can see you're having a problem with that."

"No, it's not that," Peter replied. "It's just hard for me to believe Nicholas gave his life for nothing—superstition."

"To Nicholas, it was as real as anything this mortal world could offer."

Peter understood her point of view, even if he did not agree with the assessment.

"Perhaps you should take a look for yourself?" Kea mused.

"Look—at what?"

"Where Nicholas lived."

Peter's curiosity soared. "He lived nearby?"

"But of course. Nicholas was a resident of San Cielo for many years."

Peter reminded himself of the collapsed church, and his excitement waned. "There's probably not much left."

"Not much," Kea agreed. "Perhaps you will see something others have missed?"

Peter's breath left him momentarily as he struggled to find the words he wanted to say. "I would like to go—although it would be better to have someone knowledgeable show me the site," he said and then sheepishly backpedaled. "I'm sorry, that's not what I meant."

Kea blushed. "I would like that very much; however, I think you have other problems," she said, pointing to Peter's wedding band.

Peter spun the worn, white gold ring around his finger. "It's not what I meant," he said. Then hoping to deflect her train of thought, he added, "Which way do I go?"

Kea pointed down the side street, away from town. "Not far," she replied. "A few kilometers. Nicholas's house is part of a nature preserve now. You should have no problems if you follow the signs."

"Thank you for everything," Peter said, packing up the manuscript and making his way to the front door.

"It was my pleasure to meet you, Peter," Kea said, extending her hand to shake through the open door. "You must come back and tell me everything."

"Yes, I will."

Kea closed the door behind him and waved goodbye through the glass.

Peter cursed at himself for his blunder. He could not help but feel a little bit dejected at the way things had gone. The whole situation did nothing but remind him of his current marital problems.

Chapter 8

Regardless of what opportunities life presented, it would always find a way to beat him back down. He adjusted his daypack, waved meekly back to Kea, and started his journey.

The paved side street out of San Cielo turned into a rural road that ambled its way through the low hills of the countryside. Narrow shoulders and inattentive drivers made the hike dangerous. Cars raced by and forced him off the road several times, but Peter persevered and after more than an hour, he arrived at his destination.

It was not much to look at. Crumbling walls about waist-high were all that remained of the small, rectangular building. The old dwelling sat in the middle of a meadow lined by tall trees. Beyond the tree line, Peter could hear day hikers taking in the trails of the nearby park. He approached the ruin and surveyed the site.

The remnants of the building were about the size of a small bedroom. The ground around its exterior resembled a moonscape. Holes of various sizes had been dug all along the dwelling's perimeter. Peter sighed at the damage. It was commonplace to find that looters had ransacked an archaeological dig site before proper studies could take place.

Within the building's crumbled walls, Peter found the same pattern of digging along the dirt floor. The only interior structure remaining that he could discern was a set of stone blocks that may have been a table or bed that had once existed in antiquity.

Peter was disappointed. He thought there may have been something in the dwelling that could have given him more insight into the mysterious book—some telltale inscription or hidden alcove. It seemed that everything having to do with the monk Nicholas was ordinary and commonplace.

Peter leaned against a broken wall and contemplated his long walk back to town. Raised voices coming from the trees behind the ruin got his attention. He did not give the voices much consideration, but several yards away he could see what appeared to be a person standing in the undergrowth. Low tree branches obscured Peter's vision, but the figure of a person was unmistakable. He moved to get a better angle on the interloper, but the individual backed away from the clearing and went deeper into the woods. A familiar feeling ran through Peter as he walked to the area to investigate.

Peter pulled the branches back and stepped through the first line of foliage. The light from the clearing dimmed and he adjusted his eyes to see within the shaded, darker recesses of the forest. There, on the other side of the brush and staring back at him, was the little boy.

Peter stopped dead in his tracks. He was several miles outside of San Cielo and was certain no one could have followed him. The mountain road Peter had traveled on to the preserve contained several long stretches in it where he was able to look back for approaching cars, and he never saw any sign of the little boy.

The child stood a few yards away with his hands at his sides. His demeanor was one of quiet delight. He grinned at Peter and made no effort to move deeper into the woods.

Chapter 8

"So you followed me out here, huh?"

The young man offered no response.

"Do you speak English?"

The little boy adjusted his standing position, but did not reply.

"Look, I don't know what you want from me, but leave me alone."

Again, the child did not give any indication that he had heard or understood anything the older man was saying.

Peter stepped closer to the child and immediately felt his senses start to rebel. He retreated and shook his head to clear it. Keeping his distance, he pulled out his wallet and held a few Euro notes for the boy to see. "Money?" Peter asked, shaking the bills. "Is that what you want?"

The young child nodded and moved toward the man.

The familiar ringing noise returned and clouded Peter's mind, but he held on to his senses in order to rid himself of the young menace once and for all. "That's right," he said, losing some focus in his peripheral vision. "You want some money and then you'll go away."

The boy stepped to within a stride of Peter's outstretched hand.

Peter sweated profusely. He was lightheaded and his knees were beginning to buckle, but he persevered. "Go on—take it," he said. "Just leave me alone—please."

The little boy grinned and raised his arm, but instead of taking the money, the boy snatched Peter's wallet. He retreated a few yards, holding the billfold up for the older man to see.

"Really funny, little man," Peter said, fighting the urge to pass out. "Give it back."

The little boy smiled and opened his mouth to reply, but nothing audible emerged. He turned away and darted off, deeper into the forest.

Peter realized it was not a game. He had been the target of the child all along. "Stop, you little thief!" he yelled, but the words did nothing to slow the young man's pace. Peter mustered what strength he could and began his pursuit.

The forest floor was rolling and uneven. Dry streambeds and shallow glens broke the terrain at irregular intervals, while trees and thick brush blocked most avenues to pedestrians. The only dedicated access through the woods was the well-worn trail system used by hikers.

Peter panted heavily as he chased after the little boy. His daypack pounded against his body making the effort even more laborious, but the longer the chase lasted, the more he was gaining on the child. He used his bigger strides to win out over the speed and stamina of the youth. Ahead of Peter, the little boy veered onto one of the designated paths and sprinted past an elderly couple. "Stop him!" Peter cried out. "He stole my wallet!"

Not understanding English, the couple turned to see what the commotion was, and too slow to react, did nothing to stop the child as he ran by.

Chapter 8

Feeling a bit better, Peter pushed himself faster. He managed a small, "Sorry," as he bypassed the couple and continued after the thief.

Ahead, the young man diverged from the trail and made a beeline to a blind hillock. He bolted up the small slope and launched himself into the air and out of sight below the crest.

Peter slowed as he neared the crest. When he saw the boy running along the floor of the glen below, he jumped off, landing in the soft earth. The boy obviously knew the woods better than he did, and Peter could not allow him to get the upper hand.

The boy slowed at another hillock and turned to see if Peter was still chasing him. He smiled and threw himself to the forest floor below.

Peter was willing to take a chance to gain distance on the boy and bounded off the rise, landing heavily on the ground. He stumbled, losing his footing momentarily, but continued on.

Panting himself, the little boy stopped on another rise and stared back at Peter. The child smiled grandly as if toying with the older man.

Peter stopped short of the child and held out his hand. "Just give me back the wallet, and we can forget the whole thing."

The little boy nodded and mouthed inaudible words to his pursuer. He turned nonchalantly away from Peter and leapt over the crest.

Peter ran after the boy. Reaching the top of the hill, he took a mighty leap into the air and immediately wished he had not. The gentle dell he thought would be on the other side of the rise was instead a deep defile. Once Peter was in midair, there was no turning back. Below him was a downed tree with broken shards of wood jutting up from its massive trunk. Standing next to the tree, and grinning ear to ear, was the little boy.

Peter tried in vain to adjust his course, but there was nothing he could do. His slight frame slammed into the stump with great force. He screamed out in agony as the broken wood pierced his chest and broke through his ribcage. In shock and immobile, Peter came face to face with the boy. The ringing returned with a vengeance and he experienced a euphoric lightheadedness that coupled itself to the severe pain of his injury. He lay helpless, impaled on the stump of the tree as he went into shock.

The little boy nodded and smiled at the older man. He bent close to Peter's ear and whispered, *"Me sequere."*

Peter gasped for breath. The cacophony in his head grew more intense as he tried to comprehend what the child was saying. He knew the phrase, but could not give it meaning.

The little boy laughed at the stricken man. "Follow me," he said in perfect English.

There, on the tree and amidst the complete confusion of his embattled senses, Peter drew his last breath and died.

Chapter 9

Peter was numb to the unbroken wall of blackness that surrounded him. His consciousness floated in an immeasurable state of nothingness. He had no working senses and it was as if everything about his physical being had been suspended. Peter reasoned that since his brain was functioning properly, he must still exist, but the nature and state of the medium he currently occupied was a mystery.

Peter's accident in the forest blazed forth in his memory. He relived the fall and the pain over and over until it seemed utterly surreal. He attempted to rein in his thoughts—tried to bring them back from the brink of madness. Peter focused on what he knew. He was severely hurt in a mishap—that much was certain, but what took place after he blacked out? Peter did not know. His mind started to replay the accident again and he rebelled, forcing himself past it. He could remember the incident and that meant he must still be alive. It made sense to him, but why could he not move his arms and legs? Why could he not see or hear anything?

Peter had heard stories about people spending years in a coma after a serious accident and awakening to find their family members, having aged dramatically, standing over them. Doctors often talked about brain function while being comatose and identifying an individual who might survive a coma versus someone in a persistent vegetative state. Relief flooded Peter's consciousness. He must be in a coma brought on by his mishap in the forest. He was seriously injured and his body had shut down, placing him into some kind of suspended animation. He used that information to quell his mind and to channel his concentration on the blackness. He searched for any sign, familiar or otherwise, that may shed light on his current predicament, but he lost focus and drifted.

After hours amidst the unbroken oblivion, the smallest of sensations niggled at Peter's brain. It started out so small that he barely realized it came from somewhere external to his own being. He could not make it out clearly, but he could definitely *feel* something. Peter received the faintest impression that he was falling. Not fast, but slowly. He redirected all his efforts on that fleeting, vertigo-inducing effect. The speed at which he fell was gently increasing. There were no physical markers in the realm of blackness with which to gauge his rate of passage, but somewhere deep within his consciousness, Peter knew that he was falling and that it was happening at an ever-quickening pace.

Little by little, Peter's eyes adjusted to the darkness. Dim and blurry at first, his sight sharpened and fixed on a faint white smudge against the backdrop of black. It was faraway and almost imperceptible at first, but the bright light grew in intensity as he fell toward it. Peter strained to see the area surrounding the light. He tried in vain to make out the origin of the brilliance, but the light overwhelmed everything around it. It was as if the darkness ended where the light began. As Peter neared, he could tell that the illumination was projecting an immense amount of power—more so than that of the sun. Yet, the off-white light was not blinding. There was no warmth from the glow; everything about it was cold and devoid of feeling.

Peter's momentum slowed and his aspect changed. He was no longer falling; instead, Peter was flying in an upright position, fully standing, toward the light. He attempted to determine what force was guiding him, but everything about where he was remained elusive.

Slowly, the darkness began to change. The black nothingness morphed into a rough, rock-hewn appearance similar to that of an underground tunnel. The faceted edges of the stone glinted like diamonds as Peter's position changed with every passing moment.

A reflection of light off the rim of his glasses caught Peter's attention. He crossed his eyes to see the nose bridge of his eyewear. With a little more effort, he found himself able to scan his immediate area.

Peter inspected his body. There was no sign of the injury to his chest; the telltale vestige of his accident in the forest was missing. His clothes on the other hand were foreign to him. They were the same as he remembered, but the fabric's colors were muted. It was difficult to tell exactly in the peculiar light, but the colors exhibited all the signs of being subdued with a gray dye or some opaque overlay.

Peter shifted his attention to his appendages. All his limbs were present and articulated correctly. His legs and feet hung underneath him as he flew forward. They were unmoving and lifeless, but remained attached to his body. Held tightly across his chest was another curiosity: the old, leather-bound manuscript of the monk Nicholas. He had trouble believing what he was seeing and blinked his eyes slowly in an effort to clear the image, but the book remained. Peter had no doubt it was the same manuscript, but how it wound up in his arms was vexing. He concentrated on his hands and tried to let go of the tome, but nothing happened. The sight of the book was troubling, but Peter quickly rationalized a plausible theory: during the violent and stress-laden incident with the tree stump, he latched on to his most recent and intense memory, which was the old manuscript. He had been working at trying to figure out the book's origins and it must have lingered with him into his unconscious, coma-like state.

The light ahead dimmed and then brightened back to its original luminescence. After a few moments of steady brilliance, the light dimmed again and then flickered with an irregular pulsing pattern. As Peter drew closer, the light's perturbation grew more frenetic with fewer long-duration interruptions. Strange shapes and shadows moved across the light causing the variation in brightness. He saw the shadows approach the source of the illumination and then fade away to nothing. It was disturbing to witness and he could not be sure, but it looked as if the light was consuming the mysterious figures.

Peter's momentum slowed and he found himself no longer flying forward. The unseen force deposited him, standing upright, on the rough-hewn rock of the tunnel floor. Still lacking sensation in his extremities, Peter forced his mind to reconnect to his limbs. At first, his arms and legs were nonresponsive, but after several attempts, he managed to regain some control.

Peter's first task was to release his hold on the book. He struggled to move his hands, but found it nearly impossible. He could feel the book touching his fingers, but could do nothing about it. It was as if the same unseen force that had influenced his journey through the tunnel was swaying his will. With effort, he moved his legs and tried to back away from the light, but again, his body failed him. Peter found he could walk forward under his own power, but any step backward was met by an unyielding resistance. Frightened by the obstinate force, he stopped moving entirely. It was decidedly more agreeable to simply stand firm and watch the bizarre forms move into and out of the brilliance ahead than to actually partake in their strange behavior.

Peter's noncompliance was short-lived as he found himself buffeted and jostled from side to side. Startled, he turned his head to discover an old man smiling back at him. Peter panicked and tried to back away but bumped up against another individual behind him. He turned full-circle looking for an escape route, but every possible avenue was blocked by hundreds of individuals moving forward through the tunnel and toward the cold light.

A hand touched Peter's arm. He jumped and tried to spin away, but could not. The wrinkled and weathered hand belonged to the old man walking beside him. "Nothing to fear, young man," the old man said in a weak and scratchy voice. "This isn't the end."

"The *end?*"

"Death," the old man answered, reassuring Peter with a gentle pat on his arm. "It's a new beginning for all of us."

"No, no, no," Peter replied, shaking his head. "I'm not dead—I'm in a coma." He gestured to the old man. "You," he started and then pointed to the entire crowd. "They're simply manifestations of my injured mind—nothing more."

The old man laughed. "I had a heart attack and passed right there on my front porch. I knew it was my time to go, that's why I was sittin' there."

An old woman walking behind them chimed in, "I had pancreatic cancer—at least I said goodbye to my family before I went."

Many nearby lauded the woman's mention of that fact.

"No," Peter said, shaking his head. "I can't believe—"

"See there," the old man said, gesturing to the only other young person in the crush: a gruff young man about twenty-five years old, covered in tattoos and minding his own business while trying to make his way forward through the crowd. "Young man, what's your name?"

"Butch," the twenty-something answered hoarsely.

116

"Do you believe you're dead?"

Clearly annoyed, Butch did not answer.

"Might I ask how?" the old man pressed.

"Liquor store robbery—owner had a gun," Butch snorted.

"Don't worry," the old man replied. "Redemption lies ahead—it's not too late."

Butch shook off the inspirational talk. "Too late for me, old man."

The old man laughed lightly at the reply and turned back to Peter. "He'll be okay. Forgiveness is at hand for all of us."

Peter could not respond—he did not know how to respond. He was sure this entire scenario was part of some dream—some nightmare caused by his injuries back in the forest. Peter looked down at the manuscript. If he were dead, why would he be carrying the old book? The answer quickly came to him: it was an illusion. There could not be an afterlife, and even if there was, he would not be able to take something from the physical world into the spiritual realm. It was not possible. This was a simple hallucination that he was undergoing while incapacitated. Peter had been thinking about Nicholas's book when he was injured and his mind extended his reality and created a new one. Soon, either he would die or he would find himself waking up. It was a simple solution, but he needed to be cautious and keep his wits about him so as to not become part of a self-induced, reinforcing fantasy.

The crush of the crowd forced Peter closer to the source of the illumination. He could clearly see the cause of the distortions.

Throngs of individuals moved into the brilliance and temporarily blocked the light as they passed through it, which caused the variations in output. It was a doorway of some kind and Peter thought it might subconsciously signal an end to his life. He did not want anything to do with it. He tried to back away, but the push from the others was too great. The light was cold and uninviting. It brought a sense of foreboding to Peter. He felt naked and alone, as if his troubles were about to be exposed for all to see. One by one, the individuals around him disappeared into the radiance. As Peter drew nearer, he clutched at the book and held it in front of him to stop his advance, but the mass of people drove him forward and over the threshold.

The tunnel opened onto a large square in the middle of a huge city. Tall buildings constructed from rough stone blocks rose higher than anything Peter had ever seen before. The buildings went on, street by street, in every direction for miles. The sky above the mass of congested cityscape glowed in a twilight hue that was not quite day and not exactly night.

Peter lowered the burden of the manuscript to a more comfortable position near his waist and took in the awe-inspiring sight in front of him. The first thing that stood out was the color variations. He noted that not everything was as dull and gray as the mass of people that streamed from the tunnel exit. Splashes of intensely colored fabric highlighted the otherwise lifeless rock façades of the town's buildings. Drab individuals who milled about the town's square also bore vibrant multihued swatches. All around him, Peter's eyes met with a chance encounter of vibrant color. A banner draped over a wall, a deep brown cloak, leather boots, even bright jewelry. It was difficult to process, similar to an incomplete colorization of a famed black and white movie. Yet, the entire setting made sense to him in a strange, convoluted way. In an effort to normalize itself, Peter's brain conjured a complete medieval town along with citizens to fill it. He was in San Cielo recently so the surroundings were familiar to him. The lapses in color were simply incomplete or jumbled information associated with his traumatic event.

Peter shrugged off the discrepancies of his delusions and investigated the source of the brilliance. To his disbelief, two glowing angels stood several yards away. Their robes and skin were awash in the same joyless light that bathed the tunnel exit. At nearly ten-feet tall, the angels towered significantly over their human counterparts. Their wings were partially visible over their heads and tucked in neatly behind them. The angels had nondescript facial features and appeared neither male nor female. Their stoic demeanor made it hard for Peter to discern any underlying emotion; however, their eyes told a different story. The angelic beings threw piercing gazes at each new arrival passing into the town square as if weighing the worth of each newcomer based upon their appearance.

Peter slowed his pace and watched the interactions of the crowd. Some were in awe of the two angels and paid homage to them, shouting and rejoicing as they entered the town square. Others, frightened by the sight, withdrew from the main flow of arrivals. Two men, both wearing purple tunics over underlying medieval garb, stepped in and guided the wayward individuals back into line before resuming their positions marshaling the crowd off to the left of the overseeing angels. A woman standing to the side of the two men grabbed Butch out of the crowd and spoke to him. Peter tried to eavesdrop but could not make out the woman's words. Whatever was said, Butch seemed pleased and was taken in a different direction than the rest of the new arrivals.

Peter's misgivings about the whole situation swelled at the odd behavior and he stopped moving forward. The crowd buffeted him, but he stood his ground and angled his way to the fringes of the main flow to let the faster individuals by. In that position, Peter had an unobstructed view of the two angels with which to study them. They showed little concern that Butch had been removed from the throng or that several newcomers were being denied responses to their seemingly innocuous questions. The angels' single interest seemed to be with the ongoing crush of people exiting the tunnel.

Standing to one side and very near the two angels was a middle-aged man wearing a brown robe. Peter studied the man's features. He was no more than fifty years old, but the man's broken posture and profoundly furrowed face belied his short lifespan. He had a full head of gray hair that curled at its unkempt ends. His brown eyes were contentious and angry.

Peter recognized the man as the monk Nicholas. It was not an exact match since the man standing before him was much older and more haggard than the image detailed within the illuminated text in Kea's bookstore. Still, the man was indeed the suicidal monk. Peter rubbed his eyes with one hand and shook his head. He had a difficult time believing his illusions could have penetrated so completely into his comatose state. The accident in the woods must have done more damage than he had previously thought.

Peter did not know how to proceed. The old manuscript he clutched was the monk's property. His instincts screamed to keep walking and ignore Nicholas, but Peter's unquenched curiosity won out and he held the old tome up for all to see. He tried to rationalize his actions, thinking that if he could not force himself out of his coma, perhaps he could end it by giving the book back to its rightful owner. By willingly removing the reason for his illusion, Peter might close the loop and allow himself to wake from his nightmare. Holding the book aloft, he stepped from the periphery of the moving mass of individuals and toward the angels.

The mood changed dramatically and a sense of despair and suffering descended over the square. The angels and the monk noticeably stiffened at the sudden emergence of Peter from the crowd.

Witnessing the newcomer step out of line, one of the men in medieval garb tried to intervene, but Peter persevered. He held the manuscript high and called out to the monk, "I have your book."

Nicholas eyed Peter and nodded affirmatively to both of the angels.

Not wanting to insult his delusionary characters, Peter gestured with the old manuscript and said, "You can have it, so I can end this." He adjusted his glasses and took a step forward. "I want to go home, and I think this is the best way to proceed."

Nicholas opened his palms and beckoned Peter closer.

Peter held the book out and stepped forward to close the distance to the old monk, but before he could reach Nicholas, a crystalline spire erupted from the square's cobblestone surface. The translucent structure twisted and contorted its way to loom over the angels and the individuals around them. Once the apparition reached its full height, it grew tendrils that snaked in all directions away from the main trunk. Together, the main trunk and tendrils spawned delicate branches of transparent crystal that sprouted fractal formations resembling leaves. As the metamorphosis slowed, the trunk and branches changed, becoming deeply grooved. The transformation only took a few moments, but there, standing directly in Peter's path, was a life-sized tree made out of crystal.

Peter gawked at the wondrous formation. He thought back to his mishap in the woods, trying to reconcile the apparition with his injury-induced condition. He shook his head and attempted to bypass the blockage, but the tree shuddered and vibrated as he drew near. A high-pitched noise rang out from every branch and leaf. It grew in intensity and forced all those within earshot to retreat.

Peter felt lightheaded and queasy. His vision grew blurry and his knees started to buckle. He fell against the tree, his face pressing into the crystalline grooves of the bark. Panting, he pushed away from the solid mass and peered through the translucent surface to view Nicholas on the opposite side. A distorted and deformed reflection of the monk showed through the uneven structure of the tree's rough outer covering.

Nicholas glared back and frustration coalesced on the middle-aged monk's face. He sheepishly glanced at the angels, as if asking for an explanation, but the angels ignored him and maintained their gaze on Peter. Nicholas lowered his arms and shackles slid into view from beneath his robes. Chains, affixed to the monk's wrist cuffs, trailed behind him and out of sight. Nicholas was not a protected confidant of Peter's imaginary angels but their prisoner.

A strong, meaty hand pulled Peter away from the tree and a deep voice commanded, "Run!"

Disoriented, Peter staggered backward and turned to see who was accosting him.

A large man wearing a dark cloak forced himself between Peter and the tree. The man drew a sword from under his cloak and held it in front of him. He extended his free arm and pushed Peter toward a side alley at one end of the town square. "Run, you fool!"

Unable to support himself, Peter stumbled to the ground. "Who—"

The cold light filling the square ceased. The angels' white exteriors darkened and their features contorted and grew grotesque as they turned into demons. The fine robes that adorned their stately and picturesque physiques gave way to dark leather coverings that hung loosely over their vile and twisted bodies. Their once white and gossamer wings became black and fleshy, stained with age and worn ragged at the edges.

The demons thrust forward to apprehend Peter, but the crystal-line tree's considerable girth stymied their progress.

Peter pointed an incredulous finger at the transformations. "What the hell's going on?"

The larger of the two demons raised a gnarled finger at Peter and barked out in a venomous voice, "That one carries the book—do not let him escape!"

The new arrivals screamed at the sight of the infernal creatures and broke ranks, running in every direction. The clashing of metal reverberated between the buildings. Heated voices shouted orders over the cacophony. Men and women aligned with the demons rushed in, trying to contain the newcomers as well as counter the intruders. Complete chaos enveloped the area around the tunnel exit.

Before Peter could get to his feet, two more cloaked men hoisted him up and ushered him through the pandemonium of the crowd. As they approached the edge of the square, he resisted forcefully and brought the escape attempt to a stop. "Where are you taking me?"

"Danger lurks here," one of the men answered and produced a cloak similar to his own. "Clothe yourself."

"If I refuse?"

The man gestured back to the demons. "They will be your bane."

The burly man who had originally intervened was lashing out with his sword in every direction. He fought the demons head on, trying to keep them occupied while simultaneously dealing heavy blows to humans unfortunate enough to stray within range of his blade. More cloaked men appeared from side streets and alleys. They helped keep the leathery beasts occupied while also slicing down any guards who got in the way. In retaliation, the demons conjured red and green energy and hurled it at the cloaked figures. The intruders took cover wherever they were able and pressed on valiantly, ignoring all dangers.

Peter found the scene unfathomable. History was filled with bits and pieces of the exhibition now on display before him, but he had never personally experienced anything like it. He had no idea whether the conflict was real or imagined, but Peter's sense of fear ratcheted up significantly and he decided to choose the lesser of the two immediate evils. "Fine, I'll play along for now," he responded and donned the cloak over his clothes.

"Now with haste," the cloaked man said and guided Peter at a run into a nearby alley.

The two men took up positions in front of and behind Peter as they made their way through the narrow space between the buildings. This section of the city was dense with tall structures, and only a thin strip of twilight sky peeked out above them. Most of the doors and windows of the stone edifices were shuttered. As they darted past a small intersection, Peter caught a glimpse of what appeared to be a rather strange statue or carving on one corner of a building.

Human heads jutted from the wall, with several sets of arms and legs fused to the rock surface below them. Their posture and positioning suggested that a group of individuals had been melded into the stone of the structure as a decoration.

Peter slowed his pace in an attempt to study the monstrous effigy. As the trio got closer, the sculpture's appendages moved and the hollow and haunting eyes locked with his. As they passed, Peter heard a chorus of weak voices plead, "Save us." His breath left him and his heart raced at the sound. He could not rationalize the grotesque and deformed statuary. Nowhere from his memory could he have conjured the sick and twisted scene. Terrified, he quickened his pace, forcing the two men to run faster.

From behind the three runners came a terrible, high-pitched screeching that echoed through the narrow alleyway.

The lead man hissed, "Sitri!"

The blood-curdling noise only served to increase Peter's level of fear. He searched the area around them, but saw nothing.

The cloaked figure running behind Peter gestured skyward, "He is there."

Silhouetted against the twilight sky was the blacked-out form of one of the demons. He was tracking them, flying just above the building's rooftops. Fear and panic gripped Peter. His muscles tensed, forcing the out-of-shape professor to slow his pace. "I—I can't run anymore."

The lead man ordered Peter forward, "The road ahead is your salvation!"

The alley in front of them made a lazy turn, blocking their view of what lay beyond. The buildings near the corner leaned precipitously over the narrow street to the point of forming a faux ceiling to the corridor. The dim light made the street of the alley dark and the corner darker still.

Their pace slowed as they approached the turn. Peter saw movement between the buildings, but before he could ask what it was, another cloaked individual jumped out and grabbed him. Peter resisted, but the attacker was too strong. He forced Peter to the side of the alley and through an open doorway. Peter lost his balance and fell heavily onto the building's stone floor. The man snorted humorously at the sight and slammed the wooden door shut behind him.

Chapter 10

Exhausted and disoriented, Peter lay quietly listening to the collective clamor outside. The sounds of footsteps, voices, and clattering iron rose to a crescendo and then diminished as the pursuers passed by.

After a few minutes of relative calm, Peter felt it was safe to move around. He righted his glasses and stared into the darkness. The only illumination available in the building came from the twilight sky filtering weakly through the gaps in the wooden door and window shutter. Cradling the book, he got to his feet and pushed on the door—locked. He rattled the shutter—locked as well.

Peter's eyes followed the faint streams of light to the cobblestone floor. It was clean, as if having been recently swept. He scanned the interior space. It was empty, devoid of the usual trappings of a home or an inhabited dwelling. The room was long and narrow—so long in fact, that Peter could not see the other end of it. There were no stairs. The roughly-hewn ceiling continued unabated throughout the structure with no inkling of how one might climb to the floors above.

A weak scratching noise caught Peter's attention. He followed the sound to the floor and picked up movement with his eyes. He squinted through the gloom and brought a large, silver-white rat into focus. It stood on its hind legs and squeaked at Peter. He bent down to get a closer look, but the rodent barked a shrill alarm and retreated to the corner.

The rat trembled and shook violently. High-pitched retching sounds shrieked out from the creature's lungs as its appendages elongated and deformed. The quivering rat stretched and distorted until it morphed into a flat, fur-covered disc. The disc lay in the corner of the room pulsating with each breath. The mass of fur continued to change, growing in thickness and diameter until it resembled an overstuffed pancake. The transfiguration slowed, but as equilibrium seemed assured, the disc lost cohesiveness and melted into an iridescent pool of liquid.

The shimmering fluid spread out thinly on the floor, filling the low areas of the stone surface. Peter knelt warily over the shiny puddle. The pool rose and fell as if it were alive and breathing. Opalescent colors flashed across the aqueous substance, seemingly keeping in time with its physical undulations. Cautiously, Peter stretched out a lone finger to touch the unknown goo.

Sensing the intrusion, the liquid ceased its colorful display and took on the look and consistency of mercury. Waves undulated across its surface creating peaks where slender shapes grew and protruded from the puddle. The forms separated as they rose in height. Delicate filaments of fluid joined together forming thin rivulets that moved hauntingly through the air. Swinging softly and growing in length, they coalesced into a set of proto-limbs around the main trunk of a body. The entire structure found equilibrium half a foot or more shy of Peter's stature. Slowly and deliberately, the self-morphing liquid took on the physical characteristics of an old woman.

Peter gasped. He fought the urge to disconnect himself from his senses and collapse in a broken heap onto the stone floor. For the sake of any possible recovery, Peter knew he had to soldier on and give his illusions some type of context. If he failed to do so, the nightmarish dream might consume Peter, forcing him to wander in his psychosis for all eternity. He took deep breaths and calmed himself. He resolved to meet any adversity head on and not allow anything to sway him. Peter steadied his stance and faced the old woman.

To say the frail-statured woman was old was an understatement—she was ancient. She stood around five-feet tall and her slumping posture only added to the illusion of her diminutive scale. The woman's silver hair was nothing more than an unkempt band of white wisps that ended in ragged ends near the stone floor. The wrinkles in her face, long ago turned into weathered canyons, further attested to her advanced years. Peter found that the woman's eyes were her most striking feature: piercing dark blue with a fierce determination shining within them. Tattered, torn, and wearing through at every seam, the old woman's clothes were nothing more than rags. They were made of coarse brown wool that bore no pattern or even the remains of another color whatsoever. The demeanor she cast was warm, and aside from her extreme age, she could pass for anyone's great-grandmother.

Sensing that the woman posed no threat, Peter relaxed.

The old woman cackled loudly, exposing her decaying teeth. "Not what you were expecting?"

Peter grimaced and shook his head.

"Boo!" the old woman spat.

Peter jumped back.

The old woman gurgled out a laugh. "Frightened of me?"

"Should I be?"

"I'm the least of your worries here," the woman chirped and tottered to the windowsill where she picked up a candle that had been lying hidden in the crook of the shutter. She cupped her hand over the wick and whispered, "I'm sorry." Then, as if on command, the candle flamed to life.

Peter saw no ignition source, but reasoned the old woman probably held a match or lighter in the hand that was hidden from his view. The candle burned normally but made a very faint, strange hissing sound. Peter bent closer to listen and could hear a tiny scream.

The woman took note of Peter's concern and turned her back on him. Unsteadily and under all the power her small frame could muster, the old woman ambled into the depths of the dark room.

"Where are you going?" Peter asked. "I could use a little help here."

"Help?" the woman asked incredulously. "You would ask others?"

Ask others? Peter thought.

"I wanted to see if the stories were true," the old woman grated.

"What?"

The woman cackled loudly in response and continued on her slow journey.

Peter watched the candlelight fade into the distance. He gave a passing thought to staying put, but as she made her way deeper into the building, he felt more alone and afraid than ever. At the very least, Peter thought he could use the woman as a source of information. He gripped the manuscript tightly and chased after her. "Excuse me, do you have a name?"

The old woman stopped and faced Peter. The candle's flickering light cast shadows that danced in the crevices of her wrinkled face. "They call me Isla Dora."

"Okay." Peter nodded. "I'm Peter."

Isla Dora chuckled softly. "Of course you are," she said, returning to her quest to find the end of the room.

"Could you at least tell me where I am?"

"You've arrived where all eventually do."

"Where all—" Peter thought for a moment and his heart leapt. "I'm dead?"

Isla Dora coughed out a hearty chuckle. "*That* is for you to decide."

"You mean I'm not dead; I'm just dreaming?"

"What is death," Isla Dora replied, "if not but a dream?"

Peter did not initially understand the cryptic response, but took it to mean that he was still in his own reality: not dead. Whatever the case was, he needed to press on for the sake of his sanity. Losing his mind in this place would certainly mean an end to his mental faculties once he woke from his medical state.

A wall signaled the end of their journey and Isla Dora knowingly turned to her right, leading Peter down a corridor that ended in a small room bathed in soft white light.

Peter became apprehensive and stopped. The light emanating from the room was similar in shade and color as the light from the faux angels that tried to apprehend him. He did not know Isla Dora and was not sure he could trust her. For all he knew, she could be leading him straight to his would-be captors. Peter ignored his instincts and shook the feeling off. If Isla Dora was working with the demons, they certainly would have found him by now. Slowly, he set his distrust aside and followed her into the antechamber.

The room was the about size of a large bedroom and contained the only furnishings Peter had seen in the entire living space. A heavy wooden table with chairs occupied the main area of the floor, while a bookshelf-hutch type of arrangement sat against one wall. Odd knickknacks cluttered the entire space. Some were on the shelves, others rested on the table, with still more gathered in groups on the floor. There was no theme to the trinkets. Small toys, every-day household goods, sporting gear, and an unusual assortment of clocks made up the bulk of the items, but Peter's heart skipped a beat when he pinpointed the source of the illumination. Glowing children were perched among the knickknacks, on the furniture, and in the corners of the room. They sat with their legs drawn up to their chests in a fetal position. They spanned the gamut of races. Some of the children were from eras long past and none appeared to have reached their teen years. They stared forward with unblinking eyes. None of the children seemed to notice the presence of the two adults whatso-ever.

Peter inspected the nearest youngster. "Hello?" he said, waving a hand in front of the child's face.

"Do not trouble yourself," Isla Dora remarked.

"They're children?"

Isla Dora ignored the question and blew out the light. She cradled the wax taper as a mother might a baby and laid it down on the table. "You can rest now," she said softly to the candle.

Peter cocked his head at the old woman's strange behavior but shook it off and went about studying the rest of the room. While some of the objects sat lifeless in their positions, others moved of their own accord. Some vibrated and bounced in place while others rolled haphazardly within the areas they occupied. On the floor in front of the hutch were two objects. One of them was a box of colored pencils that flipped over from side to side in what appeared to be an effort at moving forward. Stopping the pencil box's efforts was an old toy robot moving in the opposing direction. When they met, the objects would simply bounce backward and resume their attempt again unaware of the other's presence. They seemed to be stuck in a perpetual loop. Peter looked for wires or controls behind the motion of the two items but found none. The painted tin robot was of a type too old to run on batteries, and the pencil box was exactly that—an old, cardboard box containing colored pencils.

Isla Dora picked up a leather shoulder bag hanging from the back of a chair and handed it to Peter.

Peter took the bag and held it between them considering it curiously.

"For the book," Isla Dora affirmed, gesturing to the old manuscript.

"Good idea," Peter replied, placing the tome inside the leather satchel.

"Your life, was it worth living?" Isla Dora asked.

"What?"

"Your life, did you live it well? Did you make the most of it?"

Peter shrugged. "Sure, I guess I did okay."

"Did you fight for the weak and frail?" Isla Dora inquired pointedly.

Peter cocked his head.

"Did you come to the aid of those in need?" she asked slowly, as if Peter had a comprehension problem.

"I'm sorry, I don't—"

Isla Dora waived him off. "The decisions you make here will matter greatly—there's still time."

"Time for what?"

Isla Dora cackled at the young man's naiveté. "To save those who are in peril, of course." Before Peter could ask another question, she took hold of the shoulder bag firmly. "Do not allow others to possess the book. Free will is key."

"Key?"

"Strength does not serve you well," Isla Dora replied, gesturing to the young man's obvious lack of physical fitness. "You need to believe in yourself and serve those who would sacrifice all for you."

Peter cocked a brow at the crazy old lady.

Isla Dora pointed to the moving objects in the room. "Do not trust what you see."

"Oh, I won't," Peter assured, sheepishly giving a wide berth to the seemingly possessed items.

"Do not fail or we will all suffer the doom of creation," Isla Dora warned. Her demeanor became alarmed and she backed away from Peter. She began to tremble and shake. "They're coming."

Peter reached out to Isla Dora in an effort to help, but the old woman evaded him by morphing into a small white kitten. She continued her transformations through various objects and everyday items. With each metamorphosis, her body changed shape sharply and violently. Her mass expanded and shrank to unbelievable sizes. After a multitude of variations, Isla Dora arrived at a diminutive ball of sliver-white yarn.

Chapter 10

Peter took stock of the yarn that was once the old woman. "Isla Dora?" he asked. As if in response, the ball of yarn rolled peacefully toward him and bounced gently off his shoe. He shook his head in disbelief.

A loud *SNAP* reverberated through the small space of the antechamber. Peter whirled to see the joints between the hewn rocks expanding in size. A lone finger appeared within the ever-widening fissure. As space permitted, more fingers appeared in the gap until they eventually formed a complete hand. Shortly after, another hand appeared and together, the hands worked to move the stones out of the way. As some blocks moved forward into the room, others were withdrawn to an empty void behind the wall. The heft of the stones was obvious, but they parted effortlessly, without conferring visible strain to the pair of hands manipulating them. Within moments, a large opening exposed the empty space beyond.

Without hesitation, a black-haired, blue-eyed young man in his early twenties stepped into the room. He was a bit shorter than Peter and of an even slighter build. The young man's clothes were straight out of the era for sock-hop dance or some sort of mid-twentieth century play. He sported a pair of well-worn blue jeans and a white tee shirt. The ensemble was rounded off with a pair of black boots reminiscent of the 1950s. The young man studied Peter and unenthusiastically extended his hand to shake. "Thomas."

Unnerved, Peter retreated a few paces. The day had gone from strange to bizarre, but the laid-back youth seemed genuinely friendly and his gesture was a welcome one. Peter put his fears aside and stepped forward to shake Thomas's hand. "Peter. Glad to see you."

"Yeah, same here, pops."

"Pops?" replied Peter, adjusting his glasses. "I'm not that old."

Thomas chuckled. "Yeah you are." He pointed at the shoulder bag the man was carrying. "Is that the book?"

Remembering Isla Dora's advice, Peter cradled the attaché. "Why do you want to know?"

Thomas gauged Peter's response and nodded his appreciation. "Good answer. Never let that book out of your sight, got it?"

"How do you—"

Thomas shook the question off. "It's why I'm here."

"Why you're here?"

"Yeah," Thomas replied, smacking his lips dryly, "to get you and that book out of this place."

"Sorry." Peter said. "I don't understand what's going on. All of this is really strange to me."

"Ain't that the truth," Thomas agreed, studying the interior space carefully. "I ain't ever been in this room before." He pushed past Peter to study the hutch and knick-knacks. "I've been all over and never seen some of this stuff." Thomas picked up a few of the items. He scrutinized them before moving onto the candle resting on the table. "Incredible," he said, turning the candle over in his hand. "This is somethin'."

"They don't have candles where you come from, *kid*?"

"Sure," Thomas replied, smiling at the sly retort, "but none like this."

Peter gestured to the collection of inert and moving objects. "What are—"

A sharp pounding echoed down the hallway.

Peter stared nervously into the corridor. "That's coming from the front door."

"The heat—I knew they wouldn't be fooled for long." Thomas pulled Peter toward the opening in the wall. "We've got to split!"

"Through there?"

"It's either this or with them," Thomas said, motioning down the hallway. "Trust me, you don't want to go with them."

"What about the kids?" Peter asked, gesturing to the glowing children.

"Nothing we can do."

The banging on the front door grew louder until it became a splintering of wood. Voices barked orders and footsteps grew into a cascade of running.

Thomas pulled on Peter's arm. "Now!"

Peter followed the young man into the dark opening and watched as Thomas manipulated the stones back into place. Like magic, the gaps between the blocks narrowed and then disappeared. Peter placed his hand on the stones. "That's amazing."

Thomas shushed Peter. The young man breathed anxiously as he listened to the intruders ransacking the small room. He kept his hands at the ready, awaiting any movement in the blocks brought on by the pursuers.

Peter whispered, "Can they move the wall?"

"It depends if a demon came with them or not."

The sounds from the other side of the stone barrier diminished.

"Sounds like they're gone," Peter said.

"Yeah—let's go."

Peter followed the young man through darkened passageways. Thomas was surefooted and knew the tunnel system well. When the two came to a fork, Thomas did not hesitate to take the appropriate passage. Glowing children similar to the ones in the small room sparsely illuminated the narrow corridors at regular intervals. All the children were unique and their expressions were different as well. Some bore sadness or terror on their faces, while others appeared to be blissfully ignorant of the things transpiring around them. None of the children seemed to be aware of the two men running past.

After several miles of keeping pace with Thomas, Peter stumbled to a halt. "I'm old, remember," he said, gasping for breath and collapsing heavily onto a dislodged block of stone in the passage. "I've got to take a break."

Thomas slowed to a halt. "It's been a while—I'm sorry."

The young man displayed none of the signs of the extraneous journey. He was not even breaking a sweat. On the other hand, Peter felt like he was going to pass out with his heart beating outside of his chest. "You're not tired?"

"Nope."

"Why is that?"

"Things work differently here," Thomas replied. "Don't worry, it'll happen to you."

Peter wanted to know more, but an all-consuming thirst parched his throat. "Is there anything to drink?"

Thomas guffawed. "That's what I mean."

Peter was bewildered at the young man's rude behavior. There must be sources of water nearby. Even if he were in a comatose state, Peter's brain would create the resources to fulfill the basic requirements of everyday living.

Thomas licked his lips dryly. "Did you bring gum?"

"Gum?"

Thomas shook his head and gazed at the ground dejectedly. "I lost mine."

"What?" Peter asked, not sure if he had heard Thomas correctly. Gum was a triviality compared to the necessities of clean drinking water, and the young man was completely disregarding everything for his own whims. In a snarky tone, Peter asked, "Can't you get more?"

"Not likely," Thomas replied, squatting next to Peter. "You only bring with you the things you can't live without—like your glasses."

Peter took off his glasses and scrutinized them. He tried to understand what the young man was saying but could not.

"Yeah," Thomas said, "you don't *need* them, just like I don't *need* gum."

Peter put his glasses back on and felt his stomach growl. "I could use something to eat too."

"Double cheeseburgers," Thomas said, ignoring Peter and speaking hollowly to the empty air of the passageway. "There was this place down the road called Franks—they had the best burgers. I can almost remember what they taste like."

"You don't eat?"

"Like your glasses—no reason. Don't get me wrong, I want to eat—man, I miss it—I miss a lot of things."

Peter removed his spectacles once again to test Thomas's supposition. His vision blurred as it always had.

Thomas saw the concern on Peter's face. "It takes a while. You'll get over it."

Peter furrowed his brow and replaced his glasses. "But without food, how do you live?"

"Live?" Thomas laughed out. "What do you mean *live?* We're dead."

Peter involuntarily touched his face. He felt his skin and the day-old stubble on his cheeks. Everything was as it was supposed to be. His mind reeled. The evidence of his demise was all around him, but Peter could not—would not—let himself succumb to the idea that he was dead. It had to be a trick of his subconscious trying force him to let go of any semblance of the life he once possessed.

"Sorry, I thought you knew."

Peter did not respond.

Chapter 10

"It was pretty obvious to me when it happened," Thomas said. "Everyone experiences it differently. Some people can't handle it."

Peter fought to suppress his emotions.

"What's the last thing you remember?" Thomas asked, attempting to guide the man to his own epiphany.

"A tree stump."

Thomas giggled. "That's a good one!"

"No," Peter replied. "I fell onto it. I was hurt pretty badly, but I was alive—I know I was."

"It seemed pretty real, huh?" Thomas asked. "I was in a car wreck racing this guy in a bent-eight deuce trying to impress this girl." He shook his head. "I didn't even know her name."

Thomas spoke from the heart with sincerity and Peter could not detect the slightest hint of deception or malice from the young man. Peter was afraid and withdrew to let his academic training take over. It would not behoove him to make guesses. He needed to use straightforward reasoning and logic. If he was dead and this world was real, the paradox of it all must answer his questions with answers that lead to concrete conclusions. Peter took a deep breath and thoughtfully asked, "If we're dead, why are we able to function—move around and think?"

"I don't know. It's this place."

Peter glanced up and down the tunnel, surveying the stone and architectural curve of its ceiling. Everything *seemed* real.

"Your clothes," Thomas said, gesturing to the same outfit Peter was wearing when he fell onto the tree stump. "Eating, drinking, breathing—they're all leftovers from your real life."

"*Leftovers?*"

"The stuff you can't let go of—the things you clung to in life."

Peter followed Thomas's rationale as best he could. He absorbed the information and looked for weaknesses in the logic that may point to the slightest flaw or oversight.

"It'll take a while, but you'll forget soon enough," Thomas said. "When I first got here, I thought I was in Hell." He scoffed. "This place is much worse."

"Worse?"

Thomas gestured to the block Peter sat on. "You could be one of them."

Peter studied the stone. He ran his hand across the roughly hewn surface. "Them?"

"Sure," Thomas replied, pulling the strap on Peter's shoulder bag. "All this stuff, this entire city is made of the people who come here. Crazy, huh?"

Peter took a moment to understand the implications of Thomas's statement and then leapt to his feet. He tugged frantically at the shoulder bag in an effort to take it off, but he also realized he was wearing the cloak that had secreted him away. He whirled about, trying to remove both items at the same time.

Thomas placed a calming hand on Peter's shoulder. "It's okay, there's nothing you can do."

Peter took a series of deep breaths and sat back down on the stone block. He gestured to a nearby glowing child, resting in a fetal position against the wall. "And them?"

"Ankle biters," Thomas said. "They're too young so they freeze up like that. I've tried to talk to them plenty of times—nothing."

"Back in the room, there were these things—stuff—moving by themselves?"

"Animas. People like you and me, only insane, off their rockers—crazy. They have power—I've seen it. They can change into anything but can't control it. They go back and forth, from one thing to something else."

Peter felt nauseous. The information contained things he had never heard of before and it was too precise to be a hallucination. He did not want it to be true, but it was becoming harder for him to cast this world aside. There was no denying it—he may be dead. Indeed, if that was his new reality, there would be no reason not to embrace it. His survival here depended on his ability to process information rationally. His surreal surroundings were disquieting, but Peter needed to stay focused. The individuals chasing him were after the book, but for what purpose he did not know. Slowly, Peter came to terms with his predicament.

"We've got a ways to go," Thomas said, gesturing down the corridor. "Can you make it?"

"Yeah," Peter replied, shaking his head remorsefully at the turn of events. "Let's keep moving."

After several hours of trekking through the tunnels, Peter and Thomas arrived at the thick outer wall of the city. A long channel under the heavily burdened stone led to the world outside. A dim glow from the exterior breach penetrated the narrow passage. Thomas led the way, squeezing his small frame into the cramped space. Peter followed, wriggling past the uneven and jutting rocks.

As the pair neared the far end of the fissure, the stone floor gave way to a dark, granular, earth-type substance. Peter stopped and scooped up a handful of the black soil. It was lighter than sand and made up of extremely irregular particles. He sniffed the sample. The soil was pungent and fetid. Peter knew what the unique odor was: ash that was foul smelling beyond any other he had encountered. He threw the handful down and wiped his hands clean on his trousers. Ahead, Thomas moved through the opening and out into the open air. Peter followed behind, advancing the remaining distance and exiting the passageway.

What lay beyond the city was far more than anything Peter could have imagined. The ash was everywhere. A thick layer of pungent black earth covered the gently rolling hillside as far as he could see. In several places, the burned and skeletal remains of trees and plants stood defiant against whatever raging inferno had long ago destroyed them. There was no wind. The air was as stagnant and stale as that of a sealed tomb. The cloudless, twilight sky loomed above, casting a disquieting pallor over those unfortunate enough to dwell under its influence. The bleak landscape coupled with the ash's foul odor woke Peter from his denial-based stupor and filled his senses with dread.

Standing nearby was a group of seven individuals. They all wore a derivation of the cloak that was passed to Peter during his escape. With their hoods pulled back, he could see three of the individuals were women. They were of various ethnicities and the clothing beneath the loosely fitting cloaks pointed to differing time periods from ages past.

The exterior wall defending the city was massive. Built of hewn stone, the wall stretched out of sight to both sides in a subtle but noticeable arc. If complete, the overall circumference of the barrier was incalculable. The height of the wall was nearly as staggering as its circumference. It was over fifty-feet tall and buttressed at regular intervals. Garish and monstrous gargoyles and effigies of twisted humans and demented forms adorned the wall around its perimeter. The defensive structure was impregnable and designed to invoke fear into anyone foolish enough to assail it. Above the fortification, a mass of buildings and tall towers rose into the twilight sky. Windows and colorful banners adorned some buildings, while others were plain and inconspicuous.

From the assembled group, an imposing man emerged and made his way toward Peter and Thomas. The man was in his early sixties and carried himself confidently. He appeared to be of North African descent. He was taller than average and his muscular build displayed the characteristics of strength and stamina. The man had the same stature and bearing as the individual who forced Peter out of the square earlier in the day.

The man wasted no time in asserting his authority over Thomas. "Where is Valentinius?"

Thomas studied the group and glanced back to the escape passageway under the wall. "He's not with you?"

"We have no time for games, Thomas."

"Sorry, Hannibal," Thomas said, shaking his head. "I never saw him again after we split up."

Hannibal pursed his lips and furrowed his brow at the response.

"We didn't wait. The guards came in right after I got there."

Two more cloaked individuals approached the group from a location much further along the wall. When they got within earshot, the taller of the two called out to Hannibal, "Valentinius fell." The man pulled back his hood revealing his Chinese features. "He's been taken."

Noticeably troubled by the news, Hannibal grew angry and cast a glance around the group as if searching for a scapegoat. "Guan, which demon?"

"Asmodeus himself."

Hannibal's rage bubbled to the surface. He pointed at Peter. "You," he rasped. "What is your name?"

"My—my name?" Peter stammered. "It's Peter."

"Do you possess the book?"

Peter rotated the shoulder bag into view and nodded, "I do."

Hannibal scoffed. "Do you know what it is for—can you read it?"

Peter felt cold, as if his blood had suddenly drained from his body. He had no idea what the manuscript was for and he could not read the book as it was. Peter needed a primer—some sort of clue about its function or printed workings. Without the proper tools, the book's knowledge would be lost forever. "No," Peter answered meekly, "but I might be able to if I had more information."

Hannibal's consternation was obvious and he scrutinized Peter and Thomas. "How is it that the world of men is now weaker than any old woman from my age? Are there no conflicts with which to cull and wean the timid and sick from their mother's breasts?"

A hearty laugh echoed from the parapets above the group. "Hannibal, my old friend, still inspiring your men, I see!"

Hannibal turned to see a huge man standing on the wall. "We are not friends, Asmodeus."

Peter recognized the name from biblical accounts, but the human resembled nothing like a fallen angel. Asmodeus took the form of a mundane looking, albeit massive, man. He was as tall as the demon Peter witnessed upon entering the city and dwarfed all those around him. Asmodeus's broad shoulders and proportional build made his presence seem more like an illusion in a fun house than a flesh and blood reality, but seeing him walk among the humans in his charge proved otherwise. The demon wore ancient leather armor similar to that of a Roman legionnaire. Even from ground level, Peter could see Asmodeus's blood red eyes. They were unnerving and gave credence to Peter's fear.

"I am saddened by your change of heart," Asmodeus said. "It was not so long ago that you were my most trusted lieutenant and favored of all the nephesh."

"Much has changed."

"Changed?" Asmodeus scoffed. "Nothing has *changed,* Hannibal Barca of Carthage. You stand as a murderous soul to thousands, or have you forgotten?"

Hannibal lowered his head. "You know I cannot."

Asmodeus bowed, mocking the man below. "Your brutality is legendary still."

Hannibal cast a stern glance back to the demon. "We fought for our freedom—our right to exist. It was not mere folly."

"Do you believe your reasons give your acts clarity?" Asmodeus asked. "That your wisdom in the matters of men has any meaning here?"

"What then would be the purpose of this place if not to test our fortitude, our true self and our soul?"

"We own this realm!" Asmodeus spat. "You are nothing but a weak nephesh and a wicked one at that!"

Hannibal chuckled. "You are as much a prisoner of this place as I, Asmodeus. You would be wise to remember that."

"Ah, yes," Asmodeus agreed, "and that is precisely why I have sought you out—so that we may come to an agreement."

"To what purpose?"

Chapter 10

Asmodeus gestured to a small band of human guards standing in the shadows behind him. The motley crew of henchmen brought forward a cloaked captive and prodded him to stand on the edge of the wall. Asmodeus pulled the prisoner's hood back, revealing a man of European descent.

"Valentinius," Hannibal muttered emptily.

"An exchange. You give me that one there," Asmodeus said, pointing to Peter standing near the base of the wall, "and I'll return this nephesh to you."

Hannibal cast a dark gaze at Peter, but said nothing.

Asmodeus sensed the conflict within his old friend. "Also, as a gesture of my benevolence, I'll allow you and your band to roam free for as long as I control the city."

Peter listened intently to the exchange. These men had risked themselves to save him from an unknown fate, but the group of saviors had no ties to Peter whatsoever. His wellbeing now rested on a decision made by someone he did not know for a comrade the group obviously knew well. Peter felt his chances of survival dwindling by the second. He scanned the horizon for an escape route and backed away from the group.

The men and women of Hannibal's team were listening to the conversation as well. They monitored Peter's movement and when he made a change in stance, the assembled members drew their weapons.

Disgusted with the group's behavior, Thomas stepped between them. "This is what it has come to?" he asked them, looking to Hannibal to intervene. "We did all this for nothing?"

Some in the company showed signs of being conflicted, but they held their ground and kept their attention focused on Peter.

"You can't let this happen," Thomas pleaded with Hannibal.

"Be quiet!" Hannibal ordered. He lowered his head in shame at the guilt he felt even for considering the demon's offer. "We will not yield."

One by one, the individuals of the company nodded their approval and stowed their weapons.

"*You* would free us?" Hannibal mockingly asked Asmodeus.

"I give you my word."

"What of Lilith, your queen? Has she been supplanted?"

Asmodeus cast a nervous glance behind him.

"Truly, the book would be *hers*, not yours!"

Asmodeus grew angry and morphed back into his demon form.

Hannibal locked eyes with Valentinius standing on the edge of the wall. "I am truly sorry, my old friend."

Valentinius nodded and adjusted his posture to stand at military attention.

Asmodeus touched Valentinius on the shoulder and released his demonic power. The prisoner shook and his features turned dark, almost black. His face contorted and changed until he was unrecognizable as a human being. The prisoner's mass grew until he rivaled that of a hot-air balloon, silhouetted like a stain against the twilight sky. The sphere burst and dispersed into a swarm of bees.

Asmodeus raved maniacally and swept his arms through the air, commanding the swirling cloud of stinging insects to attack Peter. The bees organized into a pointed formation and flew directly at the cowering human.

Alarm gripped the members of Hannibal's company. A refrain of "Retreat!" echoed off the city's outer fortification.

"Hold!" Hannibal ordered. "Their power is diminished beyond the wall!"

Gripped by fear, Peter wanted to run, but Hannibal's command calmed him. The warrior's confident voice was like a rock that Peter could hold on to in a swift current. He concentrated on the surety of Hannibal's words and used them to shore up his diminished courage to stand firm.

The angry bees closed the distance and descended on the group. Their buzzing filled the air, causing some members of the company to raise their weapons. As the swarm got within striking distance, the bees burst into flame. For a brief moment, they sang out in a chorus of agony before their charred bodies turned to ash and rained down upon the mercenaries.

Peter fought against his paralyzing panic and labored to breathe. "What *is* this place?"

Hannibal grieved the loss of his friend as he watched the ash accumulate on the ground. He looked at the newcomer squarely. "Welcome to the Garden of Eden."

Peter contemplated the man's words. His mind was unable to process the totality of events that were transpiring before him. Things were happening too fast. At some point in Peter's immediate past, he had died. There was no denying it or rationalizing it away. Now he found himself in a strange place with his whole existence being nothing but a fleeting dream. Everything he had known was gone and there was no going back.

"Gather your things," Hannibal said, breaking the long silence. "We march."

Chapter 11

Sitri flew above the outer wall's parapet and circled in a slow arc to land next to Asmodeus. The demon stretched his leathery wings fully before withdrawing them to a resting position behind his back. Sitri's anger was plainly visible, contorting his already maligned face. He gestured to the meager band of humans making their way up the ashen hillside outside of the city's perimeter wall. "You let them escape?"

Asmodeus hid his frustration and waved off his fellow demon. "What would you have me do? They are well beyond the limit of our power."

"Lilith will not be pleased."

"They had help from the inside," Asmodeus retorted. "Not even *she* could have foreseen that."

"Nevertheless, you should have followed her plan."

"The circumstances changed. What does it matter? She's blind to what goes on here. We do the work, while she plays her juvenile games."

From behind the two demons, one of the human guards attending Asmodeus began to transform. The guard pulled away from his comrades and dropped to his knees. His body stretched and distorted. The guard's purple tunic and breeches were absorbed into his body and replaced by blackened robes. He increased in height until he neared that of the two demons. Gray wings, weathered and frayed, grew from the guard's back as his facial features contorted into the she-demon, Lilith.

Lilith leapt at Asmodeus and unleashed a fiery attack. Lavender energy poured from her hands making the air crackle as it enveloped the caught-off-guard demon. In an effort to counter the attack, Asmodeus ignited a blood red defensive field, but Lilith flung it aside and tightened her grip. She forced the demon to his knees. "Blind, am I? But I see you all too well!"

"Forgive me, my Queen," Asmodeus said, his voice quivering in pain.

Lilith focused her power further, drawing gasps and whimpers of compliance from the demon before finally releasing him. "And they eluded you how?"

Breathing heavily, Asmodeus gestured to Sitri. "He lost them over the city."

Sitri shrunk from Lilith's gaze. "They executed an elaborate deception, but we did capture Hannibal's lieutenant."

"Hannibal's lieutenant?" Lilith asked with playful amusement. "The one whom we cannot interrogate because his ashes are now strewn out of our reach—is that who you speak of?"

Asmodeus rose to his feet. "Valentinius knew nothing, my Queen. I am sure of it."

Lilith raised a grizzled hand to quiet the demon. "You know Hannibal so well that he evades you still?"

"He had help—something unforeseen."

"I know," Lilith said, pacing back and forth on the parapet while eyeing the group diminishing into the ashen hillside. "Are you sure he was with them?"

"There," Sitri said, pointing to Peter bringing up the rear of the procession.

Lilith studied the frail human struggling to forge a way through the heavy ash. "I see him."

"We could send a cohort after them," Asmodeus proffered in an effort to rebuild his lost trust.

Lilith grimaced at the thought of her much-needed guards aligning with Hannibal, or at the very least being crucified and hung up for display at the city's doorstep. The incident would cause immeasurable morale difficulties and make her remaining henchmen hesitant to follow orders again. "Too risky."

Lilith extended her wings and propelled herself into the air. She circled slowly over the parapet, her concentration fixed on the retreating humans. "We still have the advantage," she said and pointed a twisted finger at Sitri. "Post sentries at every access point into the city."

Sitri bowed his acknowledgment of the queen's orders.

"Asmodeus, find the traitors dwelling among us. Question the animas—be *persuasive*. Sort out those who would be so defiant."

Asmodeus nodded.

"Under no circumstances can we risk damaging the book," Lilith said. "Do not transfigure or use power of any kind. We must capture them unharmed."

Chapter 12

For the most part, the pallid landscape remained unchanged since the group left the base of the city wall. The travelers labored through the rolling terrain, occasionally encountering a deep defile or steep hillock that made their journey even more arduous, but the signs of the hellish fire that once consumed the Garden of Eden continued to permeate their surroundings. In some areas, the ash was so thick the group navigated around it for fear of becoming ensnared by its fine particles. Charred remnants of large trees lay scattered about, their trunks hollowed and blackened. The vestiges of smaller plant species were visible thanks to their placement by outcroppings or fortuitous topography, but the conflagration reduced those to a wisp of cellular residue forever stuck in a near facsimile of their former existence. At several junctures along the way, Peter reached out to touch the haunting umbrage only to have it disintegrate and crumble to the pungent ground.

The sky was unchanging and persisted in its twilight state all through the company's trek. A white glow hung around the horizon. Indirect gray light bathed the landscape weakly, but it did little to assuage the absolute black of the heavens above. It was as if the Garden of Eden were a separate world all unto its own and forever stuck in a perpetual solar eclipse.

The long hike through the bleak landscape gave Peter ample time to think. He wanted to ask a multitude of questions, but the most prevalent was *why*? The group had sacrificed one of their own for him. Peter found that unbelievable given the circumstances. Never in his wildest dreams would he have given up a friend for an unknown quantity—a newcomer no less. Yet, this group of battle-hardened mercenaries did exactly that. The manuscript Peter carried must be important, that much he guessed, but why not just take it? He posed no threat to them. Instead, they risked everything to whisk him away from the city. What did the members of the company expect in return? Peter mulled the question, but deep down, he did not want to know what the true answer was. Whatever the reason, the reward must be significantly more than what the group had lost, which, as a revelation all unto its own, gave him great pause.

Peter stowed his feelings and lurched after Thomas, as both trailed behind the main group by a wide margin. Hannibal set a fierce pace and the gap between them and the rest of the company had been steadily widening for the last hour or so. Unaccustomed to the physical strain, Peter's stamina was at its end. Breathing laboriously and unable to take another step, he stopped and sat down on a blackened rock. "I'm sorry, I've got to rest."

Thomas whistled out to Hannibal.

A murmur drifted through the group replete with snickers and subdued references to the frail newcomer. With audible exasperations, the company stopped, and various individuals took up positions along the high ground above Peter. Most sat down and immediately went about retrieving personal objects from their pockets or bags slung under their cloaks.

Visibly irritated, Hannibal made his way back to Peter and Thomas. "You cannot rest here," he said, gesturing to the trail behind them. "We know not what pursues us."

Peter said nothing. He got to his feet and with Thomas's help, climbed the steep slope to arrive among the resting mercenaries.

The members of the company were each busy with their own interests. Seated and standing, some played dice, others meditated, while a few stared into the distance in deep contemplation. Several acknowledged Thomas with a smile or a nod, but most made it a point to ignore Peter.

The small knoll gave Peter the perfect vantage from which to survey the city beyond. The group arrived about ten miles from the outer wall, and even at this distance, he was hard-pressed to see the city in one view. The hewn-stone metropolis was enormous. Its curved walls stretched in a large arc to the edges of his peripheral vision. Buildings of various shapes and heights jutted above the surrounding fortifications. Some structures supported chiseled faces that stared out blankly, across the barren landscape. Others were nothing more than platforms for enormous effigies that stood like sentinels against the black heart of the twilight sky. It was unsettling to see the twisted and hideous figures on such a monstrous scale.

"*This* is the Garden of Eden?" Peter wondered aloud.

"What's left of it," Thomas answered.

Peter shook his head in disbelief. "I thought all those stories were superstitious nonsense."

Hannibal dropped into a squatting position near the two youngest members of the company. "I lived in a time infested by fanciful tales and superstitions," he said, smiling at the thought of his former life. "I could scarcely believe it when I arrived—the city was much smaller then as well."

Peter sat down in the ash next to the old warrior. "What happened?"

"Lucifer was envious of humanity and grew angry," Hannibal replied. "He vowed to imprison the Almighty and destroy the last vestiges of our immortal souls. To this end, he recruited an army of angels and attacked God."

"Attacked God?" Peter mused, trying hard to remember his biblical history and struggling to remain in the moment. The tenuous hold on his new reality was slipping away. He did not want it to be true, but he was being confronted with an undeniable set of facts. He was dead and the afterlife was fraught with extreme danger and paralyzing fear.

"Unfortunately for Lucifer," Hannibal continued, "his ego was greater than his tactical prowess. In short, he failed. God cast Lucifer and his followers into the very prison Lucifer had created."

"Prison—Hell, you mean?" Peter asked.

"It has many names," Hannibal replied, ruminating on the knowledge he had gleaned from all the souls he had spoken with since his own demise. "Before his fall and as scathing testimony to his loathing for humanity, Lucifer sent three of his most trusted brethren to capture the Garden and control the Two Trees."

"The Tree of Life and the Tree of Knowledge," Peter interjected, remembering at least that much from the stories told to him as a child.

"God sent the guardian of the Two Trees to counter Lucifer's lieutenants." Hannibal gestured to the ashen landscape. "War between them lasted ages and consumed everything."

"And the angel?" Peter asked, still having a hard time accepting the story as genuine.

"He fought valiantly but was finally overcome," Hannibal replied, his eyes solemnly scanning the evidence of devastation around them.

Peter took the story in. Biblical accounts and ancient stories meant to backfill the history of God and his angels were sparse and disjointed at best. Hannibal's interpretation seemed to be a sincere retelling, but it left out key components vital to the current state of the Garden. "Why are we here then?" Peter surprised himself with his impetuous, authority-laden tone and rephrased his question. "I mean, why does anyone come here at all? It makes no sense."

"Humanity's fate is inextricably linked with the Two Trees. They shepherd our souls and provide for our wellbeing. Since they reside here, we are forever drawn to this place." Hannibal pursed his lips in disappointment. "Once our promise was broken, the Almighty cast humanity out of the Garden and sought to sever our ties with the Two Trees, but Lucifer had other ideas. He wanted humans to worship him, so he intervened."

"Adam and Eve ate from the Tree of Knowledge," Peter pondered. "Original sin and all that."

"That was the catalyst—the reason we are mired here today."

Peter's mind conjured up images of the battle between good and evil. Armies of angelic beings fighting against God for the subjugation of humanity—each side trying to impose their will on the other. If everything around Peter was the result, the violence must have been intense. He gestured to the burnt husk of a tree trunk lying nearby. "But with the trees destroyed—"

"They persist," Hannibal assured. "Heavily guarded within the center of the city, the Two Trees live to this day." He swung a muscular arm in the sprawling city's direction. "That place exists as a defensive barrier for the trees. The she-devil queen, Lilith, and her demon factotum constructed the city over several millennia. She was meticulous in her methods."

"I think I understand," Peter said. "People come here and she turns them into building materials to make it impossible to destroy the trees. But," he paused, contemplating the circumstances, "what does any of that have to do with me?"

"Do you know the monk Nicholas?" Hannibal asked.

"I know *of* him. He died hundreds of years before I was born."

"The book you carry," Hannibal said, gesturing to the satchel slung around Peter's shoulders, "did he give it to you?"

Peter thought back to the antique store. There was a strange figure in the basement. It could have been Nicholas, but he was unsure about everything now and had dismissed that encounter as a phantom—an illusion of the dark. "I don't know."

An audible groan escaped from the eavesdropping mercenaries on the hillock. They were sorely disappointed to hear those words.

"It must be him," Thomas insisted. "Why would she have had Nicholas with her at the Gate?"

Hannibal scoffed. "To deceive us, of course."

Peter reached into the shoulder bag and produced the leather-bound manuscript. "This is his book—I'm certain of it."

"But you can't read it," Hannibal countered.

Peter shook his head.

"But he can learn," Thomas said, making eye contact with the old general. "He's a smart guy—he can figure it out."

Hannibal stood up and glowered at Peter. "The knowledge contained within that book is the key to this place. I heard her speak of it many times. The queen desires that book above all else." His stance eased and his voice took on a lighter tone. "Undoubtedly they have tortured Nicholas for its secrets and now have witnessed you carry it through the Gate." He chuckled softly. "What fate awaits you if you fail?"

The copper taste of fear filled Peter's mouth. "I didn't ask for this."

"Nevertheless," Hannibal said, "the burden is yours to bear."

Chapter 13

Lilith stood on the highest point of her nearly finished amphitheater and smiled approvingly at her most recent endeavor. The
building sat above the level of the city's perimeter wall and gave an
extended view of the landscape beyond. The focal point of the
theater was a rectangular stage flanked on both sides by angled
walls. In front of the theater's floor was an orchestra pit with access
to all seating levels provided by steps cut at regular intervals into the
large blocks of the semi-circular amphitheater.

Throughout the structure, gangs of workers used ropes and
pulleys to move immense loads of building materials into position.
Once lowered onto the proper tier, the stones, beams, or accoutre-
ments were distributed to more finely skilled artisans for final
finishing and placement.

Although the ordered chaos of construction was progressing
toward completion, it was not without its complications. As with all
substantial construction projects, critical management of the labor

force was required and a few privileged human overseers stood out in that regard. The gang bosses were made up of men and women alike, former guards pulled from the rank and file of henchmen at the queen's disposal. They wore simple purple tunics and wielded whips, swords, and an assortment of iron weaponry. They showed outright contempt for the non-initiate neophytes, beating them remorselessly, oftentimes until there was a work stoppage due to severe injury.

Lilith yawned with indifference at the brutality. There was little the nephesh could do about the violence. There was no better place for the souls to go and her methods were justifiable given the circumstances. To her, humans were nothing more than a nuisance. They were a means to an end, and she could not let them get in the way of the ultimate prize.

Sitri flew up from below and landed next to Lilith on the uppermost course of stones. He knelt on one knee and bowed his head in reverence. "My Queen."

"News?"

"Hannibal leads them to the vale."

The air of confidence surrounding Lilith vanished. Her face contorted in consternation, but she waved a hand through the air, dismissing the report. "He is a fool. This changes nothing."

Noticeably concerned with Lilith's apathy, Sitri added, "But the book, Mistress—"

"Does them no good," Lilith snapped. "Perhaps you have forgotten? Combined, our power is now greater than that of any potential assailant."

Chapter 13

"My Queen," Sitri responded, measuring his words carefully, "the threat exists nonetheless."

"You doubt my judgment?"

"Never."

"Rest easy, Sitri," Lilith said. "Hannibal and his miscreants are in no position to unravel the book's mysteries—that zealot monk did his job all too well."

The demon's tension eased and he backed away from the queen. "As you wish," he said, turning to fly away.

"Be vigilant, they have few options."

Sitri acknowledged the orders and took to the air, beating his blackened wings as he thrust himself into the twilight sky.

Below, Asmodeus waded through the mass of humanity in the amphitheater. He cut a sizable swath through astonished workers and guards alike. Having a reputation for random violent outbursts, the souls averted their eyes and gave him a wide berth. Asmodeus relished in his ill repute and stared down all newcomers hoping for a chance to punish any wayward gaze. Several times, he changed paths deliberately, forcing some to abandon their tasks in an effort to avoid contact with the demon. He found amusement in the laborers' fear and laughed heartily.

"Enjoying yourself?" Lilith asked, watching her lieutenant approach.

Being imperious to the point of showing disrespect, Asmodeus answered, "Greatly, my Queen."

Asmodeus's arrogant and disingenuous tone irked Lilith, but she let it pass. She was not in the mood to discipline her subordinate, and granting him leeway kept him in line for bigger tasks. "Do you have something to report?"

Asmodeus stopped one step short of Lilith's perch. "Our interrogations have not borne fruit. We search for the more ancient of the animas now."

Lilith struggled to contain her displeasure. "I gave you a job!"

Asmodeus checked his attitude. "As you know, the animas are beyond number. As yet, none have presented a state of mind capable of admission, let alone collusion."

Lilith wanted to scream but knew the information that Asmodeus relayed was true. The animas were elusive and random creatures. They seldom presented themselves to outsiders and when they did, their nature was not one conducive to reasoning.

A thought piqued Lilith's interest. Throughout the centuries, one anima stood out above the rest as it had tried to thwart Lilith at every turn, and when the opportunity arose, it recruited other anima to stymie any progress the demon queen made in finding the guilty party. The guile, wherewithal, and total lack of fear made Lilith think of only one person. "I smell the stench of Isla Dora in all this. She and her followers have been a thorn in our sides long enough. Use all the resources you need to find her."

Asmodeus's mood noticeably improved at the order. "Absolutely, my Queen."

"Before you go, I want you to see something."

Chapter 13

Curious, Asmodeus nodded his acknowledgement and stood by.

Lilith called out to the nearest overseer and ordered they round up a large portion of the menial laborers.

The female guard ran down to the lower levels of the amphitheater and relieved the other crew bosses of their charges. Some, angry that they had been stripped of their workers, protested, but they soon obeyed without question when the female guard pointed back to the queen. Slowly, the female guard began the lengthy task of herding a large number of souls to the upper portions of the amphitheater.

Lilith greeted the hundred or so slave workers with a curt smile. She spoke overly loudly to the group, ensuring all within the bounds of the construction project would hear her words. "Do not be afraid!" Lilith assured. "Rejoice with me as your days of toil and tedium have ended!"

Smiles and faint words of encouragement broke out among the assemblage. Their slumping and beaten postures straightened, affirming their impression of hope.

"You have been chosen for a very special endeavor indeed," Lilith continued in a familiar and warm tone. "Please step forward," she commanded, gesturing to the group to come closer to her position along the upper edge of the amphitheater.

The group clambered higher. Weakened by their earlier labors, some sought help from others to climb over the hewn rocks. They stood on the precipice of the structure and marveled at the seldom seen landscape beyond the walled city.

Lilith gently glided through the group of souls, stopping at the exact center of the upper course of stones along the rearmost portion of the amphitheater. There, for no obvious reason, was a large hole in the finished row of blocks. The opening was several yards in diameter and its interior edges were finished in voussoir-type masonry. The hole was deep, continuing down through the entire depth of the theater's supporting infrastructure.

One by one, the workers drew closer to the hole and peered into its gaping maw. The high spirits that once permeated the group gave way to gasps of apprehension.

"Behold!" Lilith proclaimed. "Henceforth and forevermore shall you shine as a beacon extolling the virtue of this great city!"

Frightened, the slaves backed away from the queen and instinctively formed small groups. A few souls at the edges of the assemblage ran, attempting to navigate the steep staircases on either side of the amphitheater's centerline. Others standing near the upper boundary of the amphitheater threw themselves off the precipice in an effort to escape.

Lilith's response was swift. A wave of lavender energy poured from her body. It surrounded the group and stopped the fleeing souls in their tracks. Power clutched the running individuals and forced them back to the gathered throng of slaves. Thick loops of opaque electricity caught the persons in freefall, stopping their momentum and lifting them back to the top of the amphitheater.

Once collected, Lilith raised her arms and turned each human into a fiery, screaming mass. She swept her hands through the air, deftly combining the individuals into a fountain of fire. She held the writhing conglomeration of burning souls aloft for all to witness, scanning the area menacingly, daring the remaining slave laborers and their overseers to gaze upon her. Her point made, Lilith deposited the column of fire into the hole atop the amphitheater.

The fountain of fire raged high into the twilight sky. Near the geyser's apex, the flames cooled slightly, allowing the souls contained within a scant moment to coalesce into their former beings. Unearthly screams escaped from them as they descended back into the fire's turbulent, roiling center to begin their journey anew.

Impressed with the powerful and highly technical display, Asmodeus bowed reverently. "My Queen."

Chapter 14

The first thing that stood out to Peter was the change in terrain. Marching through the landscape slowly became much easier than the previous day's journey. The demanding trek between the hills and dales of the Garden gave way to the welcome comfort of level ground. As the company progressed, hills spread out on both sides of the company and ridges rose to create a narrow valley. The glen snaked ahead, making it impossible for any in the group to see the other end.

Once again, Peter found himself bringing up the rear of the column and struggling to maintain the taxing pace set by Hannibal. He felt guilty asking for another respite as previous requests drew extreme irritation from the members of the company as a whole. Peter kept his mind off his exhaustion by learning as much as he could from Thomas. "Where are we going?"

Chapter 14

"I don't know—I've never been out here before," Thomas called back to Peter from some thirty yards or so in front of the professor.

Burnt rocks and charred foliage littered the valley floor just as it did throughout the rest of the Garden, but something ahead made Hannibal and the rest of the group take pause. Each member of the group halted their progress to study an object that lay in their path and in turn, each shook their head before moving on. Peter maneuvered to see what had garnered their attention, but he trailed too far behind to get a clear view.

Peter watched closely as Thomas reached the mysterious spot in the path and stopped. He knelt to a squatting position and extended his hand to touch the object. Despite his fatigue, Peter stepped up his pace and covered the remaining distance as quickly as he was able. There, to his disappointment, was a semi-translucent, yellowing slab of an unknown substance lying on the ground. It was about one foot wide and six feet long. Peter could not tell how thick the slab was as the ashen floor of the valley swallowed it in depth, but it appeared to be no more than six inches through at its midpoint. The irregularly-shaped slab was roughly square at its base, with the upper end jagged and split. It looked like nothing more than a broken piece of yellowish marble. Confused, Peter could not fathom the reason for all the interest. "What's the big deal?"

"I don't know," Thomas replied, "but this shouldn't be out here."

"It's just some piece of quartz or something."

Thomas gestured to the landscape around them. "Have you seen one like it anyplace else?"

Peter thought back to the many miles of hiking the group had accomplished. This slab was the first object he had seen not showing signs of the great conflagration that consumed the Garden of Eden so long ago. Everything green and alive at the time of the fire was now ash while the more stubborn geology, such as the rocks, had been superheated to the melting point. This slab was bright in color and there was no reason for it to be so pristine. "Not around here," Peter answered.

"Not anywhere," Thomas corrected. He ran two fingers across the back of the slab and noticed a buildup of residue under his nails. The substance was granular in nature and stuck to his fingers like wet sand. Thomas sniffed the yellowish compound several times and grimaced at the foul smell. He stuck out his tongue and cautiously tasted the material. Immediately, Thomas's face soured and he spit out the substance. "Salty."

Peter guffawed at the foolish stunt, but quickly sobered up at the mention of the chemical compound. "What?"

"Really salty."

Peter bent down and swiped a lone finger across the slab. He cautiously tasted the substance. "You're right," he said, rubbing the residue between his fingers. "That's what it is, a slab of salt—as if I wasn't thirsty enough already."

"What's that mean?"

Peter sniffed his fingers and wiped them off on his pants. "I don't know."

A distant call to reassemble echoed dully off the valley's walls. Ahead, the trail veered sharply to the right and the company was out of sight.

Peter checked his belongings and adjusted his glasses. "I guess we should go."

Thomas nodded his agreement and together, the two set off after Hannibal and the others.

Peter counted no less than nine slabs of salt lying prone in the ash by the time the two of them had caught up to Hannibal and the mercenaries. The proportions of each slab were different. Some were thin and long, while others were fat and stout, with one being oddly shaped and disproportionate in every regard. Peter could not make rhyme or reason of the anomalous chunks of salt.

While Hannibal and the others waited for the two stragglers to arrive, they formed a circle around a standing blackish-blue stone stele. They discussed the various features of the rock, pointing and running their hands across it. Mostly, the group placed wagers as to how long it would take the precariously-leaning stele to finally topple over.

Peter entered the circle of mercenaries and studied the standing slab. He rubbed a finger across its surface and tasted the residue. "Covered in ash," he said, spitting and wiping his mouth at the unpleasant taste. The group broke into laughter and Peter humored them by smiling at his own misfortune. The top of the stone was elongated and shaped like an oval. Horizontal edges ran from both sides of the oval where it joined the main body of the stele. Peter scrutinized the circular top of the stone slab. He scanned the surface for an inscription, as the stele closely resembled that of a gravestone, but he found no indication the rock had ever been engraved.

Hannibal mustered the troupe and led them onward. Along the switchback path through the floor of the valley, stele of salt and stone alike made their appearance. The first upright salt stele drew limited curiosity from the group, but faded soon after as the company found several of each variety in differing postures throughout the glen.

Peter was keenly interested in the rock and salt formations, but his overtaxed physical state dampened his enthusiasm considerably. His joints screamed in pain and his thirst was all-consuming. At each turn in the path, Peter desperately searched for any source of water and was distressed to find the same dry environment ubiquitous within the Garden as a whole. It was not until Thomas poked him that he regained his senses.

"Look," Thomas said, pointing ahead.

Peter gazed in the indicated direction and saw that the valley angled right and widened considerably, but that was not what drew his attention. There were thousands of upright steles located within the vale. The slabs were spaced at regular intervals throughout the basin and were made of both salt and stone. Some individual steles faced off against each other, salt versus stone, while others were in formations matching against opposing columns of roughly the same

Chapter 14

number. It was as if time had stopped with the slabs locked in mortal combat.

As they neared the outer edge of the arrangement, the company broke apart into small groups and waded into the phenomenon. Each member studied the slabs, trying to decipher their meaning.

Thomas approached a pair of salt and stone stele. They stood within a few feet of each other and lined up evenly from front to rear. He knocked on the stone slab to test it for soundness and studied its array of cracks and crevices. Once Thomas was certain of the composition, he turned to the salt stele and ran his fingers along it. He sampled the results to ensure it was the same substance as they had previously found. He stepped back from the salt slab and cocked his head. A pattern began to emerge along the upper end of the salt. Thomas's eyes grew wide and he drew his hands back, close to his body. His features contorted and he fought the urge to vomit. He spat several times and rubbed his lips with the back of his hand. "Not cool."

Peter examined the salt stele more closely. Carved in relief at eye level was a human face. Some unknown process in the Garden caused a heavy amount of erosion, but there was no denying the face's existence. He spun around to study the opposing stone slab. It contained no discernible facial features, but a careful inspection around the perimeter of the stele showed the remnants of arms and legs still visible as independent protrusions from the otherwise smooth stone surface. Peter followed the outgrowths to their jagged ends. What he once thought was simply the splintered stone ends of crumbling rock he now knew were the digits of long-encased hands and feet.

Peter made his way through the forest of monoliths. He moved past Hannibal and the others while scanning each stele, looking for any identifiable characteristics. After several examples confirmed his findings, he turned back to the group and said, "They're people."

The company looked to Hannibal for confirmation and, as if in response to a ridiculous question, he laughed. "Of course—what would you expect in a place such as this?"

Numb at the revelation, Peter stood staring into the sea of steles. "What happened?"

"The death of hope," Hannibal answered, looking solemnly at the ancient battlefield. "This place is known as Uriel's Vale."

"Uriel," Peter said, thinking of the previous day's story. "He was the angel sent to fight the demons?"

Hannibal pointed deeper into the valley. "He is there."

Not far off, erected among an army of salt and stone pillars, was a marble statue of the angel Uriel. It dominated the landscape, standing over everything around it. His pose was one of defiance. His wings stretched from his body in different directions. The left wing was forward of the angel and positioned to shield Uriel from incoming danger, while the right wrapped behind him. Uriel's left arm and hand pointed forward as if signaling his army, while his right held a long sword in a guarding position. The angel was clad in breastplate armor. He sported shoulder spaulders with a knee-high filigreed tunic and caligae-style footwear.

Chapter 14

"Incredible," Peter muttered, attempting to grasp the significance of everything he was witnessing.

Hannibal led the company closer. The valley floor containing the steles was oblong in shape. It was about fifty yards from edge to edge at its widest point and several hundred yards in overall length. Uriel's statue was in the leftmost end of the valley from the group's approaching vantage. The upright steles showed more organization the closer they were to the statue. Stone slabs radiated out to some distance away from Uriel and then suddenly, as if an imaginary line had been crossed, they changed to their salt counterparts.

In the midst of the forest of salt were three large, vacant areas. The roughly circular areas were at the far end of the glen opposite the Uriel statue. As with the area surrounding Uriel, the number of salt steles increased in density the nearer they came to the vacant areas.

Thomas stopped at a mound of yellowish salt and called on Peter to join him. "Put your eyeballs on this."

Peter studied the heap of salt. At first glance, the pile looked fairly innocuous and nothing more than a large gathering of salt steles smashed into a six-foot tall mound, but upon closer inspection, Peter recognized the eroded lines of human extremities.

Thomas pointed to a set of parallel lines on top of the pile that resembled legs. The legs were complete and joined to a hip and then to a torso wearing a semblance of ancient leather armor. Where the head should have been was nothing more than a mass of indistinguishable salt with a set of legs protruding from it.

Peter followed the chain of human parts, never able to find an end or a beginning to the extremely eroded remains. "They're stuck together."

Thomas nodded. "That's off the wall."

"Uriel was charged with protecting the Garden." Hannibal projected the words through the still air and gestured to the statue. "He now stands as a testament to his failure."

Peter looked up to Uriel. The statue was on a slight area of high ground that increased the effect of the sculpture's height. The marble was awash in a strange and unnatural light, more so than the ambient illumination of the Garden could explain. He concluded that the strange glow must have been coming from the statue itself.

"He was outnumbered three to one," Hannibal said, pointing to the three vacant areas amongst the salt-stele side of the valley floor. "Today, after a multitude of lifetimes, we have the power to change fate and fulfill his promise to free the Garden."

The company listened to Hannibal's words, nodding and approving the valiant deeds done by a hero long gone.

Peter listened as well and tried his best to visualize what Uriel's final moments must have been like. He found himself swept up by the angel's bravery and wanted nothing more than to aid the company in any way he could.

"Fellow warriors," Hannibal called out to the group, "we have sacrificed much: our friends have fallen, our souls have been made forfeit, and yet our resolve has never been greater!"

The mercenaries cheered Hannibal's words and Peter followed suit with a stirring round of applause.

"We are strong!" Hannibal yelled. "But strength is not enough! Courage is not enough! Our destiny demands a new weapon in this war against evil—one that will make the she-devil herself recoil in fear!"

The group rejoiced in Hannibal's inspiring speech.

"I vowed I would not fail you!" Hannibal exclaimed. "Today, I give you the means of our glorious victory!" He extended a stern finger and pointed at Peter. "The book-bearer! He will level the battlefield and bring us our much-needed salvation!"

The company fell silent.

"Me?" Peter replied, backing away from the gathering.

"You carry with you something the world has never seen before," Hannibal said. "The divine words of the Creator himself— sent here to save us all."

"You believe that?" Peter asked, knowing there was a good chance the ancient manuscript was nothing more than a jumble of incoherent gibberish.

"We believe in nothing else," Hannibal replied, guiding Peter to the back of Uriel's statue. A stone stele, similar to the others but much less worn, was the object the angel protected behind his right wing. The slightly worn rock encased an unremarkable man wearing a rough-woolen tunic. His facial expression was one of staunch determination.

Peter studied the man's face. "He's better preserved than the others."

"You will read from the book," Hannibal directed, "and tell us his name."

Chapter 15

A detachment of guards ambushed Isla Dora while patrolling a chokepoint between two heavily built-up districts. The area was a narrow alley with high walls and a small, diamond-shaped courtyard at its midpoint. The long, confined space and lack of exits made it the ideal location to corral wayward animas. Asmodeus's henchmen were under orders to apprehend anyone or anything that traveled through the passageway. The two men held the frail woman pinned to a wall while Asmodeus looked on.

"Release me!" Isla Dora hissed at the demon standing a few feet away. She lashed out sprightly with her legs and tried in vain to bite the hand of one of the demon's henchmen. Her wispy hair whipped through the air as she swung her head from side to side in a failed effort to weaken her attackers' hold.

"Tell me of Hannibal's intentions and I will consider your freedom," Asmodeus ordered.

"Hannibal—who's he?" Isla Dora mocked. "Sounds like a nice fellow if he got under your skin."

"Don't test me, old woman!" Asmodeus yelled as he struck Isla Dora's face with the back of his hand. "You and your ilk of animas are merely perpetuating a calculated illusion designed to give us pause. Nothing escapes you—least of all Hannibal's feeble attempts."

Isla Dora adjusted her jaw, contorting her weathered features in an effort to mitigate the pain. "Even if I knew of whom you seek," she stated, staring unflinchingly into the face of the demon, "my fate would be no different."

With one hand, Asmodeus snatched Isla Dora away from his guards and held her aloft by her throat. Red energy enveloped the old woman and she shook violently as jolts of electricity echoed throughout her ancient frame. The demon held the torturous force steady before letting it subside. "Perhaps you did not understand my question?"

Isla Dora turned her head to one side and fought feebly to free herself from the demon. Her hair covered her face and she blew it away, casting a wary eye at the demon. "You seek that which would destroy your own destiny?"

Her words startled Asmodeus and he stepped back. He did not want to fall prey to her guiles, but she was among the most ancient of the animas. He thought for a moment and shook it off. If Isla Dora knew something he did not, then it was all the more reason to break her now. Asmodeus reasserted himself. "I have no time for riddles, witch."

Isla Dora's respiration labored as she struggled against the demon's hold. "Do you believe your queen tells you everything?"

The old woman's assertion again caught Asmodeus off guard. Lilith rarely informed him of anything. He simply did her bidding, and failing or questioning the queen brought severe punishment.

Before the demon could respond, Isla Dora added, "Does Lucifer tell her?"

Although Lilith could contact Lucifer, she seldom did. The effort required was not inconsequential, and oftentimes, there was little need. Only a few standing orders existed between the demons of the Garden and Lucifer. They mostly dealt with casting down souls into the waiting clutches of the demon king and his fellow Fallen. Troublesome and rebellious nephesh were to be sent, with Hannibal high on the list of those Lilith sought to bestow this pleasure upon. At odd intervals, Asmodeus witnessed scores of newly-arrived souls being delivered, but paid no attention to her behavior and reasoned that Hell was in need of new entertainment, nothing more.

Once in a great while, Asmodeus unknowingly interrupted clandestine sessions between Lucifer and Lilith that seemed to serve no purpose. The demon wondered if he had ever been the topic of conversation and whether his ongoing performance was being judged. It was no secret that there was tension between Asmodeus and his queen. He was a stalwart ally of Lucifer and had been there for him at every turn, but once Lilith became involved, the dynamic changed. Asmodeus thought he would be the ruler in Eden, but the directions from Lucifer were clear. Once the nephesh started arriving, he became subordinate to Lilith in all respects.

Asmodeus became wary at the thought of his dismissal. At any time the queen wished, she could cast him out the same as any other human. Once an individual was cast down, be they demon or human, there was no possibility of return. Hell existed in its own space and the Garden of Eden, suspended just outside of Creation, proved to be the only conduit to access its vile depths. Over the millennia, the Garden of Eden had become a complex organism in its own right. Lilith needed Asmodeus, and he knew that she could not run the city without him.

Isla Dora saw the demon's distrust. "Hannibal is not the one you should fear."

Asmodeus's rage flared at the old woman's continued attempt to cast doubt at the demon trio's loyalties to each other. A deep red aura emanated from the demon and brightened to a blinding hue. The two guards covered their eyes and backed away from the spectacle.

Isla Dora screamed in agony. She began morphing her shape in an effort to escape. Her human form gave way to an inanimate broom. From there she changed to a small rodent and then went on to several other objects, both large and small.

At each turn, Asmodeus countered the old woman, holding her with increasing amounts of energy. His anger flared and his resolve

Chapter 15

to break her grew greater than ever. "Tell me of Hannibal's plan," he commanded.

Isla Dora stopped resisting and changed back into her human form. She raised her arms skyward and elongated her body, growing tall and thin. "I will do no bidding of yours!" she cried out and exploded into a blinding iridescent cloud of mist. The concussion knocked the demon backward and threw his guards to the stone floor of the courtyard.

Asmodeus's sight reeled in a kaleidoscope of color. He flexed the hand that had firmly held Isla Dora and found it empty. He stumbled a few steps and attempted to focus on the surrounding area. The old woman was gone. The demon grabbed the guards by their necks and yanked them to their feet. "She tricked us—find more men and search the area immediately!" he ordered, pushing them in opposite directions, toward either end of the alleyway. "Stop any animas—let none escape!"

The guards hurried off and disappeared into the darkness.

Asmodeus scoured the diamond-shaped courtyard for any sign of the old woman. Satisfied that he had not overlooked anything of significance, the demon leapt into the twilight sky and flew in low circles over the courtyard. He increased his search pattern with every pass until he disappeared out of sight.

The mist settled on the surrounding stone and formed a thin layer of shimmering water vapor. Almost imperceptibly, the damp rock shone with rainbow hues reminiscent of oil mixed with a light summer rain. The liquid drew together, retreating from the rock and gaining volume until it formed a pool on the floor of the courtyard. The pool flashed through a series of colors, growing in density until it solidified into the form of a silver-white rat. The rodent contemplated both passageways and then climbed to the top of the wall where it scampered away.

Chapter 16

"Rise," Hannibal ordered, kicking Peter in the chest. "We have much to do."

Peter awoke and rubbed his eyes. He had fallen asleep in the sheltered confines of the space between Uriel's statue and the stele he was studying. What seemed like an entire day came and went during which he tried to read the ancient manuscript—attempting to understand its nuances, but ultimately, the long bouts of prolonged boredom finally settled in, causing Peter to lay his head in the ash and fall into a deep slumber.

Hannibal loomed over Peter. "I hope the progress you have made is enlightening for us all."

Peter hoisted himself up to a sitting position and adjusted his glasses. He opened his mouth and ran his tongue across his dry lips in an effort to replenish their lost moisture. "I could really use some water."

"So could we all," Hannibal mocked. "It is time to introduce you to your benefactors," he said, striding off to join the company gathered in a clearing near the edge of the small valley.

Peter leaned back on Uriel's statue and brushed the ash away from the manuscript. He looked up to see the face of the stele and stared into its unblinking eyes. The test to see if Peter could gain insight into the man frozen inside of the rock had failed miserably. Translating the manuscript was a futile task. The mysterious tome was as indecipherable now as when he obtained it from Edda's trinket shop. He did not know how to tell Hannibal and others about his shortcoming, let alone the truth about how he came to possess the book. Peter was drowning in guilt. The band of mercenaries seemed intent on helping him, but there was nothing he could do to reciprocate their gesture. Despondent, he rose to his feet and ambled off in the direction of the gathering.

The individuals of Hannibal's group assembled loosely along the edge of the field of steles. Some stood while others sat on rocks or on the soft ashen ground. The mood was light with laughing and chiding amongst its members. Peter weaved his way around the steles toward the group but failed to make out what the levity was all about.

At some point during Peter's slumber, the members had removed their cloaks and stowed them into the personal satchels each carried. Without the burden of their outerwear, he was able to see their faces clearly for the first time and was struck by the diversity of the group. Altogether, there were seven men and three women. Three of the company were of Asian or Eurasian descent; one was African, with the remaining individuals, aside from Thomas, being of far-flung European heritages.

Peter attempted to gauge their ages, an extremely difficult task since each and every one of the men and women gathered was in exemplary physical condition. They exhibited the muscular structures and defining characteristics of athletes in the prime of their lives. Never before had Peter glimpsed a group of middle-aged men and women with such awe-inspiring physiques.

In his early twenties and easily the youngest of the group was Thomas. Beyond that Peter guessed the next-nearest age to be roughly early forties, with most of the group ranging into their fifties. Hannibal, by far, seemed to be the oldest of the bunch, perhaps in his early- to mid-sixties.

Peter recognized the various historical uniforms they wore. Most donned armor covering some sort of underclothing, but each was wearing a wholly different version depending on the origin and context of the particular member. Some wore ancient leather armor, replete with embossed filigree and shoulder spaulders, while others sported a more recent mixture of materials, such as chain mail and metal plate. The women's version of armor, for all intents and purposes, was of the same quality as the men's with one woman having a standout exception. The mercenaries' footwear ranged from sandals to heavier enclosed shoes, again, each depending on the historical context of the individual. Aside from Peter, the only deviation to the warrior dress code was Thomas and his 1950s greaser garb.

Peter closed in on the gathering and could finally see the cause of the amusement. At the group's center was Thomas, clumsily wielding a sword to attack the largest member of the assembled warriors. Dressed in leather armor over a dark-green silk robe, the defender was Chinese and a brute of a man. At well over six-and-one-half feet in height and close to three-hundred pounds in weight, the man dwarfed all who opposed him, but his physical size was not his most distinguishing attribute, as that honor went to his facial hair. Roughly two-feet long, the warrior's coarse beard fluttered through the air as the man easily deflected Thomas's haphazard blows.

Hannibal acknowledged Peter's approach and gestured to the large Chinese man, "This is Guan."

"Guan," Peter said, bowing his head.

Without giving the fight a second thought, Guan reciprocated the bow with sincerity and then continued to amuse himself with Thomas's innocuous assault.

Hannibal pointed to two men standing off by themselves. "Godfrey and Verus."

Godfrey was European, French from what Peter could deduce. Covering the man's aristocratic and slight frame was a fanciful thigh-length tunic emblazoned with a Cross of Lorraine. Under the tunic, Godfrey sported a full complement of steel armor along with a broadsword at his side.

Chapter 16

Standing next to Godfrey was the gladiator Verus. He was a little taller and much stockier than the Frenchman. Dressed in minimal clothing, he donned a leather manica on his right arm with a large metal galerus as a high shoulder guard. A short sword in a scabbard hung on Verus's hip secured by a wide belt around his waist. A knee-length leather skirt covered the gladiator for modesty.

Peter raised his hand in a friendly gesture to the two men. They smiled curtly in response and promptly returned to their conversation.

Hannibal put his arm around a beefy man of Norse decent standing next to Peter and gave the Viking a manly hug. "This is Gunnar."

Gunnar picked Peter up in a bear hug. "Welcome!" the Viking said loudly. "You must forgive me as I had my doubts, but Hannibal never wavered."

"Thanks, I guess," Peter responded, gasping for breath while extricating himself from the strong man's embrace.

In his forties, Gunnar was a big man with unkempt blond hair and a scraggly beard. Everything about him was rough. He wore a long, rusted chainmail shirt cinched in at the waist by a tattered belt. His leggings were in need of mending and his boots were open to the air in places. Gunnar carried a halberd-type weapon for combat and a round wooden shield. Both needed repairs, making Peter wonder if they were able to take more damage before falling apart.

Hannibal motioned to a Japanese man alongside the Viking. "Musashi."

Peter bowed deeply and flourished his arms. "*Konnichiwa.*"

Musashi chuckled at Peter's dialect, but bowed in response, replying, "*Yōkoso.*"

"Sorry," Peter said sheepishly, "that's the only Japanese I know."

"You honor me," Musashi said, smiling.

Musashi, in stark contrast to Gunnar, was compact and lithe. The only one of the group wearing no outer protection, Musashi was impeccably dressed in a samurai *Kamishimo*. His linen robes were all white with a red, wing-like shouldered vest. Carried in scabbards at his side were two samurai swords paired in the traditional *daishō* style. Musashi's balding head, spotted with tufts of graying hair, lent the man a trusting, grandfatherly air, but his keen eyes gave away the ruthlessness of his true nature.

After the introduction, Gunnar and Musashi went back to the fight before them. Both pointed at Thomas's footwork and mimicked his lack of proper technique. They shook their heads when Thomas was in danger and yelled at him to retreat before Guan could spank him with a sword. Gunnar and Musashi found comical relief in Thomas's failure, but they also offered encouragement and praise.

Peter was surprised to see the camaraderie between the two men. Gunnar and Musashi seemed as different as night was to day, but their rapport was one of admiration, respect, and family.

Hannibal guided Peter to the last three members of the assemblage. The women sat in a tight group conversing amongst themselves and paying little, if any, attention to the duel between Thomas and Guan.

Hannibal bowed. "Ladies," he said with the utmost of graciousness.

Almost in unison, the three women nodded their response.

Watching uncomfortably, Peter could not help but notice some form of political concession happening, but for the life of him, he did not know what it could be.

"Peter, the book bearer," Hannibal said. "Please extend him every courtesy."

The three women snickered at the request.

Hannibal waved his hand across the three from left to right. "Khutulun, Amanitore, and Elizabeth."

"It's nice to meet you," Peter said, mustering all the charm he could.

Khutulun was a trim woman from the Asian Steppe region. In her early forties, she had long and dark wiry hair pulled back into a simple ponytail. She wore leather armor over a more colorful blend of billowy pants and a blouse. Aside from a dagger, Khutulun carried a longbow with a quiver of arrows slung over her back. She nodded at Peter, but he could tell right away that she felt him unworthy of being in their company.

Amanitore was African, probably Ethiopian from what Peter could tell. She was in her fifties and sat with all the grace and poise of a Nubian queen. Amanitore was dressed similar to everyone else, with the exception of a very short skirt peeking out from under her armor plate. At her side was a curved, sickle-type sword and slung across her back was a longbow. Amanitore held her head high and reluctantly acknowledged Peter with a wry smile.

Even among the strong, the brooding, and the calculating, Elizabeth stood out like no other. The woman was a petite, raven-haired beauty, but her physical appearance was not what set her apart from her peers. She wore a shimmering, sleeveless dragon scale dress made of solid gold. It ended just above the knee and was held in place at the waist by a silver belt. Covering her arms were jewel-encrusted gauntlets that ended in grandiose rings gracing every finger. An ornate hilt protruding from behind Elizabeth's neck signaled a sword and scabbard that rode high on her back so as not to interfere with her range of motion.

Elizabeth's demeanor was more welcoming than the other two women. She seemed curious about Peter and made unflinching eye contact. She rose to greet the newcomer and performed a respectful curtsy. "Welcome indeed, book bearer," she said in a playful, almost flirtatious Eastern European accent.

Surprised at the overtly sexual greeting, Peter nervously adjusted his glasses and clumsily stammered, "Um—thanks."

Elizabeth took Peter's hand and turned it over to study his palm. She carefully felt along his arm assessing his physical strength. "Unspoiled," she judged, winking at the other two women. "Tell me, Peter, what did you do in life?"

"Do?"

"Your trade—your profession."

"I'm a—" Peter started, but then corrected, "I was a professor."

Elizabeth grabbed Peter by both shoulders and pulled him close to her. She sniffed the air around his face and chest. "I knew many professors as a child," she said, eliciting giggles from the other two women. "I study many subjects," she purred. "Which is your preference?"

"History, actually," Peter answered, respectfully trying to pull free of Elizabeth's grasp.

"I love history," Elizabeth teased, using her superior strength to immobilize Peter and forcing a drawn-out, sloppy kiss upon him.

Peter turned his head away. "I'm sorry—I don't know you."

"You want to though, yes?"

Peter looked to Hannibal for guidance.

Hannibal sneered at the woman's undisciplined behavior. "You are interfering."

Elizabeth released Peter. "I just want to speak to him; he knows history."

"I do," Peter interjected, straightening his glasses. "In fact, I recognize most of you."

Elizabeth dropped her alluring charade. "Tell me."

"Your last name is Báthory," Peter responded. "History remembers you as the Blood Countess."

"Lies!" Elizabeth spat, diverting her eyes from Peter.

Peter gestured to Hannibal. "You're the great general from Carthage." He motioned to Guan who was still sparring with Thomas. "He was also a general—China still reveres him."

Guan was paying more attention than he let on and said to Hannibal, "I told you."

Peter waved his hand across the entire group. "You're all there—in the pages of history." As he processed the ramifications of their respective careers, a feeling of dread came over him. He sat down on a rock next to the three women and without thinking, mumbled aloud, "You're all killers."

Collectively, the members of the company released a heavy sigh and murmurs filtered through the stagnant air.

Guan laughed at the news. "I told you that as well," he said, then used his sword to slap Thomas's butt, eliciting a yelp from the younger man.

"I'm sorry," Peter apologized. "I shouldn't have said anything."

"No," Hannibal said loudly so the others could hear. "We cannot run from our past. Every one of us endures today because of who we were."

Peter cast a quizzical glance back to Hannibal.

"The queen," Hannibal answered. "She pulled us from the multitude of new souls and gave us a purpose—without which, we would have been turned to stone."

Although he was curious, Peter did not reply. He could tell the mere mention of Hannibal's previous actions was too unpleasant for any conversation. It was simple enough: these individuals were saved from the queen's wrath because they could serve a purpose. There was no one better to oversee thousands of new arrivals than trained mercenaries and battle-hardened military personnel. They were good at what they did, and the queen appreciated their unique skill set.

Peter's thoughts went back to the day he arrived. He found it odd at the time that the young hoodlum, Butch, was plucked from the incoming flow of souls. Now Peter knew why. The queen was rewarding his lack of deference to the law. Butch would find a position within her guard that suited his capabilities. He would be free to continue his reign of terror while good people were turned into building materials.

"Ouch!" Thomas screamed and dropped his sword into the ash. He hopped around the center of the gathering holding his finger all the while being laughed at by the others. "It's not fair—he's too tall."

Hannibal retrieved the sword and thrust it back into Thomas's injured hand. "Do you believe you will be able to choose an opponent on the battlefield?" he asked, staring into the young face of the trainee. "Life is unfair; death is even more so."

Penitent, Thomas shrugged. "I understand."

"I don't think you do," Hannibal said, holding his hands up in a surrender position. "Strike me."

"You don't even have your sword out."

"Strike me!"

Not wanting to hurt the old general, Thomas swung his sword lazily through the air.

In one swift motion, Hannibal pulled his weapon and blocked the young man's weak attack. He sheathed his sword and ordered, "Again."

More serious, Thomas took another more energetic swipe at his opponent, but the older man simply stepped out of the way.

"Concentrate," Hannibal instructed.

Attempting to catch his teacher off guard, Thomas turned his body slightly to mask his attack and swung forcefully at Hannibal. The old warrior drew his weapon late and the upward trajectory of the incoming sword nearly cleaved through Hannibal's throat. The awkward impact was enough to push Hannibal off balance, forcing him to fall backward into the ash. Seeing his opening, Thomas pressed the advantage and thrust his sword in for the kill. Expertly and with little wasted motion, Hannibal swept Thomas's legs out from underneath him causing the young trainee to fall into the ash.

"Well done!" Hannibal congratulated. "Your awareness is greatly improved!"

Thomas picked himself up and in a hopeful voice, asked, "I'm better, right?" Immediately, he could see the frown on Hannibal's face, so he followed with, "I've been training—I almost beat you this time. That's got to be worth something."

Hannibal got to his feet, loosened a strap under his breastplate, and handed Thomas a sheathed knife. "This has been with me since the beginning."

Thomas studied the knife with disappointment. "You're pulling my leg, right?"

"In the proper hands, a knife can be a formidable weapon," Hannibal said, but seeing that Thomas's feelings were hurt, he added, "Your unique gift to move the stones is what has made our success possible. Without you, our endeavors would have failed years ago."

Disappointed, Thomas handed the training sword back to Guan and took a seat at the far edge of the gathering.

Peter followed the interaction closely. He felt for Thomas but could see the lesson Hannibal was trying to teach. There was no rule of law in Eden. To exist here, as Hannibal and his group had done, you needed to fight. You must be able to defend yourself and lend aid to those around you. There was no place for someone who would be a hindrance during battle. Resources needed to protect a weak link were resources lost toward the advancement of the final goal.

Peter knew all too well where he stood in the scheme of things. He was no fighter—no warrior. He was dead weight around the necks of the entire group. If a battle were to break out, Peter would have no recourse except to seek shelter. Hiding was something he could do. His only use up to this point had been to carry the ancient manuscript: a simple task recently burdened by the pressure of actually reading it.

Hannibal extended an arm in Peter's direction. "Tell us, what news from your examination of the book?"

Peter now understood the reason behind Hannibal's intention of bringing the book into the presence of Uriel. Hannibal hoped the manuscript would reveal something, but nothing, as of yet, had presented itself. Peter hoisted himself upright from the rock and stood before the company. He scanned the expectant faces and lowered his gaze in shame. "I have nothing to report. I'm sorry."

The mercenaries let out a collective breath and looked to their leader for support.

Hannibal met their stares and asked Peter, "Is there nothing you can do?"

Peter's courage retreated even further. The appropriate words to articulate his failure vanished from his mind. He struggled to find a balance between what he knew and what this world wanted. He felt lost, like a ship foundering on a tumultuous sea. The problem at hand required a thorough investigation. Parameters needed to be set, guidelines published, and a clear goal established. Peter could not work in the dark and he could not make progress by guessing. Then, as if by chance, he found what he was looking for: a direction. His scholarly instincts kicked in. Moving the problem forward required more data, something he was lacking but was more than eager to discover. If Peter could frame this problem in an academic fashion, he stood a better chance of finding the resolution. His posture straightened with his newfound confidence. "I don't know enough about the book," he said. "If I had a primer—somewhere to start—it would help immensely."

Hannibal considered Peter's words. "The first time I heard of that book, I was in the presence of the demon-queen herself. She referred to it as the Book of Souls."

Chapter 16

Peter recognized the name from historical references and various religious texts. The Book of Souls was a variation on the Nice List. If your name appeared in the Book of Souls, you were considered a moral person and allowed to enter Heaven. Peter's thinking all along had been that the Book of Souls was a fictional story meant to keep wayward individuals in line. Even with that knowledge, encountering the real manuscript simply provoked more questions about its purpose. Skeptical, Peter asked, "Why would God need a physical book—I mean, doesn't he know who's been good or bad?"

The contemporary reference elicited a small chuckle from Thomas, but the rest of the group remained stoic and looked to Hannibal for answers. This gave Peter the impression that the mercenaries were in the dark when it came to their actual objective.

"It contains more than a mere list of the righteous," Hannibal responded. "The volume is powerful beyond measure. Used properly, it will end this wretched existence and restore the original paths to salvation," and after a moment of hesitation, he added, "or damnation."

Peter absorbed every word Hannibal had to say about the book. The ancient manuscript could rectify what was happening in the Garden by unfettering the souls in their journey to the afterlife. He hefted the tome and turned it over in his hands. "And if it's used improperly?"

"I remember the day Lilith received news of the book's existence. She was jubilant," he said with disgust. "The queen believes the words written within will destroy the gates of Hell and allow her brethren to invade Creation."

"And you wanted to stop her?"

"We," Hannibal started and then paused for a moment. "I have done many things in my life I wish to atone for, deeds so despicable I can scarcely recall the warrior who committed them."

A chorus of sympathetic affirmations murmured through the group.

"It is said that the book was dictated to the monk Nicholas by angels," Hannibal said. "He was entrusted with its secrets because he was pious, because he was *worthy*." He motioned to the assembled mercenaries. "We want to be found worthy as well. We cannot change the past, but we can proceed more enlightened into the future. Our goal is to deny the queen her prize and release these souls to their rightful place—to whatever outcome awaits each of us."

Although he had lingering doubts, Peter found Hannibal's words compelling. He had assembled a team of like-minded individuals willing to sacrifice everything for a chance at redemption. They wanted to live on in the afterlife without fear of retribution from their wrongdoings.

"Can you not help us?" Hannibal asked.

Peter scanned the group to find every set of eyes upon him. "Of course," he responded, "but I'm not sure how much help I can be."

"Surely, Nicholas must have given you some instruction?"

Peter thought back to the day in the antique store basement. "I found it," he confessed.

Chapter 16

"He did not give it to you willingly?"

"He was there," Peter answered to a swell of relief from the group. "He never said anything, but he wanted me to take the book—I'm sure of that."

From out of the crowd, Musashi broke the awkward silence. "Perhaps it was not bestowed properly?"

Hannibal mulled the samurai's idea. "Perhaps."

Peter asked the obvious question. "How would we know?"

"The Book of Souls would manifest itself with the power of Creation," Hannibal responded. "Only a true believer or divine soul may wield it."

Peter's enthusiasm along with his newfound courage waned. Even when confronted with the reality of the Garden of Eden, he still had a difficult time believing that an almighty being created everything. Deep within his subconscious, Peter held out hope for an ending that found him waking from an injury-induced coma. His belief system was taxed enough already and he was certain the failure existed not in the book, but in himself. Peter considered his options. The only person in Eden that could use the ancient manuscript was Nicholas. The monk was there when Peter had arrived at the Gate; surely, Nicholas must know all about the old tome. With that in mind, he asked, "What about Nicholas?"

"He is guarded at every hour," Hannibal replied. "The queen seldom leaves him unattended." The old warrior withdrew in thought. He was a fierce leader, but hearing that his initial plan had been for nothing affected Hannibal's confidence noticeably. The men and women of the company respected him and relied on his absolute knowledge of the inner workings of Eden's political structure to succeed in their operations. Proof of Hannibal's leadership was all around them. The company had managed to snatch Peter away from the demon queen and leave the city—a feat none of them had thought possible.

Hannibal thoughtfully measured all the facts before him. "It is a risk, but if Nicholas were to possess the book, his actions should be swift. The operation would require a diversion of sufficient length—something we could provide."

A series of groans elicited from the company. They spent days traversing the relative safety of the countryside to find Uriel's Vale. Although there was only one city, it was massive. Any attempt to approach Nicholas would mean up to a week of crossing enemy territory to covertly seek out the monk. The odds of the mercenaries being captured would grow exponentially with each step they took.

No one knew the odds better than Hannibal. He raised his hands in a calming gesture. "Would you stay here?"

The members of the company looked to each other for support and nodded.

"I understand your fear," Hannibal said. "It is pleasant to dwell on these surroundings. We are known, but not yet hunted. The queen would find a way to reach us in this place. It is a fact that she will not rest until we have been found. We cannot hide here forever."

The mercenaries looked away to conceal their guilt.

Chapter 16

"The queen will never suspect something so rash. If we can find the monk, we can end this. All I ask is for a small amount of the support you have already placed in me."

One by one, the members of the company nodded their approval. Some detested the idea of running away, while others murmured their preferences of being the hunters and not the hunted.

"My friends, gather your belongings; we will move into the city," Hannibal said.

The group rose to standing and begun the task of stowing their gear.

Peter scanned the area for anything he might have dropped. He checked his glasses and placed the book in his shoulder bag. As the group got ready to leave, he was still curious about the stele of the man behind the angel and asked, "Who *was* Uriel protecting?"

"Adam," Hannibal responded. "The first of us all."

Chapter 17

Peter's body was still in the first stages of acclimation to the Garden. His physical fatigue remained, but his thirst had quelled somewhat over the previous days. The march back to the outer wall of the city was not as difficult as the initial trek out to Uriel's Vale, and Peter found the time very therapeutic. The burned landscape was calming, almost serene, especially compared to what awaited him inside the city.

Hannibal's approach to the wall was cautious and took nearly two days. He stopped the group well short of the fortifications and sent Elizabeth and Khutulun ahead to reconnoiter the area. Godfrey and Musashi were set as sentries, rotating out with Gunnar and Verus. The remainder of the company simply bided their time. The entire operation played out according to Hannibal's exacting and overly-deliberate plan.

The final advance on the city's fortifications was done quietly and in pairs. Every individual was assigned a partner and each grouping took different routes to the destination. The area Hannibal had chosen was littered with debris from the final battle of Eden. Dead trees and burnt brush, coupled with massive rock formations, reached out of the surrounding hillside and piled against the wall, forming a well-concealed gathering point hidden from wayward eyes. The once spacious niche became increasingly cramped as the individual members of the company filed in. Hannibal was the last to enter and stood in the confined space eyeing an uncovered portion of the city wall.

"Make quiet," Hannibal whispered to the chatty group. "Thomas, your skill is required."

Thomas knelt and studied the stone bulwark. The wall disappeared into the ground as it did all along the city's outer perimeter. There were no lintels, pillars, or any obvious indication that an entry point may exist along the local stretch of fortifications. "Are you sure there's a way in here?" Thomas asked. "The whole wall could come down on us if there isn't."

"It is here," Hannibal assured. "The perimeter has since encroached on the original structures."

Not entirely sure of the general's claim, Thomas proceeded with the utmost of care. He touched the hewn stones gingerly, as if he were caressing a woman. He worked the blocks back from the encasement and off to one side.

Peter watched the demonstration with great interest. Each block fit the wall snugly, but when Thomas placed his hands on them, they contracted. Once free of the load they carried, each stone seemed to breathe a sigh of relief, and Thomas simply guided the blocks to a new location to one side of the passage he was creating.

Peter placed his hand on the hard rock. "How is he able to do that?"

"Each one of us brings something to this place," Hannibal answered. "In all my years here, his gift of the stones is unmatched save that of the demons themselves."

"They're suffering," Thomas interjected.

"You can speak to them?" Peter asked.

"No," Thomas said, shaking his head, "but they were human once—men, women. They still feel things—they want to help me. I don't know how to explain it."

Thomas finished moving the stones and stood up, showing the company a large, arched doorway just inside the outer casing of blocks. The rock of the hidden entry was rougher and smaller than that elsewhere in the city, signaling its more ancient construction.

"Torches," Hannibal whispered.

From rucksacks and pouches, several members of the group produced short wooden staves with a sticky resin at one end. They cupped their hands around the end of the torch and whispered something. Peter was not sure what was said, but it appeared to be some kind of prayer. The torches flamed to life and gave off a warm glow, each hissing like a burning log with too much moisture trapped in the wood.

Peter drew closer to one of the flames and noticed the same screaming he had heard earlier from Isla Dora's candle. The sound disturbed him and he backed away.

"We must stay together," Hannibal ordered. He took one of the torches from Gunnar and led the group of mercenaries under the archway and into the bowels of the city.

Peter's eyes were accustomed to the perpetual twilight of the Garden, but the city's underbelly was as black as tar. He stepped cautiously and allowed his sight to adjust to the low light levels. Through the scant, flickering light of the torches, Peter discerned a maze of cells and holding areas separated by iron bars.

The prison complex was large and extended into the darkness on all sides of the company. The jail was in disarray and seemed to have not been in use for hundreds, if not thousands, of years. More than a few cell walls had collapsed in on themselves. Strewn about as if a riot had taken place were heavy iron doors that once attached to hinges now left vacant on most of the holding pens. Detritus from the ceiling occupied every space and in some cases made the way impassable. It seemed the prison was unplanned and its space reused when the city grew in mass above it. Multiple corridors ended at walls, and large columns took over old cell space to support the weight of the streets above.

The group's footsteps echoed dully off the rock of the old prison. The trip through the derelict lockup gave Peter the chills, and he tried to calm his nerves by studying the architecture. It was reminiscent of the Roman era but was less refined and far earlier than anything documented within historical texts. Some portions of the jail were recognizable, while others were without context—haphazard and poorly made. Peter could see distinct changes in the construction methods as they continued. The older styles gave way to more contemporary building techniques the farther the company ventured into the labyrinth. The floor makeup caught Peter off guard as it was made of dirt—plain brown dirt. It was somewhat refreshing for him to see that the ash was not as pervasive as it was outside the wall.

Hannibal guided the company resolutely through the convoluted warren of abandoned cells. Along the way, the path forked frequently, but his confidence was unshakable. He navigated the corridors and stairways expertly, choosing the best possible route as if he had done so countless times in the past.

Peter attempted to memorize the way through the dungeon, but gave up soon after the first few switchbacks left him believing the company had turned in the direction of the perimeter wall. It gradually became clear to Peter they were heading deeper into the city, rather than back outside. The ceiling changed from stone blocks supporting the foundations of buildings to earth and rock similar to an underground cavern. He sensed the burgeoning mass of the metropolis and that of the physical Eden growing above him. Not only were they moving closer to the city's center, they were descending far underneath it.

Peter attempted to keep track of the number of days that had come and gone since his arrival. Initially, he relied on his circadian rhythms to help him count by adding a day when he got tired enough to sleep. At first, Hannibal would allow a respite for the company on the newcomer's behalf, something for which Peter was eternally grateful, but which brought much chagrin from the mercenaries. As his acclimation to the Garden progressed, the need for sleep dwindled until only a short nap sufficed. As a result, Peter had no idea how long the company had been roaming the depths of the city. Despite his every effort to keep a mental note, he came to the realization that time did not matter in Eden. It was a static place and the pure essence of things that had transpired meant nothing.

The jumble and arbitrary confusion of the original detention area gave way to a more orderly and thoughtful organization of holding cells. The numerous paths coalesced into a single avenue with bars lining both sides of the corridor. The debris-strewn footpath was narrower than before so the company found themselves marching single file.

The passage wound its way around several corners and through various straight stretches until the group confronted a blockage preventing them from moving forward. The ceiling had given way, clogging the corridor with dirt and rocks.

At the head of the pack, Hannibal immediately went to work clearing the debris. The two strongest, Guan and Gunnar, came forward to help. The rest of the members gave the men room by standing out of the way, against the iron bars.

Peter leaned back and watched the three men work. Flickering torchlight cast ghostly shadows on the façades of the cells. The light was weak and did not illuminate the interior spaces fully, but with the ebb and flow of the flames, Peter got a chance to see what life must have been like within.

Each holding chamber was slightly different from its neighbors. Dirt floors seemed to be the norm throughout, but the appurtenances were unique for each. Some cells contained raised beds made of the natural rock and earth of the Garden; others contained crudely made benches or chairs, with a few being devoid of furnishings entirely.

Fascinated with the living conditions, Peter turned to look into the cell directly behind him.

A man's face appeared from the darkness and his hands shot out to grab Peter by the straps of his shoulder bag. The man drew Peter closer and held him against the cell door.

Peter tried to pull away, but was unable to break free and screamed out in terror.

A chorus of clattering iron and warriors adjusting their footing greeted the newcomer's cry, but the first to respond was Musashi. In one swift motion, the samurai unsheathed one of his swords and struck down through the narrow gap between the iron bars and Peter. Musashi sliced through the man's forearms with great force, causing the prisoner to recoil violently. The man released Peter and withdrew back into his cell.

Chapter 17

Shocked, Peter stepped back and scanned the floor for the man's severed limbs. He knew the evidence of the carnage should be right there in front of him, but he saw nothing. Anxious, Peter patted the front of his shirt for blood, but found that his clothes were dry. It was as if the prisoner suffered no wounds at all.

The man came forward into the wavering light and grabbed the bars with both hands.

Peter was aghast; the prisoner's hands were still attached to his forearms. No blood or other signs of injury were evident. Peter could not fathom how the man could have escaped significant trauma—he witnessed Musashi's blade slice cleanly through the prisoner's flesh. Slowly, a realization dawned on Peter. Why would a soul bleed if they were never alive to begin with? The man obviously felt intense pain, but his injuries were not permanent. It made some sense; you could not kill something that was already dead. No doubt, the ability to inflict pain to any degree without the subject dying came in pretty handy in this place. The demons could do anything they wanted and the souls would endure the pain repeatedly if they did not relent. By default, Eden had become the perfect venue to conduct torture.

The prisoner pressed his face against the iron door, his thick beard and filthy black hair protruding from the gaps between the bars. His large brown eyes stared out from their sunken sockets and gauged each member of the group. "Hannibal?" he asked meekly of the old general.

Hannibal stepped forward bearing a torch. He approached cautiously with his weapon drawn and bathed the man in light. "Darius?"

A smile brightened the prisoner's cracked and withered face. "I knew you would come back for me."

Hannibal sheathed his sword and the others in the company followed suit. "The queen released you," he said. "She told me herself."

"Naught but a ruse to quell my followers," Darius replied, wiping his hands across the few scraps of material left covering his slight and meager frame. "I have been imprisoned ever since."

"It has been centuries," Hannibal muttered.

"Yes, a long time," Darius said, unable to suppress his lifted spirits, "but now you can rescue me."

In the faint light, Peter peered through the bars and scrutinized the floor. The few inches of dirt had been removed exposing a foundation of natural bedrock underneath Darius's cell. A multitude of claw and scratch marks were clearly visible on the surface of the stone. Peter surmised the man had tried to escape his fate only to find the geography of the Garden against him. He could not imagine the solitude and hopelessness Darius had experienced alone and in the dark for so long.

The Nubian stepped out of the group and placed her hand on Darius's arm. "It is I, Amanitore."

A tear flowed down Darius's face. "Yes, I remember." He pointed to the gladiator. "And you, Verus."

Verus nodded.

Hannibal reached out to the Viking. "Gunnar, your halberd."

Gunnar relinquished his weapon into Hannibal's waiting grasp.

Hannibal jammed the business end of the steel halberd between the door and the iron hinges of the frame. He put his full weight into prying the cell open and then, abruptly, stopped. "We cannot free him."

Thinking that the issue lay with a lack of physical resources, a few members wedged their swords into the gap and proceeded to apply force, but Hannibal waved them off. "No," he ordered. "We dare not free him."

"Hannibal?" Amanitore asked "What is this?"

"If the she-devil were to find him missing, we would be at a tremendous disadvantage."

Various members of the company shook their heads in disgust, but they knew Hannibal's wisdom was sound. Saddened, the group stowed their weapons and in turn, placed a hand on Darius's as if to bid farewell.

"Would you leave me here for another eternity then?" Darius asked of the mercenaries.

"It will not be that long," Hannibal replied. "Whether we succeed or fail, this existence will end and you will be free."

"We have an opening," Guan called from the front of the procession by the blockage.

"Move out," Hannibal commanded.

One by one, the individuals of the company moved through the opening in the debris.

Darius grabbed the old general's arm and pleaded, "You cannot leave me—our friendship was one for the ages, or do you not remember?"

"We cannot jeopardize our campaign," Hannibal replied, breaking free from Darius's grip. "You will not be forgotten, I promise."

"Hannibal!" Darius shrilled into the darkness.

Hannibal nodded solemnly to his imprisoned friend and made his way through the breach. He sighed heavily and ordered the company to seal the route behind them.

The company followed a simple path through the underground caverns of the Garden. It had been several hours since the company had witnessed any signs of the metropolis above. Once they left the prison area, the symmetrical blocks symbolic of the city grew in scarcity until all that remained was the natural soil and rocks of the Garden itself.

The mood among the mercenaries was a somber one. Hannibal seemed more determined than ever to fulfill his quest, but leaving Darius behind had cut him deeply. The leader of the company kept to himself and only spoke to hush any banter as the noise could lead to discovery by enemy forces.

Chapter 17

Peter followed along. He found the trek through the caverns excruciatingly boring. The flickering torchlight revealed no signs of active geologic formations, or anything else of interest normally found in caves—just miles upon miles of barren earth. He was not surprised. Eden was a barren and lifeless place. Regardless of the stories of old, the contemporary Garden offered no vestiges of its once glorious past.

Ahead, the mindless stupor of the mercenaries changed. They began speaking in low voices and waving their hands excitedly through the air.

Peter strained to see what the fuss was about but saw nothing. He pulled on Thomas's shirt and asked, "What is it?"

Thomas shrugged. "I don't see anything."

After a few steps, Peter felt the source of the jubilation waft across his skin. It transformed the members of the company, energizing their spirits and charging the atmosphere with hope. It was the simplest of things. Peter might not have noticed had it not been for Thomas's look of amazement. It was a breeze. Warm, moist air blew through the confines of the cavern, reminding Peter of a summer's day at the beach.

The group moved forward carefully, navigating several turns around fallen boulders and squeezing through the tight spaces left between the rocks and the walls of the cavern. Ahead of them, light streamed in from the backside of the last boulder, bathing the passage in a soft, opaque glow. The company's anticipation grew as they snuffed out their torches and pressed forward.

Peter pushed his way past the last obstacle and stood in awe of the sight that greeted him. The floor of the cave behind the large rocks had collapsed long ago, revealing the open-air underside of the Garden of Eden.

The path around the gaping maw was narrow and treacherous. The opening was long enough to accommodate all the members of the company side by side with room to spare, but jagged rock and overhanging earth made navigation tricky. Bright daylight streamed in from the outside making it difficult for the group to view the exterior directly. A humid breeze rustled clothing and elicited words of pleasure from the mercenaries.

To Peter, the hole was nothing more than a minor nuisance— something to hinder their progress, but the rest of the company perceived the sight as nothing short of miraculous. It was interesting for Peter to find that the twilight sky that pervaded the city above was gone, but anything more significant was lost on him. To get a better view, he kneeled and held on tightly to the rock floor of the cavern. He hung his head below the rim of the opening and took a long look. His breath left him. A mile below was a sea of crystal-blue water spanning nearly the entire horizon. At its furthest reaches, the inland sea offered a tantalizing glimpse of a rocky, desert coastline. It was remote, but Peter could discern the coast following the water for a short distance before trailing off, out of sight. He could not make out the source of the sunlight, as it appeared to be coming from directly over the Garden.

Chapter 17

As Peter searched the rocky underside, he noticed the most astonishing thing of all: the Garden of Eden was floating in midair. There were no signs of supporting structures, either from the water below or the sides of the Garden. The mass seemed like a fixed point within the cloudless sky. He gazed to the sea's surface and saw no shadow cast against the serene waters. The Garden sat suspended, high above the inland ocean. It did not intervene or obscure the light from above in any fashion. He shook his head in disbelief at the concerning sight.

Not far off from the group's location was another oddity that only added to Peter's amazement. A river of water poured from a small hole in the misshapen underside of the Garden. The water fell in a great torrent, slowly turning into a heavy rain on its journey to the sea far below. Peter attempted to focus on the river's entry into the vast body of water. He wanted to see if the disturbance influenced or created waves of any kind on the clear, flat surface of the inland ocean, but the distance was so great he could not tell if the two ever touched.

Peter raised his head back into the cavern. His thirst, once a waning thought at the back of his mind, now came to the forefront. By the look on the group's faces, he was sure the same thought had crossed all their minds. "Why don't we jump?" he asked to no one in particular.

Licking his lips, Thomas seconded the thought. "We can't die, right? We just take the book with us—she'd never know."

Peter pointed in the direction of the remote shoreline. "We can swim—it might be better down there."

Hannibal chuckled. "Do any of you share in young Peter and Thomas's sentiment?"

The mercenaries mulled over the question. A few nodded, while others raised their hands in agreement. Giddy chatter broke out amongst the company.

Hannibal looked forlornly at the glimmering water. "I too share in your dream," he admitted, "but it is a cruel deception."

The playful banter died down.

"It is the sea of Avernus," Hannibal said, gesturing to the sea below. "Those shores you speak of, Peter, they are the shores of Hell. Once you have fallen, there is no hope of redemption—none who have ventured there ever return. Neither demons nor humans can cross the boundary again after it has been fully traversed."

The members of the company sighed and stowed their fading emotions.

"You would be taking the Book of Souls directly to Lucifer himself," Hannibal said, trying to prop up the morale of the men and women in his charge. "We have the advantage here, and we must use it while we can."

"Is there any hope?" Peter asked.

"Yes," Hannibal replied, pointing to the treacherous ledge that circumvented the gaping hole in the cavern. "Our path leads us to the queen's throne room."

The group raised their voices in opposition to the route.

Chapter 17

"Our only hope is to create a diversion while Peter gives the book to Nicholas," Hannibal said, quieting the dissent. "The monk dwells in the throne room most days, and he will be lightly guarded."

"And if the queen is there?" asked Godfrey.

"We will not proceed if demons are present," Hannibal replied. "We can easily hold the guards at bay for as long as necessary—the book bearer will not fail us," he assured, looking sternly at Peter.

Peter put on a good face and acknowledged his role, but deep down he was frightened to death.

"Retreat?" asked Guan.

"There is none—we must succeed."

Chapter 18

Hannibal guided Peter and Thomas up through the interior supporting structure of the queen's throne room to an access point in the floor between two walls. Before leaving the small void, Hannibal gave them explicit instructions to stand fast until the obvious intervention by the mercenaries had begun. Hannibal had faith in the young men, but nonetheless found himself second-guessing his overall plan. Put simply, the company's entire effort lay in the hands of their two weakest members.

The cramped space Peter and Thomas crouched in was nothing more than a cavity between old, roughly-made stonework and that of a newer, more elegant finished wall. The area was dark with only a smattering of light entering through small gaps in the stone from the well-lit hall beyond.

Peter and Thomas were on edge and doubting their abilities to fulfill their obligations to Hannibal and the group as a whole. Peter restlessly shifted his position several times, trying not to appear anxious while Thomas fidgeted with his hands, placing them on the stone wall and removing them quickly as if a false start had been announced.

"You've probably done plenty of this stuff, huh?" Peter asked.

"Hardly any," Thomas answered, shaking his head timidly.

Peter's voice heightened as alarm pervaded his tone. "But you've been with Hannibal for a while, right?"

"Some, I guess."

In his mind, Peter recounted what he knew about Hannibal and the others. They seemed sincere in their quest, but their historical personae were fraught with violence and despair. Peter wondered if he had unknowingly fallen into a trap—if the only reason for his rescue by Hannibal's group was to deliver the book directly into the waiting arms of the demon queen herself. Suspicious, he asked, "How did you meet Hannibal and the others?"

"Meet?" Thomas asked, surprised at the question. He thought back to the day he entered the Garden. "I was scared, you know?" he said, looking expectantly through the near-total darkness at Peter. "I split as soon as I came through the Gate. I didn't know what else to do. There was so much going on—so much I didn't know."

"You didn't get caught?"

"Not right away. A couple of guards saw me leave, but they didn't say anything. They must've thought they were going to get in trouble or somethin'."

"You were lucky."

"Yeah." Thomas chuckled quietly, remembering the events. "I wandered around—tried to stay hidden. That's when I found out I could move the blocks. That was a cool feeling—and scary at the same time."

"And then you met Hannibal?"

"More than a few years passed before I did," Thomas answered. "I'd been all over this place. I was doing okay on my own, but one day I got caught." He took a breath. "The guards were taking me to Asmodeus—that's when Hannibal rescued me." Thomas said, poking at the dim beams of light coming through the imperfections in the joints of the wall. "I left with him—I didn't know what else to do."

"Did he ever say why he rescued you?"

"They'd been watching me. Hannibal asked how I had managed to never get caught." Thomas giggled. "They must've thought I was some kind of boss warrior or somethin'." He cast his gaze to the floor and muttered sadly, "But when I moved the stones, they knew why."

The more Peter listened to the story, the more suspicious he became. "Do you trust Hannibal?"

"I trust him—I trust that he's true to his cause," Thomas replied. "The others, I'm not so sure about. It's been years, right? They hardly talk to me. I'm an outsider to them still—just a tool to help get them around."

Peter recognized the despondency in Thomas's voice. "Guan seems to like you."

"Yeah," Thomas said, his mood lightening a bit. "Hannibal, I guess; the rest of them—not so much."

Peter's apprehension was at an all-time high. The fear that had plagued him since his arrival intensified. He found himself moments from a battle he could not escape with his loyalties on the verge of disintegrating. Part of him wanted to summon what energy he could and run away from the city, hide in the ashen wasteland and never come back, but his braver half wanted to fight, to prove that he was not weak.

Peter's mind raced. He saw both sides of the dilemma at once. Perhaps Hannibal's intentions were true—the renowned general only wanted forgiveness—but then again there was no way to know. Thomas had faith in the old general and that was comforting, but Peter needed proof. He felt caught in a tsunami and unable to escape. Powerless, his only recourse was to watch his fate unravel. Peter quieted the negative thoughts, as it was too late to divert from his unfolding path. He mustered what confidence he could and vowed to move forward.

Thomas placed his hands on the roughly yard-square block in front of them. With an acute tenderness, he shrunk the stone so that its edges receded from the wall around it. The gap was no more than an inch, but the fascia stones were relatively thin, making the openings adequate for the young men to surveil the chamber beyond.

The throne room was approximately two-hundred yards long and nearly half that in width. It was ostentatious to say the least. Soaring, buttressed ceilings, complete with mosaics, stone imps, and demonic faces, decorated the interior surfaces. At regular intervals along the high, white-marble walls, sturdy sconces held iron kettles blazing with smokeless fire. Around the perimeter of the black-marble floors was an array of statues. Peter knew from his experiences at Uriel's Vale that the statues were those of poor individuals caught by the queen and transformed to stone—forever hardened into a pose befitting their fear.

Peter cast his gaze to the near end of the chamber. An oversized throne rested on a raised platform several feet above the marble floor and sat empty at the focal point of the room. The chair glittered in the firelight. Although it was primarily made of gold, a strange set of silver orbs decorated the chair's numerous vertical splats. Peter squinted to see the detail more clearly. The spheres were in fact silver-plated skulls staked through with large pikes and integrated into the chair's back. Their flesh had been removed at some point, but whoever oversaw the gruesome task had left the eyes of each individual in situ. They blinked and moved, tirelessly scanning the area around the throne.

Shocked at the sight, Peter backed away from the small slit between the stones and shook his head, trying to clear the abhorrent image. "Do you think they can see us?"

Thomas spied the throne from his side of the crack between the rocks. "That's crazy!" he said in an overly enthusiastic whisper. "Can they say anything—alert the guards?"

"I don't know," Peter replied, pressing his eye back to the spy hole to renew his scan of the room.

Chapter 18

Behind the queen's throne was the monk Nicholas. The middle-aged man sat at a medieval scriptorium perched upon a long table set against the back wall of the audience chamber. A thick manacle around the monk's left wrist was chained to the floor just under Nicholas's wooden bench. The set-up allowed the monk to reach either end of the table, but not much else. Piles of papers, stacked haphazardly on the desk and table, were joined by a supply of quills and clay jars of ink.

Peter sensed Nicholas was being forced to regurgitate a copy of the Book of Souls from memory. In all likelihood, the ancient manuscript was purposefully disjointed in its authorship so as to prevent what the queen was now attempting.

"I see him," Peter said. "On the far wall."

"Lots of guards," Thomas commented as he eyed the chamber's defenders.

Peter studied the room's occupants. Gangs of workers toiled on everything from small cleaning chores to moving heavy objects into and out of the hall. Overseers used whips and swords to entice the slave laborers to accomplish their various duties and to keep them in line. Several sentries were stationed at each entrance to the throne room. Wide hallways flanking each side of the hall near the queen's throne were unguarded, but numerous individuals frequented the passages, leaving Peter to believe they led to a warren of chambers deep inside the building.

Hannibal must have known the layout of the throne room so well that he placed Peter and Thomas in the optimal location to make a break for Nicholas. They were no more than one hundred feet or so to the monk's table. Peter gauged the security to be much less at the throne-end of the hall than anywhere else in the chamber. He would have to run fast and maneuver around the throne, but otherwise it was a straight shot. The only complication would be the sentries at large or personnel coming from the hallways on either side of the scriptorium table. If he were able to give the book to Nicholas, perhaps the monk would be able to end this world before Peter was even discovered.

"There they are," Thomas said, gesturing to the opposite end of the hall.

An opulent vestibule provided access to the interior of the throne room. No doors were present in the antechamber that Peter could see, but he guessed more corridors and buildings stood in the way between the city streets and this inner sanctum of the queen.

Hannibal and his mercenaries came in through the vestibule. They wore their cloaks and did their best to blend in as another gang of workers. The gladiator Verus, donning a purple guard's uniform and holding an unfurled whip, stood over them as their overseer and led the mercenaries deeper into the hall. The company mimicked the work of other laborers within the great throne room by holding cloth rags and diligently scrubbing the already spotless floors.

Peter snickered to himself. The audacity of Hannibal and his friends was unimaginable. They played their part well and did a marvelous job of convincing the other overseers of their legitimacy. Whenever Verus felt the glare of scrutinizing eyes, he cracked his whip and yelled at Hannibal and the others to work harder. Likewise, some of the group purposefully lingered behind, forcing Verus to put on a show of scolding the stray members.

The company had not quite reached the midpoint of the hall when Peter spied a familiar threat. Butch, the tattooed young thug pulled from the stream of incoming souls at the Gate, was leading his own detachment of slave workers in the general area of Verus's gang. Peter could not tell what the issue was, or even if suspicions had been aroused, but Butch approached the mercenaries nonetheless.

"This is my spot," Butch told Verus, scrutinizing the gladiator's face. "I've never seen you before."

Verus smiled. "Is that so?"

"Who gave you orders to be here?"

The members of the group stopped working and listened intently.

"Why, Asmodeus himself," answered Verus.

The response gave Butch momentary pause, but his suspicions grew. "You and your men, come with me," he said, motioning for Verus's laborers to rise. "Master Sitri will need to clear this."

Behind Verus, the cloaked mercenaries rose to standing. The gladiator peered in the direction of Hannibal and picked up on the subtle head shake the old general was signaling. "Hold!" Verus ordered the company and turned to the young thug. "We do not take orders from you."

Butch loosened the grip on his whip, letting the coiled leather unfurl to the throne room floor. "I'm just doing my job."

Verus exhaled deeply and pulled his sword. "So are we."

Hannibal and the others heeded their cue. The group cast off their cloaks revealing a glittering array of armor and weapons.

"Intruders!" Butch screamed and lashed out at Verus, swinging his whip in an attempt to catch the gladiator in the face, but his attack was too late. Verus sent his sword plunging into Butch's chest. The thug grasped in agony at the bloodless wound and fell to the marble floor.

Hannibal surveyed the assemblage of guards closing in on their position. He drew his sword and took a defensive position while the others followed suit. "We must delay as long as possible," he said, slashing the first of the queen's responding minions and dodging a second.

"That was subtle," Peter said, trying to calm his paralyzing anxiety while his heart pounded in fear. It took all his resolve to extricate the ancient manuscript from its confines of the shoulder bag and clutch it to his chest. He fidgeted with his glasses and looked expectantly at Thomas. "Should we go?"

Thomas was on edge as well but dealt with his stress in a calmer fashion than Peter. He considered the unfolding situation and replied, "Not yet. We still have guards at this end."

Peter peered through the small slit in the stone. While some sentries disappeared through the corridors at either side of the hall, others were unable to decide whether to join in the fray or to stay at their given duty stations. Several remained in and around Nicholas's work area, decreasing Peter's chances of delivering the book.

A shadow traversed across the gaps in the stone, blocking the limited light entering the cramped space. Thomas pulled back. "Holy shit! It's Sitri and he's going ape."

Peter followed the leathery-winged beast on his flight through the great hall. Sitri rose into the vaulted and airy ceiling of the throne room, took a bearing on Hannibal's group, and dove headfirst into the battle.

"Demon!" Hannibal shouted over the din and wheeled about to prepare for the new threat.

Sitri's first thought was to turn Hannibal's lot into a lump of charred flesh, but his queen's orders had specifically prohibited any transformations of matter due to the risk of damaging the Book of Souls. Instead, Sitri unleashed his power on the still-injured Butch and his cowering slave laborers.

Bright green energy surrounded Butch and the nephesh in his charge. The verdant aura penetrated between the slaves, wrapping each individual in an emerald haze. Butch, lying prone and enduring the painful restorative process to his injuries, was instantly healed. Swirling mist forced the overseer and his workers to their feet. The fog penetrated their bodies and washed over them, obscuring their features. They cried out in pain as the unorganized bank of green brume grew. Pulsing energy surged through the dense cloud, knocking back combatants on every side. The apparition reached its apogee, soaring into the interior spaces of the hall, then without further bluster, quietly dissipated, revealing a giant.

Twisted and grotesque, Butch the Giant stood nearly twice as tall as the demon Sitri. The giant's massive body was made from the melded remains of slave workers. Headless bodies were fused together from ankles to shoulders to make up the bulk of the giant. Its trunk was two humans in height and several deep. The souls were merged laterally along their individual torsos, giving the giant a solid mass in his chest area. Appendages such as arms and legs were comprised of several slave bodies each. They were joined end-to-end and sprouted from the giant's main trunk forming working limbs. The worker's knees and arms served as Butch the Giant's joints while an opposing set of slave hands on each arm gave the giant a means of clasping objects. The fearsome beast's feet were little more than a mass of fleshy stumps that were flat on the bottom similar to an elephant's foot. Fused to the giant's shoulders and jutting out like a superfluous appendage was Butch. Every movement the thug willed of his new giant body brought a ripple of spasms and twitches from the souls that composed his misshapen being.

"Subdue them!" Sitri ordered to his minions at large while turning to Butch the Giant. "Bring me their leader—spare no souls!"

"Cool," Butch the Giant acknowledged and hoisted a fallen guard in each of his clasping hands. He used them like truncheons, battering his way into the skirmish, smashing friend and foe alike.

Hannibal raced to confront the monster. He placed himself between Elizabeth and the swinging arm of the giant. As Butch's hand descended, Hannibal sliced across the set of opposing wrists, forcing the gangly creature to release his grip and sending the unfortunate defender crashing into the marble wall. Hannibal lashed out against the giant and struck a crippling blow to his unnatural legs, temporarily hobbling the creature.

Hannibal glanced at the doorways. They were jammed with guards pouring into the throne room. It would only be a matter of moments before the mercenaries were overrun. "Tighten our ranks and rally!"

Peter watched helplessly from the safety of the wall's façade. The bravery of Hannibal and his mercenaries was inconceivable. They were putting everything on the line for him and the Book of Souls. Their past lives behind them, the battle-hardened warriors sought redemption through their actions against the malignancy that ruled the Garden.

Peter pushed his fear down and swallowed hard. "Open the wall—I'm going to make a run for it."

"Run?" Thomas coughed, peering through the gap. "There's a guard on the other side of the room—he'll see you."

Peter studied the solitary sentry. All the other guards had left their stations to join the skirmish. The lone man's attention remained fixed on the fight and not on the hall at large. If Peter could leave the confines of the hidden wall space quietly, he would be able to traverse the distance to Nicholas without too many issues. The real question was whether Nicholas would choose to read the Book of Souls or turn Peter over to the demons. It was impossible to say which would happen as the old monk kept his head down and barely took notice of the pandemonium unfolding around him.

Peter would have to chance it. "Open it up."

"You're sure?"

Peter calmed himself and held on to the book tightly. "Yeah, it's now or never."

Thomas touched the stone and shrank the block by a few more inches. Silently and with little effort, he pushed the stone forward and slid it to the right, creating an opening roughly three-feet square.

Peter crawled through the hole and rose to standing inside the chamber. The atmosphere was hectic. Amongst the clattering of steel, he could clearly hear the gasps of the wounded and the calls to action by the mercenaries.

Peter clutched the book to his chest and took a step forward. Behind him, Thomas peeked out of the hole. "Where are you going?" he asked of the young man.

"With you."

So his voice would not raise an alarm, Peter knelt. "Stay here and keep the door open."

"No," Thomas countered, drawing the knife that Hannibal had given him. "I can fight."

Peter considered his alternatives and then replied, "Look, if something should happen, come and get me, but stay here in any case."

"That doesn't make sense."

Peter looked around and chuckled. "None of this does."

Thomas retreated. "I'll yell if I see something."

Peter nodded and started his trek. He stepped out away from the wall and walked with purpose, trying very hard not to appear out of place in the throne room. Peter kept his eyes focused on the marble floor, occasionally looking up to the monk's table. He quickened his pace and threw a glance to the sentry. The guard's gaze remained set on the battle at the far end of the chamber.

Peter took a deep breath and drew closer to the queen's throne. The eyes from the silver skulls followed him as he walked past the raised platform. He tried not to make contact with the stares, but Peter's curiosity got the best of him and he stole a look. The eyes immediately locked with his, but instead of fear, Peter felt an overwhelming sense of sadness. The eyes were not searching for intruders; they were in pain and seeking a liberator to ease their suffering. Peter bowed his head curtly as if to acknowledge their plight and let them know he had no power to release them. The eyes answered him with a simple, yet moving, closure of their lids. Peter's nerves eased somewhat, but he maintained his rigorous pace.

Consumed in his writing, Nicholas gave no notice of Peter's approach. The old monk kept his head down, shuffling back and forth among the stacks of papers.

Peter turned to check the sentry's position once again. With his momentum moving forward and his sight fixed behind him, Peter failed to navigate the back edge of the throne's stepped platform and crashed to the floor. The Book of Souls tumbled free and hit the marble squarely. A sharp *SLAP* echoed through the hall. The noise immediately caught the attention of the sentry who screamed out a fierce alarm.

Startled by the noise, Nicholas spun around to see what the fuss was about and was surprised to see Peter sprawled on the floor so near to him.

Peter cringed. He heard Sitri's orders to fall back and to capture the book-bearer echo through the great hall. A thunderous storm of footfalls rose to replace the sounds of striking steel. In the distance, Peter heard the unmistakable rush of air passing over a set of beating wings.

"Get up!" Thomas screamed from the confines of the wall. "They're coming!"

Peter scrambled to his feet and picked up the manuscript. Too scared to look back, he ran forward holding the book in front of him.

Nicholas closed as much of the distance as he was able, straining on his chains and reaching out with his free hand toward Peter.

As Peter closed to within a few paces of Nicholas, a large crystalline tree rose from the black marble floor. The tree vibrated, creating a ringing sensation that pierced through Peter, causing him to lose his balance. His temperature flared and he began to sweat profusely. Peter's head pounded and his sight closed in around him. He could scarcely see the face of Nicholas just beyond the far side of the crystalline tree as he attempted to skirt the formation, but it was no use. He stood dazed for a brief moment before falling face first, unconscious onto the cold marble of the queen's throne room floor.

Chapter 19

Sulfurous fumes burned Thomas's eyes as he entered the octagonal room. Several doorways were present at odd intervals along the walls. Habitually, he turned back and took notice of an outstanding feature along the entrance's lintel. A block of stone to one side of the opening had a large hole in it. He instinctively marked the exit as his escape route. After years of struggling with the confounding and nonsensical architecture of the city, Thomas knew to plan ahead.

The room itself was on the small side, about thirty feet across. A small ledge, just able to accommodate one person walking comfortably, ran against the octagonal walls and provided access to the asymmetrically-placed exits. The remainder of the floor area was an open pit of active lava some ten feet below the level of the walkway. The viscous, superheated magma boiled and erupted, throwing molten rock and flames into the upper reaches of the chamber.

Thomas brushed off his surprise at the method of torture used within the room and focused on his mission. Although a stable source of illumination was hard to come by, the flames produced from the lava gave off enough light to distinguish a human hanging limply amidst a forest of chains.

Peter was unconscious. He dangled over the open pit of molten rock secured by manacles attached to his wrists. His head was slumped forward putting his glasses in jeopardy of falling into the roiling magma. Peter's clothes were drenched with sweat and draped damply over his lithe frame. The shoulder bag containing the Book of Souls hung loosely from his neck.

Thomas was bewildered at the sight of the satchel. He was sure the demons would have absconded with the book. Freewill kept the demons at bay even now. The manuscript was of no use to them if they could not acquire it by an act of freewill on Peter's behalf. The knowledge only reinforced Thomas's belief that his friend would suffer mercilessly at the hands of the demons.

Thomas leaned over the edge of the pit. A fierce blast of flames stung his face and forced him to retreat to the safety of the ledge. The young man carefully adjusted his footing, ensuring he was well on the stone walkway before slowly reaching out to Peter. He endured several waves of heat, but his efforts were for naught as Thomas found himself several feet short of his goal.

"Pops," Thomas said as loudly as he dared. "Teach—Peter, wake up." When he received no response, Thomas searched for loose stones, debris—anything he could throw at the unconscious professor, but the walkway was clean. He was too far away to jostle Peter to consciousness and he could not risk making too much noise for fear of being discovered. In addition, Thomas did not know when someone would return and by all accounting, he had lingered long enough.

Thomas grabbed a set of chains closest to the edge of the pit and pulled hard, testing them against his weight. In response, the iron fetters jerked out of his hand and a loud howl filled the chamber. Startled, he let go and backed away. The noise was loud enough that Thomas feared detection. He cocked his head toward each exit and listened carefully. The silence from the corridors reassured him that he had gone unnoticed. The young man squinted through the darkness and into the upper reaches of the octagonal room.

Slowly coming into focus was a mass of moving flesh. Thomas discerned nearly two dozen individuals fused at the waist to the hewn stone of the chamber's ceiling. A few women were among the group of men and most seemed to be asleep or unconscious. They moved eerily back and forth as if in concert to the same dream. The poor souls hung upside down like bats, heads and arms dangling into the dry heat of the room. Their facial features had lost their individuality long ago, leaving a wide-eyed, hairless, and sharpened visage more reminiscent of an elf than that of a human. Their torsos were naked. The soul's flesh dripped sweat, creating rivulets through the oily grime accumulated over centuries of servitude.

Thomas studied the nearest hanging soul. Around each of the slave's wrists was a manacle attached to a long chain that hung to just above the molten pool below. Thomas noted that Peter was elevated above the superheated magma almost to the level of the surrounding walkway. The soul that held Peter had taken in the slack and held it in his hands rather than letting the professor bathe in the molten rock. It was a curious spectacle. Either the slaves were adhering to strict orders or were allowed some form of freewill toward those they helped torture.

The sight did not surprise Thomas. There was no limit as to what the demons could manifest out of the plainness of humanity, and in his travels throughout the city, he had witnessed some of the most terrifying and bizarre things imaginable. Although the chain-bearing souls were new to him, their presence was not unexpected.

Thomas locked eyes with the hanging slave he had trespassed. He appreciated the poor soul's position, but time was short and he needed help. "Please," he implored of the disfigured human, "I need to get my friend."

Incapable of speech, the chain-bearing soul snarled a warning in reply.

Thomas held up his open palms. "I'm sorry—really—about all of this, but things will get worse if I can't reach him."

The slave parodied Thomas's gesture and chortled, rattling the chains in jest. He slapped the soul next to him and woke the creature. After a moment of hand signals and grunts, the two pointed and snickered at the hapless young man.

Perturbed, Thomas ignored the two and turned to the slave that held Peter directly. "Can you help me?"

Chapter 19

The soul nodded and, straining under the weight, began to swing Peter closer to Thomas's position along the ledge.

Now angered, the two creatures that recently snubbed Thomas were doing everything they could to hamper the rescue effort. As Peter noisily arced through the dangling chains, the two grabbed at the unconscious professor, pulling on his restraints in an effort to stop his momentum. Other chain-bearing souls arose from their slumber and joined in the odd skirmish. A few attempted to block the efforts of the two dissenters while others chanted in an unintelligible tongue, egging the renegades on.

Thomas did his best to quiet the group by waving his hands and softly trying to shush their voices, but his efforts went largely unnoticed. The amount of noise was considerable, and he feared the queen's guards would burst in at any moment. He stood by anxiously, scanning the various entrances and plotting his escape. However, after a few tense minutes, Thomas concluded that the overwhelming din echoing through the room must be a given due to the fettered creatures' constant bickering and divided loyalties.

As the soul swung Peter, he let more chain free on each pass. This made Peter dive further into the pit, but it also meant that his unconscious body came closer to the edge during apogee. Thomas used one of the friendly creatures' chains as a handhold and when Peter neared the ledge, he grabbed the professor by the shoulder bag's strap. It was precarious at first, but after a few minutes of wrangling and coordinating with the chain-bearing soul to slacken the restraints, Thomas was able to bring a slumped-over Peter to the edge of the walkway.

"Come on, get up," Thomas said, shaking the unconscious professor. "We've got to split."

Peter stirred awake, blinking his eyes slowly as he processed his surroundings. "Where am I?"

"You don't want to know," Thomas replied, tugging at the manacles on Peter's wrists. The locked bindings left scant wiggle room between the iron and the man's flesh. He studied the chains and examined the links, looking for a weakness. The restraints were secure and made with exacting precision to negate any possibility of escape.

Peter recognized the look of dread on Thomas's face. "That good, huh?" Peter said as he lifted his head and peered into the pool of molten rock. Unfazed at the sight, he righted himself to a sitting position and hefted the weight of his iron fetters. He followed the chains into the dark ceiling and their unlikely, grotesque keeper. The chamber's purpose was clear. The Book of Souls was important, more so than any one being or soul. The only way the queen would possess the ancient manuscript was by torturing the individual that carried it into submission. Once the pain was too much, the book would be hers *willingly*. An eternity of time was on the queen's side.

Regret, anger, and hopelessness filled Peter's mind, but he stifled them. "Where's Hannibal?"

"Captured," Thomas replied. "I don't know where they went, but they took Nicholas with them."

Peter pulled on the shackles fruitlessly. There was no actionable way forward. He was deep inside the city's underbelly and hopelessly chained to one of the queen's slaves. Peter grew despondent. He rummaged through the shoulder bag and produced the Book of Souls. "Take it."

Thomas reached out instinctively, but stopped himself. "What?"

"Look, you're the obvious choice. You can move around in the walls, wait it out, and when you're close enough, give Nicholas the book yourself. You don't need me or anyone else."

"Keep it," Thomas said, pushing the book away. "I'm going to get you out of here."

"How?" Peter chuckled. "They'll submerge me into the lava. Even if I lasted through that, they'll just do something else—I'm done, no matter what. The only hope we have is for you to get the book out of here." He pushed the manuscript at the young man. "Take it."

Reluctantly, Thomas placed his hands on the book. "I'll—"

A high-pitched, shrill noise sliced through the heat of the chamber. The odd and unexpected disturbance came from a silver-white rat on the ledge next to Peter and Thomas. The rodent sat back on its haunches squeaking excitedly and gesturing with its paws. All outward appearances pointed to the fact that both men were in the process of being scolded.

"Isla Dora?" Peter asked the rat.

Surprised, Thomas cocked his head. "You know this mouse?"

The rodent lowered herself to all fours and hunched her back. Her body vibrated, changing color and shape. The main mass of the rat diminished in size and morphed into a flat, furry disk. It retracted further, continuing until its shape settled on a unique-looking, multi-pronged, brass key.

"The shackles," Peter said, holding out one wrist. "Try it."

Thomas gingerly picked up the key and inserted it into the lock. The key turned easily, releasing the manacle. He moved to the other arm and freed Peter from his bonds. The young man held the key out and examined it closely. "That's something. I didn't think they could be so—normal."

The key transformed back into the rat and, in a show of defiance, bit Thomas sharply on the finger. The young man jumped up and shook his hand, sending the rodent to the stone of the walkway. The rat wheeled about, squeaking in protest.

"Damn mouse," Thomas cursed, sucking at the wound on his finger.

Peter bent down and locked eyes with the rodent. "We need to get out of here—can you help us?"

Isla Dora shifted her appearance once again, from a rat to a medium-sized, white dog. The dog whined and wagged its tail. It ran to one of the exits and disappeared through it.

"That's not the one I came in," Thomas said, noting the lack of physical characteristics on the stone.

"It doesn't matter," Peter replied. "She wants us to follow her."

"What if she's crazy?"

Chapter 19

Peter rose to standing and brushed himself off. "Yeah, what if we all are?"

Thomas nodded and together, the two men chased after Isla Dora.

Chapter 20

Asmodeus and Sitri led the procession of prisoners slowly and deliberately through the bowels of the city. The demons paraded the captured group of mercenaries through the most populated areas of the stone metropolis like trophies. The tedious route forced the company to navigate locked gates, steep stairs, and tight passages all to the sounds of jeers and taunts from most of the city's occupants.

With their arms and hands bound in front of them, Hannibal and his mercenaries were unable to give much resistance to their captors. They feigned injury and fatigue to slow their progress as much as possible, but the demons swiftly put down each action and maintained absolute discipline over the renegade band.

The monk Nicholas trailed behind the main group. His head hung low, he followed the captured fighters on their trek into the subterranean depths of the city. Heavy iron shackles made his gait labored, and he often found himself needing help to negotiate the onerous path.

Chapter 20

A small detachment of guards followed the procession, helping maintain order and watching for covert actions or gestures by the prisoners.

Lurking in the rear was Butch the Giant. He carried most of the company's captured weapons in small bundles slung over and through the various human parts that made up his oversized body. Even with the massive scale of the city's design, Butch the Giant's ungainly physical structure slowed his pace considerably. Many times, he was forced into awkward positions to navigate a doorway or to squeeze through a corridor, but after each obstacle, the giant recovered the distance lost and obediently resumed his place at the back of the pack.

Hannibal noted with keen interest that the group of mercenaries had not been completely disarmed. Amanitore and Khutulun's quivers were confiscated, but the women still carried their bows. A search of the company's personal effects should have turned up more than a few eyebrow-raising items, but the effort was haphazard and poorly executed. Numerous members of the group still carried hidden blades or objects on their person that could pose a formidable threat under favorable circumstances. Hannibal could not fathom Asmodeus or Sitri being that complacent. Either the group posed no risk or the guards were more fearsome than watchful eyes could discern. In any case, having a few weapons within reach gave him hope.

Hannibal kept a wary eye on the road ahead. He searched for anything that might be useful as an avenue of escape. With two demons present, the odds against them were long, but given their physical attributes, a set of small rooms could provide the ideal venue to shed their bonds and evade their captors. Speed would be the key in such an effort, as the demons' ability to use their powers and change shape would tip the balance back into their favor quickly. Another issue consuming Hannibal was his lack of knowledge of the newer parts of the city which they currently traversed. Any escape attempt needed an exit to go beyond the perimeter walls, and anything less would be a foolish waste of effort. To make matters more worrisome, Thomas was nowhere to be seen. The young man's talent had saved the group more than once in the past and without his abilities now, the way forward would need to be clear of all obstructions. He took a deep breath. Any chance of avoiding their current plight was near zero.

Hannibal's gaze wandered among the guards until it came to rest on Nicholas. This was the first time he had been close to the captive monk. For all the fear and uncertainty surrounding him, Nicholas seemed to be as calm as the demons themselves. Hannibal found the monk's lack of interest extremely odd. The entirety of Nicholas's stay in Eden had been as a prisoner under the heel of the demon-queen. The monk went from one confinement to the next, all the while being shackled and beaten like an unwanted animal. For all anyone knew, this could be a move to something far worse, yet the old monk plodded along, seemingly unafraid of the coming plight. The show of blitheness worried the general deeply.

Chapter 20

A massive set of double doors at the end of a torch-lit, marble-lined hallway signaled an end to the prisoner's forced march. Asmodeus stepped forward and ran his hand vertically up the reinforced seam between the two doors. With a crackle of electricity, red energy forced its way into the mechanism and unlocked the heavy iron portal. The doors swung inward revealing a world unbeknownst to all except the demon spawn.

The enclosed area beyond the doorway was vast. Among the monumental buildings of the Garden, the space was significantly larger than anything else in the city. The room itself was simple—circular and made of stone blocks. About ten stories tall, the walls were dotted sporadically with walk-out balconies accessed from corridors or antechambers not visible from ground level.

Hannibal marveled at the sight, but its sheer size was not its most impressive attribute as the hall was home to thick, lush vegetation. Vines wrapped themselves around massive columns that supported the ceiling above. Trees, bushes, and a variety of flowering plants thrived in the rich humus of the understory. The ash and debris so prevalent in the Garden of Eden was absent in the spacious chamber. It was as if the terrible conflagration spared this portion of Eden and then someone erected a building over it to keep it safe. Hannibal heard his compatriots gasp and murmur at the sight. The spectacle before them was but a taste of the Garden of old.

Despite the lack of windows or direct source of light, a strange luminescence hung over the abundant vegetation. The plants bathed in a washed-out yellow light that Hannibal could only discern as coming from the flora themselves. The amount of illumination given off by the plants was sufficient to light the entire enclosure.

The prisoners moved through the threshold, and Sitri locked the door behind them. The sharp sound jogged Hannibal from his reverie and forced him back to reality. He took note not only of the locked exit but of the balconies protruding from the walls. Some were low enough to the ground that his men might be able to reach them. Where they led was of no immediate concern, as anywhere may be preferable to what awaited them here. Hannibal used the confusion of the transition to reach for his hidden dagger but came up short when he remembered he had given the trusty knife to Thomas. Hannibal hissed under his breath to Guan and gestured for the large man to locate a blade capable of cutting through the leather cord, but the sound caught the attention of the demons.

"Silence!" Asmodeus ordered. "You and yours have been given a true gift. You should enjoy it while you can, Hannibal Barca."

Hannibal slyly shrugged off clandestine help from Guan. "I suppose you are correct."

The guards ushered the prisoners over a well-worn path through the dense foliage of the Garden remnant. The trail meandered with the uneven landscape to seemingly no purposeful destination. Without a good vantage point, the sea of green was impossible to penetrate visually so the group was blind to their objective. The only reference point any of the mercenaries had was the ceiling and walls. As the prisoners moved forward, the supporting columns grew closer together and the company knew that they were closing in on the center of the chamber.

The sound of a waterfall greeted the captives as they broke through the undergrowth and emerged into a broad, circular clearing. In the exact center of the chamber was an earthen plateau that floated substantially above the surrounding terrain. Pouring over the edge of the hovering island was a raging river of water. The thunderous noise brought temporary delight to those in the company, but dread soon set in. The water did not pool or run off through the clearing; instead, it disappeared into a wide hole below the gravity-defying hillock. The diameter of the opening was much greater than that of the plateau, and it appeared that the chasm was created as an intentional barrier to the oasis.

Outside of the ability for the small island to levitate above the floor of the chamber, there was nothing special about it—certainly nothing that warranted the extra protection given by the wide opening, but Hannibal soon realized the error in his perception. The significance was not in what he saw, but rather in what he did not. The floating, earthen mass held two ancient and twisted trees wrapped around each other on the leftmost bank of the raging water. In stark contrast to the rest of the Garden remnant, the trees appeared to be lifeless. The gnarled bark of the two behemoths had merged over the centuries and their massive roots clawed into the soil in a show of defiance against all who would seek to remove them. Withered fruit littered the rocky area beneath the trees and despite there being a river of water nearby, nothing else grew in their immediate presence. Hannibal could only come to one conclusion: they were the fabled trees of the Garden of Eden—the Tree of Life and the Tree of the Knowledge of Good and Evil.

Asmodeus was correct; it was an honor for the mercenaries to see the trees firsthand. Although they appeared dormant, the trees broadcast an air of power that flooded the hall of the Garden remnant. The fallow, circular pattern seen in the clearing surrounding the Two Trees gave evidence to something amiss with the legendary totems. Near the floating plateau, the tree's tainted energy was so great that nothing could withstand it. The negative force overwhelmed any plant life near the Two Trees' position, but with distance, the adulterated might abate enough for vegetation to grow normally.

Hannibal felt the warm air rise from the breach and immediately knew what lay below. The fissure led to the Avernus Sea and the dominion of Hell. An unfamiliar chill ran down the length of Hannibal's spine. He and his mercenaries had caused so much trouble they were being cast down as playthings for the multitude of demons that inhabited the underworld. How fitting. The company fought bravely for a righteous cause, but despite all their efforts, everything would end as their original lives had dictated. To make matters worse, their demise would come at the failed cost of their quest. No wonder Asmodeus was so willing to bring them here. The demon wanted to gloat—to prove to Hannibal that nothing they had done would change their fate. There would be no redemption for those whose stories were already written.

Peter and Thomas followed Isla Dora's dog manifestation through a maze of twisting corridors and random antechambers until the trio arrived in a room devoid of any windows or doors save the one they entered. Lit by a single torch, the space appeared to be just another empty room.

"Where now?" Peter asked the dog.

The dog whined and pawed at the wall.

"Why is this so hard?" Peter asked under his breath to no one in particular.

Thomas studied the rock. "She wants us to break through," he said, looking to Isla Dora for confirmation.

The silver-white canine barked her approval.

Thomas placed his hands on the largest of the stone blocks and slowly moved it enough for the trio to get through.

Exiting the other side, Peter stumbled forward and caught himself before falling over a balcony railing. It took him a few moments to take in his surroundings and gauge where he was.

Peter found himself three stories off the ground and staring wide-eyed into the giant circular chamber containing the remnant of the Garden of Eden. A vegetation-encrusted column of stone stood within reach of the balcony and shielded most of his view, but in the distance, Peter could see two demons directing a group of guards while Butch the Giant stood watch nearby. His expectations of a clean escape came crashing to a halt. Terror struck him like a thunderbolt. Peter's chest tightened and his mind grappled with the fear assailing his senses. He ducked below the level of the railing and whispered, "Dammit!"

Thomas emerged from the escape route and gazed in awe at the sight before him. "You know what this is?" he asked rather loudly.

"Be quiet," Peter whispered and motioned to the gathering at the center of the chamber. "Demons."

Thomas hunkered down next to Peter and hushed out, "This is the Garden—the real thing."

Peter scowled at the dog that was using one of its hind legs to scratch behind her ear. "You were supposed to lead us outside."

The dog wagged her tail and sat down obediently next to Thomas as if she were expecting a treat.

"No, bad Isla Dora," Peter scolded. "What are we going to do now?"

Thomas peeked over the railing and took a long look at the demons and their entourage. He recognized the captured mercenaries among the moving figures. The prisoners were near the edge of a precipice that Thomas concluded led to Hell. "Hannibal's over there," he said, gesturing toward the leftmost end of the gathering. "We've got to do something."

"Are you crazy?"

"He risked everything to save you," Thomas retorted. "The least you could do is help him now."

Peter could not fathom another failed attempt like the one in the queen's throne room. He was not brave. He could not superimpose a noble warrior over the weak shell of his true self. There was not enough courage in the entire world to transform Peter into someone he was not. He shifted about uneasily and his breathing labored as he struggled to find a valid reason to deny Thomas's logic. "We're not soldiers—we don't even have weapons."

Thomas pulled out Hannibal's old knife. "We have this."

"Great," Peter mocked Thomas in an attempt to put himself at ease. "You can poke them to death."

Thomas assessed the captives again. "Look, they've got Nicholas too."

Peter peered over the handrail. Standing off to the right of the gathering was Nicholas. There was no denying the old monk had the same fate awaiting him as the rest of the mercenaries, but Peter buried the thought deep and remained defiant. "So?"

"Look at them," Thomas said, staring at the mercenaries. "Everyone who can help you is down there right now. The demons are going to make this a fight between you and them. Nicholas won't be able to help—they're casting down every chance you have, and you're just going to run away?"

"Yes," Peter snapped, "and you should too."

"No," Thomas said. "I won't abandon my friends."

"Friends?" Peter mocked. "You don't trust them—you said so yourself."

"I don't, but they've saved me too many times for me to turn my back on them now."

The canine placed a paw on Thomas's arm in a show of support.

Peter turned to the dog. "You're one to talk after everything you told me about this place—not trusting anyone or anything I see?"

The dog laid her head on Thomas's shoulder and whimpered.

The visible display of unity made Peter felt guilty. Thomas knew what the outcome would probably be, and yet he was still willing to risk whatever existence he had in an attempt to save someone he did not trust or know that well. That was the definition of true courage: going willingly into the unknown regardless of your own misgivings. Peter had held the notion of bravery out at arm's length, as something that never really pertained to himself. Before the Garden, he never needed to think about such things. The real world was violent, but he had always been insulated from the vile transgressions that plagued it—they were reduced to the relative safety of published articles and news broadcasts. Here, brutality was the way of life—the norm. An individual had to act in a violent fashion for something they desired and should expect full reciprocation in return. Peter wondered how long it would take him to change his mind on the matter, to reason his way into thoughts that were warlike and barbaric. Perhaps he would be no different from anyone else in that regard. If that was the case, what might he lament about today's opportunity?

Peter mulled through his options. He knew he could not die, but that was a problem all unto itself. An immortal soul could be tortured for eternity. That was completely unacceptable. He needed assurances. The risk he was taking had to be mitigated somehow. If the end of the Garden was the prize, then there must be a fallback position, a compromise—something short of win or lose, black or white.

Thomas read the consternation on Peter's face. He could see the professor's mood swinging back and forth. Although he was prepared to give his eternal soul for a good cause, Peter was not. Thomas decided to sway the professor's opinion. "I can create a diversion," he said. "That should give you enough time to give the book to Nicholas."

Peter smiled at the kind gesture. "You don't need to do that."

"I can do it," Thomas said, pointing at the vine-laden column in front of them. "I'll just climb down and sneak in through the bushes."

"Fine, but they don't want you, the book is—" Peter stopped cold. An idea surged to the forefront of his mind. It was as if a dam had broken upstream and the raging water caught the professor in its torrential flooding. Peter waded into the thought and let his inspiration sweep him away. Perhaps the demons wanted to inflict retribution on Hannibal and the mercenaries, but it was doubtful they cared about anyone else. Peter's entire premise of being hunted stemmed from his ill-conceived theory that *he* was important. The more he thought about it, the more Peter realized how narcissistic *he* was being. The demons cared not for Peter—their interests were concentrated on obtaining the ancient manuscript, nothing more. He felt relief rise in him as he tossed his idea through several iterations. He laughed under his breath and adjusted his glasses. "Isla Dora," he said, addressing the dog, "we'll need your help."

The guards pushed Hannibal and his company to the rough edge of the chasm. They loosely arranged the mercenaries on either side of the old general and placed Nicholas to the far right, some distance away from the precipice. Butch the Giant milled through the guards, ensuring the minions were following the orders precisely as laid down by the demons.

Hannibal peered over the sheer drop. The walls of the chasm were made of rough earth and rock several yards in depth, but the face of the rift was not coarse enough at any point to form ledges or outcrops that might create a handhold or a place to land. The distance between the floating island and the edge of the chasm was so great it was impossible for any individual to jump. At best, the person may find themselves able to touch the levitating plateau beyond, but too low in elevation to do anything about it. They would fall through the hole and plunge the mile or so to the waters below.

Asmodeus paced slowly behind the band of mercenaries. The demon's red eyes scoured each captive, assessing their weaknesses and their overall value to Hannibal. The demon stopped behind Guan and motioned for Butch the Giant to step forward. Asmodeus drew Guan's sword from several bundles the giant carried. The demon studied the sword and tested its blade for sharpness. He held the weapon in front of the large man. "I gave this to you—do you remember?"

Guan nodded reluctantly.

Chapter 20

"I knew this soul," Asmodeus recounted to all within earshot and keeping his eyes fixed on Hannibal. "One of the ancient ones— so full of fear his stench made me sick."

Hannibal knew what was happening. Asmodeus wanted him to witness every atrocity committed upon the members of his charge, as if the old warrior's very existence was the cause. He found himself trapped by the demon's gaze. He did his best to remain stoic and uncaring, but it was too much to bear. "Guan—"

"Ah, yes," Asmodeus said, leaning over the hulking Chinese man to speak into his ear. "You were captain of the guard until you betrayed us for Hannibal," the demon snarled, glancing back to the old general. "How do your convictions feel now?"

"I can only ask for forgiveness," Guan answered.

Asmodeus let out a hearty laugh. "I do not think my queen is the forgiving type."

Guan snickered. "I would not tarnish my soul to seek comfort in *her* blessing."

The response angered Asmodeus. "Then I shall release you from your prison," the demon hissed, driving the blade through Guan's back until it emerged from the man's muscular chest.

Guan swallowed the pain and stiffened his posture. He deliber- ately moved his beard aside to see the end of the sword protruding from his chest. "Do not concern yourself, Hannibal; these demons are not worthy of your time."

Incensed, Asmodeus kicked Guan into the chasm. The chamber filled with gasps of outrage from the remaining mercenaries but soon dwindled to a solemn silence.

Hannibal's temper swelled. He wanted nothing more than to exact retribution on Asmodeus. He struggled with his restraints and stepped away from the edge of the precipice. He nodded to the mercenaries to make ready for a fight.

Asmodeus let out a hearty laugh and motioned for the guards to force the old warrior and his friends back into position. "You must not abandon your troops, General. After all, they are about to pay dearly for your mistakes." The demon pulled Elizabeth out of the lineup and spun her around so she could face him. Asmodeus tugged on the sleeve of her golden dress. "I see it still fits?"

Elizabeth turned away.

"You were my favorite once, and yet you betrayed me as well."

"My darling," Elizabeth responded softly, turning back to the demon and staring deeply into his eyes. "If it was not for you leaving me wanting, I would have stayed."

Giggles elicited from the women of the company while outright laughter filled the chamber amongst the men.

"Silence!" Asmodeus ordered, sweeping his hands through the air and demanding obedience from friend and foe alike. He drew Elizabeth's sword from a bundle the giant carried. "Lay her on the ground."

"Leave her alone!" Hannibal burst out and lunged at the demon, but Gunnar stopped him.

Chapter 20

"Please, old friend," Gunnar said. "All of us have had the time to envision the limitations of our freedoms." The Viking nodded slowly, making minute gestures to his hands and showing the old general he had freed himself. "I beg you. We will be ready when it is our time."

Asmodeus pushed Gunnar aside and bared his jagged teeth at Hannibal. "It is well that your subordinates know their place. I would hate for you to precede them."

Hannibal threw a glance at Gunnar and backed away. "Yes, it would be unfortunate for me to evade my sworn duty."

"I will make you suffer in due time," Asmodeus chided, staring the aged warrior down.

"You will try," Hannibal countered defiantly and reassumed his position on the edge of the precipice.

Asmodeus held Elizabeth's sword up high for all to see and said, "A gift that has gone unappreciated." He nodded to his guards and they forced the female mercenary to lie spread-eagle on the ground.

Hannibal met each one of his comrade's looks with one of determined anger. He conveyed his message of readiness to the members of his company with the utmost of covert nuances.

In response, the mercenaries gauged the distances to their nearest enemies and prepared mentally for the movements their bodies would need to make prior to the fighting.

Khutulun stood to the left of Hannibal and on the farthest end of the group. She signaled her acceptance of his orders but also her concern of the demon Sitri standing just to the rear of her position. Hannibal acknowledged the issue but had no guidance to offer. Sitri would be a wildcard no matter what precautions they were able to make.

The tension among the mercenaries rose to a heightened level and all eyes followed Asmodeus as the demon knelt in front of Elizabeth.

A sharp *CRACK* reverberated through the chamber. Dislodged building stones and broken rock rained down from the ceiling. The guards scattered, but several were caught by the falling debris and trapped. A stone slab about ten feet in diameter landed squarely on Butch the Giant's torso, pinning the ungainly abomination to the ground.

Hannibal searched for the cause of the disturbance and found Thomas clambering amid the thick vines of the supporting columns. He positioned himself above the contingent of henchmen and used his power to dislodge the blocks to send them careening to the ground. Hannibal relished in the chaos of the moment. He heard the cries of conflicting orders echo through the chamber and took the fortuitous circumstance to signal his mercenaries to free themselves. Hannibal raised his hands to Gunnar, and the Viking produced a hidden dagger that cut through the leather cord.

The members of the company swarmed the fallen giant and gathered their weapons. They immediately confronted the guards and formed a tight-knit fighting unit that wasted no time in going on the offensive.

Chapter 20

Holding the book tightly in his hands, Peter pushed through the last of the thick vegetation and into the circular clearing. Once free of the obstruction, he made a run straight for Nicholas. The old monk stood virtually alone near the outskirts of the group. Nicholas seemed curious by the commotion, but not so much as to seek shelter to avoid the falling rubble. It was not until Peter had crossed most of the fallow earth that Nicholas even bothered to notice the approaching professor, but once the old monk did, his eyes looked at nothing else.

Hannibal's heart lifted at the sight of Peter clumsily running across the open terrain toward the monk. The two least likely members of the company had managed to plan and execute a brilliant maneuver.

"The book-bearer!" Sitri screamed over the fighting while gesturing wildly at Peter. "Stop him!"

The guards wheeled away from the mercenaries and ran at Peter.

"Block their advance!" Hannibal ordered.

The mercenaries responded immediately, tackling guards that were still within reach and firing arrows to slow down all others.

Sitri hurled himself into the air over the melee. He set his eyes on Peter and dove forward.

Khutulun readied her bow and sent two rapid-fire arrows through the tough membrane of Sitri's wings. She watched as the demon spun about in midair and crashed to the ground.

Hannibal spied Asmodeus leaping into the air, intending to execute a semi-flying, low-arc jump into the unknowing Peter's path. Hannibal slashed at the demon's legs. The intense pain caused Asmodeus to retract his outstretched body and land well short of the passing human.

Fear drove Peter forward. He held the ancient manuscript tightly to his chest and attempted to stay calm, at least as calm as he could under the circumstances. The professor channeled his paralyzing fright into his muscles, calling on his limbs to carry him faster than he thought possible. In his peripheral vision, he could see the mass of men and women doing battle. He could hear the barking of orders and the clash of metal-on-metal resonating through the hall. Through it all, he kept his mind focused on Nicholas.

Due to his shackled legs, the monk had moved little from his original spot. Instead, Nicholas extended his arms and urged Peter closer with frantic gestures. His eyes were wide with excitement, yet the monk said nothing; he gave no words of encouragement or caution to the approaching book-bearer.

Peter covered the final steps in the blink of an eye. He gripped the book at one end and held it out, stretching the last few feet to place it squarely into Nicholas's waiting grasp.

Nicholas gave Peter a mordant smile and thrust the book aloft. Intense multicolored energy flowed from the manuscript and surrounded the monk. It gathered in brilliance, enveloping Nicholas until it erupted into a blast of power and blinding light.

Chapter 20

The shockwave tore through the combatants. Sitri and Asmodeus contracted their wings and clawed at the ground in order to withstand the concussion, while the humans were thrown into the surrounding vegetation. Peter was the exception. He remained unscathed as he stood scarcely a few feet away from the monk's raging power.

The light consumed Nicholas's body. His features were all but obscured, leaving only the outline of the human he once was. Energy danced upon his visage, pulsating with each breath. A light lavender hue grew at the manifestation's core. The color expanded outward, swallowing the opalescent form and forcing the underlying creature to change shape.

The moving mass of energy morphed into Darius, the prisoner Peter had met in the old dungeon of the city. Peter was able to gaze at the unkempt man's face for only a few moments until the purple vibrancy elicited another transition. The form collapsed in on itself, shrinking to a size not much bigger than that of a child. It swirled about and solidified into the little boy Peter had chased through the streets of San Cielo. He stood before Peter and smiled mischievously, bowing his head in a curt, but respectful manner. As quickly as the boy had come into view he was gone, swallowed back into the seething vortex of power. Growing in height and width, the disturbance rose to tower above Peter. It elongated, slowly condensing into the solid and visible shape of a demon holding the ancient manuscript in its burnt and scarred hands. The demon stretched its wings to their fullest extent and snickered at the stunned human before evanescing back into a nondescript mass of lavender light.

Peter did not immediately understand the implications of what was happening, but deep down he knew something was wrong. He stepped back from the disturbance and turned to find support in Hannibal and the company. Most of the mercenaries had righted themselves, but instead of continuing the fight, they found themselves transfixed by the vision unfolding before them. As the demon's form faded, Peter realized the trouble at the same time the predicament coalesced on the faces of the company. "Hannibal!" he yelled across the clearing, but was stopped midsentence by a soft, feminine hand tenderly resting on his forearm. Startled, he turned to find the bookstore owner, Kea, greeting him with a warm smile.

"Surprised?" Kea asked.

Peter noted that although Kea wore the same clothes as she did at the bookstore her voice was significantly different. She no longer bore the local accent that added to her seductive qualities. Her stance and demeanor had changed as well. She was still confident, but the genuinely caring and sympathetic woman Peter had known had been replaced by a version that was arrogant, evil, and malignant. He wondered about her transformations and which, if any, of her personas represented the true being she was.

Weapons at the ready, Hannibal's company charged the demons.

With little effort, Kea used her power to send the mercenaries sprawling back into the thick vegetation. Her display proved her dominance without question. The humans' arrayed arsenal was naught but toys when opposed to her might. "Fools!"

Peter watched his comrades fall and turned to face Kea. "It was all a game then?"

"Hardly," Kea rasped, gripping the ancient manuscript tightly. "That useless monk tried to thwart us by hiding the book, but it wasn't until a living soul—you—came into contact with it that we could put our plan into place. Only a nephesh can bring the Book of Souls across the threshold of death—didn't you know?"

Peter had been living a lie. The roads of chance and circumstance had been engineered to lead to the one place no one would willingly choose to go. The deception started the moment he took possession of the book. Everything since had been nothing more than a calculated scheme to inspire Peter to willingly turn the ancient manuscript over to the only person he thought could help. Kea and her henchmen had been choreographing every word spoken and every act committed. Hannibal and the mercenaries, although roaming free, never posed any real threat to her plans. The fact that the company had rescued Peter temporarily from the clutches of the demons had done little to influence the outcome. No matter the course, the Book of Souls would have eventually seen its way to the queen.

Kea drew closer. "You could have been here with me—shared in the glory of what's to come." She gave Peter a coy smile. "Things could have been much different between us—well, that is, until I tired of you."

"You'll destroy everything then?"

"Not all of it," Kea replied. "You see, the trees are much more than a simple link to humanity; they're a gateway to Creation itself, a door through which all of the Fallen may pass."

"Things won't be different, you'll just fail again," Peter stated, drawing visible ire from the queen.

"Lucifer has found a way to merge the realms of Creation and Hell. His power will be equal to the Almighty," Kea said, "and with an army behind us, we will not fail." She looked absently at Peter. "Where was I again? Oh yes," she said and effortlessly morphed into the demon queen, Lilith. Holding the book in her right hand, she elongated her left into a sharpened spear point and stabbed Peter through the chest. The demon hoisted the writhing professor off the ground and flew him over the chasm to the top of the outcrop and the base of the Two Trees. She pulled her hand from Peter's chest and sent the grimacing nephesh splashing to the edge of the riverbank. "Now, bear witness to your own naiveté."

Peter hit the ground coughing and clutching at his chest. He rifled through his clothes to examine the wound, but all he could catch was a glimpse of the bloodless injury closing in upon itself. He could no longer die, but the debilitating pain he experienced was far greater than what he would have expected in life. Gathering his breath, Peter pulled himself out of the stream and up onto the dry bank where he lay quietly in the soft earth, rebuilding his strength and keeping a wary eye on the queen.

Chapter 20

Lilith wasted no time in approaching the intertwined trees and opening the ancient manuscript. She studied the pages eagerly and spent long moments flipping back and forth as if trying to understand the text. The demon paced the bank of the river, growing ever more furious at the book. Lilith ignited her power and forced lavender energy through the manuscript's pages. In a fit of rage, she threw the book at Peter and screamed, "What have you done?"

For the first time since arriving in Eden, Peter felt the giddy sensation of empowerment surge through him. He embedded himself in the moment and allowed it to consume him. The ever-present fear that haunted his every step left his body, leaving only an unconquerable resolve. Peter adjusted his glasses and gingerly retrieved the book from the damp, loamy soil. "Missing something?"

Lilith's anger grew to immeasurable proportions as she made the stale air of the chamber vibrate with electricity. In one motion, the demon queen pushed her arms forward and let loose a devastating stream of energy aimed squarely at the pretentious nephesh.

Peter's close proximity to the demon and his poor reflexes did not allow for much of a defense. He held the book up as a last resort to protect his face from whatever was about to engulf him. The force of the impact pushed Peter backward several feet, but he dug in and let the energy spill around him. The strange spell made his skin crawl like a thousand ants scurrying about, but he fought the sensation off and weathered the attack.

As the glare faded, Lilith stood in disbelief. The amount of malice and anger she poured into the assault should have flayed the weak human's flesh from his bones. Peter should have been nothing more than an insignificant stain across the floor of the Garden remnant. Instead, the insubordinate soul mocked her with an ever-widening smile that grew across his smug face. Incensed, Lilith gathered her power for another attack.

Peter searched for an escape route. The small plateau the Two Trees occupied was devoid of anything that could make for defensible cover. There were plenty of knee-high boulders and tree roots, but they were not nearly large enough to protect him. All around Peter, the chasm's gaping maw presented an insurmountable obstacle to jump. The river created by the gushing wellspring was so strong Peter doubted he could take refuge in it without being swept over the edge. Out of options, he dropped to one knee to reduce his profile and held the book in front of him like a shield.

The shockwave reverberated through the chamber. The massive amount of energy brought to bear on the book began to melt its outer coverings. Iridescent, silver-white liquid dripped onto the ground and created a small puddle. The book grew heavy in Peter's hands, so much so that he was no longer able to hold it aloft for protection. As his guard fell, the disintegrating tome transformed into a shimmering, semi-solid mass that leapt forward, into the teeth of the queen's attack. Continuing to deflect the onslaught, the undulating being took on a human form, resolving into a disheveled and quite perturbed Isla Dora.

The sound of rushing water rose to the forefront as Lilith ceased her attack and an eerie calm fell over the Garden remnant. The demon queen stepped forward to stand menacingly over the frail woman. "You have interfered with me for the last time."

"I certainly hope so," Isla Dora chided.

The flash of power from Lilith was instantaneous. The queen screeched in anger as she poured might upon the old woman. Lilith enveloped Isla Dora in purple energy and lifted her off the ground to stare into the old woman's withered face. "You are nothing compared to me!"

Isla Dora quickly changed shape and melted to the ground. She reemerged in human form outside of Lilith's influence and struck back with forceful blast that sent the demon queen reeling. "I fight for the righteous and for those who would defy your rule—how could we possibly compare?"

Lilith sank her hind claws into the earth and kicked forward. She brought her wings in close to her body and flew headlong into Isla Dora. The old woman stepped to the side but was caught by the demon and forced to the ground.

Lilith sent energy surging through Isla Dora's body. The old woman shifted her appearance rapidly. Isla Dora tried every combination at her disposal, including summoning her own power to force the queen back, but nothing worked.

Once Lilith contained Isla Dora, her anger came to the forefront. She wanted nothing more than to silence the pest once and for all, but she thought better of it. The manuscript was the real prize, and if the old woman harbored the slightest piece of information that could help, then it was the queen's duty to preserve that option. Revenge could wait until the book was recovered.

Lilith increased her power and used it to squeeze the thrashing woman into unconsciousness. The demon queen rose to her feet and threw Isla Dora's limp body to the ground. She turned her attention to Peter. "Where is the *true* Book of Souls?"

Peter backed away and nearly lost his balance over the edge of the plateau. Righting himself, he stood tall and adjusted his glasses. "I don't know exactly."

Lilith flapped her blackened wings and thrust forward, covering the few yards to Peter's position in an instant. She trapped the smaller human against the gaping maw of the rift and the raging waters of the river. "Perhaps you need more incentive?"

Before Peter could reply, Lilith placed her hands on his shoulders and triggered her power. Slowly at first and then rising in intensity, she forced energy through every aspect of Peter's being until he radiated an aura of brilliant light.

The pain Peter experienced was excruciating. He swayed under the strain. His consciousness ebbed and flowed like the tide during a winter's storm. His mind wandered. He thought back to his days of teaching and his fondness at discovering a new student's desire to learn. His life had been mundane and pedestrian, but Peter found great strength in his former, drama-free existence.

With all eyes focused on Lilith's attempt to shatter Peter's will, no one saw Thomas until it was too late. His legs tucked close to his body, the young man came swinging in on a group of thick vines attached to the ceiling. Thomas gauged his arc of descent perfectly and impacted Lilith squarely in the ribcage, sending the demon sprawling to the earthen floor of the floating island.

Thomas let go of the vines and unslung the shoulder bag containing the Book of Souls. "Here," he said, forcing the satchel into Peter's hands. "It's yours."

"But the plan?" Peter stuttered out, trying to comprehend the incredulous turn of events.

"I couldn't sit by and do nothing," Thomas replied, his attention fixed on the rising Lilith. "Watch out," he said, pushing Peter to the side.

Lilith flew across the plateau at full speed. She covered the distance in a fraction of a second and reached for Thomas. Using the queen's speed against her, Thomas kicked off the ground to lessen the impact and used his free hand to grasp Lilith's wing. Fighting against the demon's considerable strength, Thomas threw his legs over her wing and used all his might to collapse the membrane. Lilith lost her flight characteristics and heeled over. Locked together, Thomas and the demon queen tumbled into the chasm and disappeared.

"Thomas!" Hannibal's scream broke the stunned silence. The grief visibly drained him, but after a few moments, the old warrior collected himself. "Concentrate on the remaining demons," he ordered. "Spare no one."

Asmodeus and Sitri were caught off guard by the unexpected turn of events. The onrush of combatants forced the two demons into a defensive posture. They hurled power at the humans in a sloppy and wholesale manner. Their attacks landed few blows on the mercenaries and instead, wrought havoc amongst the reassembling guards.

Peter removed the Book of Souls from its concealment within the shoulder bag. Casting the leather satchel aside, he gazed at the manuscript for a long moment. He found himself struggling to muster the courage to physically open the book. The loss of Thomas had dulled his resolve to continue. Peter could never have fathomed that the fate of creation would somehow hinge on his efforts—that the meaning of his existence would be forever entwined with the sought-after ancient manuscript or that his actions would cause irreparable harm to others. Now, it would seem, his worst fears had come to pass.

Peter's moment of reflection was cut short by Sitri. The demon broke free of the fight and lashed out at the professor. Sitri sent a wave of force careening toward the unheeding human. Cries of alarm rang out from the mercenaries, but Peter did nothing as he stared unfazed at the twisting, emerald energy bearing down on him.

At the last moment, a crystalline tree metamorphosed from the earth directly in front of Peter. The tree grew to full height in an instant and deflected the inbound malice. It resonated sharply with a high-pitched bell noise issuing forth, but this time Peter was unaffected. He remembered the sights and sounds of the tree. It was there at the entrance to the Garden when he arrived and then again, in the queen's throne room. Upon closer inspection, the crystalline structure appeared to be mimicking one of the Two Trees of the plateau. The only difference was the foliage. The crystal structure sported a replicated complement of leaves and fruit, while each of the legitimate trees looked as barren and lifeless as the landscape outside of the city.

Sitri poured more power into his assault until the demon was blindsided by Gunnar and Elizabeth. The two mercenaries slashed and hacked at the demon until he had no choice but to disengage and protect himself.

The threat temporarily neutralized, the crystalline tree transformed again. Shrinking in size and gaining thickness, the structure morphed into a man. Wearing tattered and torn robes, the bedraggled man stood before Peter smiling with admiration.

"Nicholas?" Peter asked, surprised to find a familiar face. "It was you?"

"Yes," Nicholas answered in a weak and timid voice.

"But what about—"

"We can rejoice another time," Nicholas said, checking the status of the demons behind him. Sitri was in the process of beating back the two mercenaries and Asmodeus had nearly freed himself from an encounter with Hannibal. Nicholas pointed at the book. "You have work to do."

"I do?" Peter looked at the manuscript curiously before extending it to the monk. "This is yours."

Nicholas cast a wary glance at the book. "It was never meant for me."

"What?" Peter asked, unsure of how stable the scruffy monk's mental state actually was. "But you wrote it."

Nicholas shook his head. "I transcribed it, nothing more."

Peter stared at the monk waiting for some sign that the disheveled man was perpetrating a cruel joke, but after several moments, he took a deep breath and lowered the manuscript. "How do I use it?"

"I do not know," Nicholas replied, laughing lightly at the question. "I had faith."

Sitri broke free of his attackers and took to the air, aiming squarely for the humans on the plateau. Nicholas wasted no time and transformed into an eagle. He took flight and intercepted Sitri. Although the bird was no match for the large demon, he was more nimble and able to deal enough damage to Sitri's eyes to significantly hinder the demon's forward momentum. The monk continued his attack, forcing Sitri into a battle of aerial attrition above the Garden remnant.

Peter took in the chaos and swallowed hard. His plan had fallen apart and his comrades were still in peril. Whatever reservations and shortcomings Peter had, he was not about to let them get in the way now. Propping up his waning courage, he stepped to the base of the Two Trees and opened the book.

Peter saw nothing unusual in the pages of uniform lettering that ran the length of the ancient manuscript. It appeared the same, but slight alterations were beginning to take place. The ink of the evenly-spaced Latin text, which once had been so dark, now seemed to be diminishing with each passing moment. The off-white parchment, thick and rife with uneven blemishes, started to lose its opacity. Peter stared into the tome thinking the effect was an optical illusion but soon realized the book was changing.

A faint outline of images began to appear on the near-translucent parchment of the ancient manuscript. Peter flipped back and forth through the book and found that each set of pages bore a different scene. Large green masses danced upon the book's parchment and the movement, similar to a playing child, swept across several scenes. Slowly, they came into sharper focus and Peter realized what the pictures were.

In one scene, Peter saw a young couple running carefree through tall grass. In another, he witnessed a hand picking fruit from a large tree. On the final pages of the book, Peter saw the Two Trees turn black and wither into their current state. He held the book up to confirm the images in the book were identical to the Two Trees in front of him. Without a shred of doubt, the Book of Souls was showing historical events connected to the objects around him.

To test his theory, Peter held the book in the direction of Hannibal. Images of battle and the hardships of a warrior's life littered the manuscript's pages. Peter traversed across the rest of the mercenaries and the demons as well; each told a unique and different story through the parchment of the Book of Souls.

The manuscript was a window that looked back in time—to things long past. Simply put, it was a record of all that had ever been. It surveyed the whole of Creation and displayed those moments that defined an individual's existence. Every event, every person, and every instant of good or evil was contained within the stale pages of the dusty tome.

With the battle raging in the chamber, Peter swung the book back to the Two Trees. He studied the images presented to him. Although he comprehended the context, he struggled with how to use the knowledge. The scenes were nothing more than snippets, hardly capable of conveying more than a visual reference to a historic moment. The object of the lesson eluded him.

Peter redoubled his efforts. He studied the imagery as it rolled by like a film. He concentrated on the patterns of any perceived meaning or series that the manuscript was trying to show him. Slowly, Latin text overlaid the movie-like sequences. With each new scene, the text changed as if it was communicating in tandem with images depicted. Peter flipped through the pages of the manuscript until he came to the scene containing the Two Trees. He held the book out and concentrated solely on the letters that appeared. The text floated to the surface from across both pages. As it came forward, regular patterns coalesced over the images to form words. Each set repeated, forming a series of phrases.

Peter read the Latin and translated, "Replace that which was taken?" He looked up to the intertwined trees and scanned the hundreds of fruit laying on the lifeless soil beneath them. The revelation hit him like a ton of bricks. The Book of Souls wanted Peter to perform a sort of penance—to atone for a sin that happened long ago. He was to locate the fruit Eve had taken from the Tree of

Knowledge and restore it to its proper place. Peter drew a sharp breath. "Oh my god."

Chapter 21

For millennia, the demon queen utilized an enormous amount of energy to create the city within the Garden of Eden. Although the metropolis gave Lilith a base of power to draw from, it did so at the expense of her freedom. The ongoing expenditure to keep the stone megacity in situ meant she could not stray far from its borders. As Lilith and Thomas fell through the bottom of Eden, she felt her energy rapidly drop off and diminish to nothing.

Left only with her physical prowess, Lilith made a series of aggressive aerobatic maneuvers designed to throw Thomas off her back, but the human held fast to the base of her wings with both his arms and legs. Each wild swing in her increasingly erratic flight path caused the queen to lose an alarming amount of altitude, dropping her further away from Eden and closer to the threshold between the realms.

Thomas looked back and caught a glimpse of the Garden hovering in the air above them. Where once the Garden had stretched to fill the sky, it was now fading from sight. Its earthen edges were beginning to blur and lose cohesion as if the greater distance was somehow causing it to recede from reality. Nearly obscured from view, the only noticeable hallmark he could make out was the massive amount of water turning to rain as it poured from the gaping fissure.

Everything Thomas had heard about the Garden of Eden was coming true. Eden existed within a nether region between Creation and Hell. The path down was unidirectional and once an individual traversed into Lucifer's domain, they could never return.

Thomas resigned himself to whatever awaited him. The decision to push the queen into the rift had not been difficult to make. Lilith was undefeatable in battle, even more so when her two henchmen were at her side. With her out of the picture, Hannibal and the mercenaries would have a much better chance at completing the mission. Thomas came to understand one of the harsh lessons Hannibal was trying to teach him: when you are free, you can act for the greater good. It was lost on Thomas during his decades roaming alone in the shadows, but now he realized what it meant. He could do nothing as the queen's captive, but given an opportunity, he could change the balance of Creation with a simple push. He sacrificed himself so his friends could succeed.

Lilith made an abrupt turn in midair hoping to throw Thomas in the direction of her momentum. The maneuver caught Thomas off guard, nearly causing him to lose his grip, but he adjusted his center of balance and held on tenaciously. The demon queen groped behind her to dislodge him, but he shifted his position to stay just out of reach.

"Fool!" Lilith screamed over the rushing wind. "Did you believe your arrival in Hell would be a welcoming one?"

Thomas paid little attention to the queen's rhetoric and instead, kept his eyes glued to the fading underside of the Garden of Eden.

"The Fallen are without number and bored beyond measure," Lilith said. "Your relentless defiling will be their utmost pleasure."

The queen's words dredged up memories of the atrocities Thomas had borne witness to in Eden. His mind flooded with the sounds of souls screaming for mercy as the queen transmogrified them for entertainment. The echoes reverberated through his being even as he tried with all his might to erase them from existence.

Lilith sensed the fear building within the human and used it to push him further into the unknown. "Shall we join my brothers and sisters then?" the queen asked, tucking her wings in behind her. She dove like a hawk, gaining speed and aiming for the center of the Avernus Sea.

Thomas reacted instinctively. He held on to the top of Lilith's wings where they emerged from her back and tried to lower his wind resistance profile by laying forward on the demon. In response, the queen increased her dive angle to full vertical. Thomas began to slip forward and quickly repositioned his grip to hold on to the bottom of the demon's wing. He glanced one last time at the Garden of Eden as it became nothing more than a silhouette within the opaque sky.

In one motion, Lilith heeled over and extended her wings. The amount of shear produced was tremendous. She felt the stubborn nephesh lighten and lose his grip. She rolled in the air and steadied her flight path. She locked eyes with Thomas and laughed wickedly as he flailed his arms and tumbled out of control toward the sea far below.

Lilith gauged her location and turned her eyes skyward. A faint outline was the only remaining visible evidence that the Garden of Eden still existed. She spied a steady rain falling from the heavens and thrust her leathery wings forward. The demon entered into a circular pattern around the column of mist and rose quickly through the atmosphere in the direction of the water's source.

Peter held the Book of Souls in front of him and scoured the ground looking for the one fruit plucked from the Tree of Knowledge so very long ago. The manuscript highlighted all the emaciated, fig-type fruit, but showed no distinction between the tree of origin or picked versus fallen through natural causes. All the while, the Latin words for the phrase, *Replace that which was taken,* continued to cycle to the forefront. "Yeah, yeah, I know," Peter muttered. "It's not that easy."

The ongoing battle in the Garden's remnant continued to distract Peter. To his eyes, it seemed to be an evenly-matched fight. Hannibal and four mercenaries kept Asmodeus at bay, while Nicholas engaged Sitri. The contingent waylaid every attempt made by the two demons to circumvent their separate entanglements and attack

Peter directly. The remaining mercenaries kept the guards occupied and dealt with attacking the recently freed giant, Butch.

Peter adjusted his glasses and turned his attention back to the problem at hand. He changed tactics and assessed the quandary as he would any other academic challenge. From his scholarly perspective, there was still a piece of the equation missing. The Book of Souls issued forth a need to be resolved, but it did not provide adequate information to find the solution. He suspected that finding the correct fruit was only half the quandary. Peter scanned the desolate branches of the Two Trees. Knowing exactly where to place the lost fruit would be the hard part. There was no doubt in Peter's mind the problem was designed to be difficult as it was a safeguard against someone using the book for ill purposes.

From behind Peter, a meek voice murmured, "Such a small thing, really—I've been asking for nothing but forgiveness ever since."

Startled, Peter wheeled about to see a young woman standing before him. She was in her late teens or early twenties. About five-and-a-half-feet tall with a slim frame, she had long, thick brown hair that fell to the midpoint of her back. Her fair complexion and rounded cheeks gave the young woman a cute innocence that was very alluring. The young woman's dress was coarse and tattered, similar to that of a vagabond. When she brushed her hair away from her face, Peter recognized the dark blue eyes staring back at him. "Isla Dora?"

She laughed at Peter with a more youthful version of Isla Dora's cackle and moved beneath the Two Trees. The young woman sat down on their massive roots and gazed at the lifeless branches above her. "I was sitting right here when it happened."

"You're Eve?" Peter said, staring at the woman incredulously. He was not able to catch a full glimpse of the women in the images the book offered, but nonetheless, there could be no denying that the girl standing before him was the first woman of Creation.

Eve smiled in response. "I had never known fear before that day," she said, penitently looking at the ground. "He came right through there," she said, sweeping her hand through the air and motioning to the bank on other side of the wellspring.

A chill ran down Peter's spine. "Who did?"

"The Creator," Eve replied, wiping a tear from her eye and managing to produce a quiet, despairing chuckle. "I knew it was wrong, but I didn't realize the consequences would be this," she said, gesturing to the battle raging in the circular chamber. "It's been so horrible for everyone."

Peter took stock of the fight. It was a delaying action, nothing more. Time was growing short and although he had a great number of questions for Eve, only one was pressing. Peter knelt down by the tree roots and held up the Book of Souls. "We have to right this," he said, gesturing to the multitude of withered fruits littered about the floor of the plateau. "Do you remember which one it was?"

"It was so long ago."

"Please, try to remember."

Eve pointed across the water to a place now bereft of vegetation. "When the Almighty came, I was scared," she said, her eyes filling with tears. "Adam wanted to leave, but—" Eve stopped, her face rife with anguish.

"But what?"

"I couldn't go because I still had the fruit in my hands," Eve said, holding her empty palm up as an admission of guilt.

Peter scanned the ground around the exposed tree root. The withered fruit were roughly the same and none showed any of the telltale signs of bite marks. "I don't see anything."

Eve put a hand on Peter's arm to calm him. "No," she said. "I wanted to hide it so it wouldn't be found—so we could escape our punishment."

"Okay," Peter replied in a soft, reassuring voice. "Where did you put it?"

Eve cupped her fingers together to make her hand as small as possible and snaked her arm into the gaps between adjacent tree roots to one side of where she was sitting. After several moments of blind groping, Eve pulled out a partially eaten, withered fruit. "There, you see?"

Peter held the book up and studied the images. The diminished fruit had the same hallmarks as the one displayed in the manuscript. "That's it," he said and scanned the branches overhead. "Where does it go?"

Eve studied both of the trees. They bark of each was twisted and fused so tightly together that it was almost impossible to tell which trunk belonged to which tree. After several long moments, Eve recognized the crook of two main branches on the Tree of Knowledge as the place where the snake had perched. "I took it from there," she said, handing the half-eaten fruit to Peter.

Peter held the fig up to the first empty stem along the trunk of the tree.

"Not there," Eve corrected. "The one next to it."

Peter moved the fruit to the next stem and watched as the connection between the fig and the tree healed itself.

A strong wind blew through the chamber. The smell of flowers permeated the Garden remnant and the long-forgotten scent caused the fighting to momentarily abate as the combatants reveled in the surprising aroma.

A noticeable sense of easing swept across the Two Trees. Their trunks released their hold upon each other, slackening to the point of separation. The bark lightened in color from a charcoal black to a deep-amber brown. Grass seedlings sprang to life beneath the trees and spread out through the dead zone that made up the clearing. Leaf buds appeared along the Two Trees' branches and grew toward adulthood at an incredible rate. The withered fruit, scattered around the plateau, greened and lifted into the air. The figs rose into the trees' ever-greening canopy and reattached themselves to the branches where they once belonged.

The relative calm that befell the last vestige of the Garden of Eden was fleeting as Lilith powered her way in from below. She twisted through the chasm, brushing her wingtips on its rocky sides and bathing the immediate area in a shower of earthen debris. She felt the rush of energy course through her veins and screeched with joy as she entered the chamber.

Lilith surveyed the situation. The first act of repentance for The Book of Souls was completed. The Two Trees were alive and thriving. The battle had taken a toll on her brethren and they appeared battered and spent. The queen recognized the tenuous position and the need for urgency. She needed to act quickly to recover the book.

Lilith made a pass above the battle and barked orders to Asmodeus and Sitri. They would be in charge of capturing the mercenaries while she would handle the Book of Souls. The queen's anger exploded at the sight of her former rival standing on the plateau. "Eve!" she shrieked through the chamber.

Lilith landed on the floating island and spat, "Insubordinate creatures!" She pointed a dire finger at Eve. "You're the whole reason we're in this mess!" A lavender flash pierced the subdued glow of the chamber as the queen sent tendrils of energy toward the young woman.

Eve summoned an opalescent shield and blocked the attack. She sensed that Lilith's power was not yet back to full strength and countered with a blast that sent the queen crashing to the ground. "Do not blame your petty jealousy on me! The Fallen's plight is one of its own making!"

Lilith rose to her feet and brushed herself off. She glared at the attractive young woman and began a transformation process of her own. Her scarred and grotesque physique gave way to the slender, burgundy-haired Kea from San Cielo.

An aura of intense energy gathered about Kea and polarized the air around her. "Enough!" she screamed. "You stole him from me and for that I will own your soul!" She threw a concentrated blast of energy that engulfed the young woman, squeezing her from all sides.

Eve used all of her might to push back against the onslaught and render it harmless. "Your pleas for affirmation are pathetic—what I would expect from a being bereft of humanity!"

Kea's rage exploded. A lavender halo grew from her body. It expanded outward, seeking to encompass the entire plateau.

Eve whispered to Peter, "We need to finish this—I can't give you much time."

"Okay," Peter said, squinting through the growing haze to pinpoint Eve. "How?"

"Uriel," Eve replied, speaking like a specter from the cloud of charged atmosphere. "He is the rightful guardian here—you must free him."

Kea's discharge of power was massive, sending arcs of electricity through the trees and across the water. Eve pushed Peter to safety behind the collective roots of the trees and deflected the brunt of the assault into the open air of the chamber.

"Quickly!" Eve screamed, countering another volley from the queen. "I cannot hold her."

Peter opened the Book of Souls and found that its pages had come alive. It was a confusing mass of incoherent images. Each scene depicted an instance from someone's life. The snippets fused together to form a never-ending roll of sequences that made him nauseous. He theorized that he was witnessing the lives of all of the souls entombed within the demon-made stone of the chamber's architecture. Each soul was trying to tell their unique story through the ancient tome. It was so overwhelming that Peter closed the book to clear his mind. He surmised that the best place to start would be with Uriel, but given the circumstances, that would not be possible. Without the physical presence of the angel, Peter would need to locate Uriel's story somewhere within the Book of Souls' multitude of unrestrained personal accounts.

Peter gauged the direction of Uriel's Vale and opened the book once again. The montage continued, but he forced himself to tune it out, trying to see the ramble of images as nothing more than background noise. The Book of Souls was a window into the past and understanding that fact gave him new insight. Peter wanted to look through the current stream of forgotten lives to see what lay behind them—beyond the souls physically entombed around him. He scanned the smallest areas of the ancient manuscript and tried to visualize the handwritten text underneath.

Peter focused on the gutter near the book's inner binding. He concentrated on one of the few Latin letters visible underneath the barrage of images. The character was inert as if nothing out of the ordinary was occurring, but after a few moments, it moved. Ever so slightly at first, it grew in thickness and began to pulsate. The text sprang to the forefront of the pages and turned ice blue in color. The scenes running rampant through the Book of Souls faded away. A new series of images depicting three demons using their collective might to subdue Uriel arose. The events scrolled through the manuscript so fast that Peter could not understand the sequence, but they replayed continuously until he grasped their meaning.

Millennia passed as Uriel fought fiercely against the attacking demons. The lush vegetation of the Garden was set aflame and burned to a cinder by the constant use of divine might. Humanity arose and entered Eden, taking sides in the ongoing skirmish. Weapons were forged and armies built. Entire forces took to the hills to do battle for the future of the nephesh. Throngs of souls clashed mercilessly. Lilith and her henchmen took the advantage and decimated Uriel's ranks. The angel tried to intervene but was caught off-guard by the demons and turned to stone.

Vertigo beset Peter as he witnessed the spectacle. The scenes became real to him. It was more than watching a film—it was as if he were living the moment. He felt each attack by the three demons as if he were the one standing against them. Power surged around Peter and he tried to move away—to regroup—but he could not. Trapped in a morass of energy, he was unable to do anything except watch the inevitable unfold. The tension in the situation rose to a crescendo, and Peter felt guilt flood through his being. His emotions were one with Uriel's as the stone encased him. The pain and anguish grew in intensity and then subsided as the angel fell. Peter's mind relived the angel's poignant agony until the cries from the battle in the chamber leaked into his consciousness. He could tell the fight was not going well for the mercenaries, but he intensified his effort on the manuscript and cleared away the distraction.

Eve fought Kea at every step. She changed into a giant the size of Butch and hurled herself to the floor of the chamber. She led the queen away from Peter and put up a fierce defense near the clearing's edge. Although she was able to keep the queen at bay early on, her power was no match for Kea's. The queen eventually caught Eve in the heavy underbrush and immobilized the animas, converting her back into a frail woman. Kea inflicted as much pain as possible through the transformation process and left the woman entombed in stone upon the earthen ground of the Garden remnant.

Sitri maintained his pursuit of Nicholas through the chamber's expansive interior airspace. The monk used every bit of cunning and guile he could, undergoing several variations and donning manifestations of every bird of prey known to him. Each time, the smaller and more agile Nicholas circled back to the demon and attacked, forcing the demon to protect himself. Ultimately, Sitri constructed a latticework of emerald energy and trapped the troublesome clergyman. The demon flew to the edge of the precipice, and with a gleeful smile, tossed the squirming nephesh through the chasm.

Freed from their assailants, Kea and Sitri joined Asmodeus to subdue the mercenaries. The demons split up and systematically attacked each group as a separate unit. They used the guards and Butch the Giant to herd the company into indefensible positions to make quick work of the mercenaries. They ravaged each member accordingly and left a trail of statuary in their wake until Hannibal remained as the lone-standing fighter.

The demons hurled pure malice at the old warrior. They toyed with the general like a group of schoolyard bullies harassing a weaker student.

Hannibal endured pain beyond measure but kept his guard high, fighting back with all the strength he was able to muster. Fatigue eventually caught up to him and he swung his sword ever more wildly through the air, trying desperately to connect with the out-of-reach demons. He grew weaker and weaker until he had no option but to lower his weapon in defeat.

The three demons pushed the old general to the chasm's edge. They spoke to Hannibal tersely, trying to goad the mercenary into jumping to save them the trouble of torturing him.

Hannibal sheathed his sword and turned away from the demons. Time had not been on the company's side. They put up a good fight, but once the queen rejoined the fray, it was too late. The old warrior stumbled to the precipice's edge and kneeled. He looked serenely on the waters below and lamented the loss of his friends, especially Thomas.

"What are you waiting for, my old friend?" Asmodeus asked. "Will you cower before us and plead for mercy?"

Hannibal's anger resurfaced, but he quickly put the emotion in check. He glanced at Peter, being careful not to arouse the demons' suspicions. The true point of his humility was to buy the professor as much time as he was able.

Asmodeus would not accept the old warrior's silence. The demon bent down and whispered into the general's ear, "I will flay your cowardly friends daily if you do not comply."

Hannibal spun to face the demon and drew his sword. He thrust it forward, hoping to lodge the blade in Asmodeus's chest, but his attack was for naught as Kea flashed a bolt of energy that encased him in stone.

Asmodeus nodded at the diminutive Kea, standing between the tall demons. "My Lady."

"Save it," Kea scoffed. "We must focus our energy on the book-bearer."

Peter sat against the tree roots, oblivious to all else around him. The rolling images of Uriel's failure repeated in his mind until Peter thought he could recount each sequence from memory. There seemed to be no correlation between Uriel's fate and a possible solution to revive the angel. Peter pressed deeper, viewing not just the scenes but feeling the remorse and anguish that overcame Uriel at his moment of failure. He concentrated on the angel's loss and there, amid a myriad of emotions, he found the root cause of Uriel's utter despondency. The angel had broken his vow to the Creator. He was to protect the Garden of Eden at all costs, but Uriel was unworthy of the challenge.

Text from beyond the rolling sequences rose to the forefront of the pages. The letters transformed into a series of phrases that cycled past the pages and stood out amongst the images. Peter translated the Latin as it solidified into a final phrase, "Languish no more in the sorrows of failure and come forth to redeem your honor to defend those who would fight for your charge, O' Uriel the Guardian of Eden."

A thunderous report shook the Garden remnant, and the Book of Souls' once lively pages went black as night.

The burnt ash of the vale rippled outward as shockwaves radiated from Uriel's statue. Evenly-spaced and slowly building in power, each wave carried through the landscape like a small earthquake. The steles of stone and salt surrounding Uriel's statue rocked with each upsurge. The frequency and vigor of the disturbance was too much for some, sending the most ancient and unstable steles crumbling to the ground.

A cold blue light crept through the crevices of Uriel's statue. The intensity multiplied in lockstep with the seismic pulse shaking the small valley. The glow grew to envelop the marble statue, obscuring its features and rendering it nothing more than a beacon of light. It continued until the vale was awash in a dazzling, cyan brilliance.

After a moment of stability, the center of the light changed. It became denser and took on a deeper, glacial hue than that of its surrounding aura. The core expanded outward, permeating the large statue and revealing the true form of the angel hidden within.

Uriel stretched his wings and sheathed his sword. As the outer edges of the angel's disturbance encountered the stones of his long-encased comrades, the hard rock melted away and released the souls trapped inside. Each of the freed humans fell to the ground in agony. They clutched at their limbs and chest, unable to give their suffering proper vocalization. He took special note of Adam lying behind him. The human was slowly reverting to his original form on the ash of the valley floor. The angel smiled warmly to his friend. Adam could not respond but nodded his acknowledgement. Uriel stepped forward through the sea of steles and with an eerie, almost gravity-defying gait, the angel glided through the desolate landscape, his radiance releasing those entombed within the monoliths of stone.

Uriel stood for a moment at the end of the vale and studied the huge city on the horizon. The angel's facial expressions broadcast his disgust at the malignant sight. The pure evil and malevolence of the city made Uriel bristle with anger. He searched the high parapets of the wall and gauged the center point of the circular metropolis. Once his bearing was established, Uriel's eyes locked in the direction of the Two Trees, and with a fierce determination, the angel pressed forward and hit the ramparts of the city head on.

Verbal alarms rose across the frontier of battlements. Guards raced to buttress the fortification, but it was no use. Every stone that was touched by Uriel's aura reverted into its corresponding trapped soul. All around the angel, humans in every state of transformation fell from the barricade to the ashen ground. The loss of structural integrity caused the upper sections of the wall to collapse into a heap near the angel's influence, further quickening the reversal of the queen's spell on the human souls.

Chapter 21

Buildings fell and structures gave way as Uriel bored into the city at ground level. Guards formed haphazard cohorts to attack the angel, but each that came into contact with Uriel's power was instantaneously turned to salt. The angel left a wake of recovering humans and salt monoliths as he unwaveringly made his way deeper into the city and nearer the Two Trees.

Sounds of the city's collapse filled the remnant's chamber. The demons knew immediately what the reverberations represented. Any disruption or deviation in the city's mean energy flow instantaneously broadcasted an alert to the demons.

"Uriel's free!" Kea shouted and gestured to Asmodeus and Sitri. "Gather those men and prepare a defense."

The demons heeded the queen's orders and positioned the humans in front of the large doors as an initial distraction to the angel. Butch the Giant was off to one side and instructed to follow up any entry with a full-on attack.

Smiling triumphantly, Peter rose to his knees and was met by a menacing glare from the queen.

"Do you believe this changes anything?" Kea asked smugly. "Once I've dealt with Uriel, I'll make you suffer until the end of Creation—whether you give me that damn book or not."

Peter swallowed hard. Although he felt some relief in summoning Uriel, he knew what awaited him should Uriel fail again.

Outside, a continuous series of deafening reports drew closer to the chamber. The ground swelled and quaked as nearby towers and buildings collapsed.

"Hold your ground!" Kea ordered. "He stands no chance against us!"

Ice-blue light penetrated the joints between the blocks of the chamber's walls. The light grew to a blinding intensity as Uriel's aura surrounded the rock and transformed each into human souls. Individuals of every era from history oozed from their former positions like melting wax. They dripped down to the earthen ground of the chamber floor and lay quietly in fetal positions as they regained their senses.

Uriel pushed through the circular breach and into the Garden remnant. His glow flooded the massive chamber with cyan light, overwhelming everything and everyone within. Perched high on the nearest pillar to the opening, Butch the Giant flung himself toward the center of brilliance and the unwary angel. A blast of energy struck out from the aura and swept across the falling giant. The power severed the bonds between the individuals who made up the giant's body and sent the freed souls plunging through the air. Uriel spun a web of glacier energy and caught the falling mortals, settling them gently into the dense undergrowth, out of harm's way. A simultaneous strike directed at Butch turned the falling thug to salt, allowing him to shatter across the indigenous rock of the earthen floor.

Chapter 21

The guards followed closely on the heels of Butch's attack. They charged the blue sphere of light, thrusting and swinging their weapons in all directions. Uriel moved forward, his aura brushing them aside and turning their diminutive ranks into a forest of salt steles.

Kea remained in the center of the chamber barring access to the Two Trees while Asmodeus and Sitri flanked wide in an effort to surround their opponent. The queen and her two henchmen let loose with their power, flooding the chamber in a dazzling array of colored energy. Their might scorched wide tracks of vegetation, turning the vibrant green into ash. The combined force of the three demons swept away Uriel's glacier aura and exposed the angel's true features.

"Ah, there you are, brother," Kea mocked. "Won't you break your vow for us—perhaps say a few words before we silence you again?"

Uriel responded with a sardonic smile and drew his sword. Orange and red flames erupted along both edges of the weapon as it left the scabbard. He held the burning blade aloft and took a battle-ready stance.

"A pity," Kea said, nodding to her two henchmen to begin their assault.

From their flanking positions, Asmodeus and Sitri advanced, throwing sustained discharges of red and green might at the angel.

Uriel used his sword to absorb Asmodeus's attack and easily dodged Sitri's. Instead of standing his ground, the angel spread his silken wings and leapt into the air. He flew at Sitri and delivered a forceful blast that sent the demon reeling. Uriel angled sharply toward the center of the chamber and Kea. He held the flaming blade high above his head and dove at the queen.

In a show of superiority, Kea calmly held steadfast. She was unperturbed as Uriel swung the blazing sword down upon her. At the last moment, the queen raised her arms and met the angel with an explosive concussion that shook the foundations of the chamber. Their might combined to form an indigo sphere of power that obscured them both.

The discharge of light was too much for Peter to take in directly. Instead, he followed the odd interactions of Asmodeus and Sitri. The demons held off their support of the queen, apparently not wanting to incur her wrath with a premature intervention.

Uriel pushed Kea back and slashed the diminutive queen across the chest, opening a gaping wound. He sensed the queen's power waning and the glow of their collective output faded. He sheathed his weapon and put all his might into a sustained blast that enveloped the woman. The angel drew the queen's energy from her, causing the woman's appearance to fluctuate between human and demon.

From Peter's vantage, Uriel's victory over Kea seemed all but assured, but a quick glance at Asmodeus and Sitri dispelled that misplaced hubris. The queen's impending doom stirred her two henchmen into action.

The two demons stepped forward and attacked Uriel at close range. The roar of power echoed through the chamber as energy arced to the nearby columns and traced lines of electricity throughout the atmosphere of the hall.

At first, the angel ignored the additional threats, but as the demons got the upper hand, Uriel had no choice but to disengage and fight a defensive battle. He drew his sword and lashed out at the attackers, but they kept their distance and continued to pour offensive might into the fray. Healed of her wounds, Kea rejoined her subordinates and their combined potency was more than Uriel could handle. He spread his wings and attempted an escape, but the queen caught him midair and forced the angel back to the ground. The attackers circled power around the struggling divine being and tightened their grip.

Peter turned away. He could no longer bear witness to the brutality that would once again be Uriel's end. He did not realize exactly how overwhelmed the angel would be against the power of all three demons. Peter needed to help, but he did not know what to do. He fumbled the Book of Souls open only to reveal its darkened pages.

Peter studied the manuscript closely. The jumbled scenes of lives past had been replaced by an unending stream of nothingness. He ran his fingers across the rough paper. The parchment underneath was still present; it was just being obscured by a field of black. Peter felt as if he were being punished—perhaps the book was choosing not to display anything because of his reckless action in calling Uriel to an unwinnable confrontation.

Down below Peter, the demons were gleefully toying with Uriel. Panic gripped him and his mind flooded with the thoughts of the torture and pain he would suffer following the angel's demise. He wanted to run, but there was nowhere to go. The chasm surrounding the plateau was an insurmountable obstacle and regardless, he was sure the demons would see him at the very least. He took an unsteady breath and looked down to the waters of Avernus. If it came to it, he would throw himself into Hell and make a run into the dunes surrounding the sea. If he were lucky, perhaps Lucifer and his army of Fallen would never find him. Peter shook his head and shuddered at the idiocy of his pointless strategy. Hell was their domain, and it was foolish to think he could outrun them to any degree.

Peter swallowed hard and returned to the Book of Souls. He held the manuscript out at arm's length and moved it about the room looking for any sign as to its usage given the current situation, but the book remained indignantly unhelpful. He was missing something—something very important. Peter closed his eyes and calmed his mind, but riotous laughter drew his attention back to the demons.

Kea and her henchmen surrounded Uriel. They poured might onto the angel, forcing him back to the ground while hurling taunts and insults with each act of subjugation. Slowly, the three attackers were turning the angel back to stone.

Uriel lashed out, but every assault came up short. The angel's strength was waning as he desperately searched the chamber for any advantage he might be able to bring to bear. In the background behind Asmodeus, Uriel spied the statue of a soldier holding a weapon. As darkness descended upon the angel, he sent a flash of glacial energy to encompass the effigy and convert Hannibal back into his human form.

Hannibal assessed his situation in one glance. "End this now!" he shouted to Peter and plunged his sword through Asmodeus's right wing and into the demon's ribcage. As Asmodeus reeled from the impact, Hannibal jumped onto the demon's shoulders and tipped them both backwards, into the chasm.

"Hannibal!" Peter screamed as he watched the pair fall in a spiraling motion through the sky below. He could see Asmodeus attempt to throw off the old general, but Hannibal was too strong. The general moved deftly across the demon's shoulders, pressing the sword deeper into Asmodeus's body to keep the demon in pain and unable to mount any serious challenge. Together, the two combatants continued their fight until they disappeared from Peter's view.

"No, no, no!" Peter cried out in anguish. Guan, Thomas, Nicholas, and now Hannibal gave their very existence to see this quest through to the end. Their sacrifice was all too poignant for Peter. They had risked everything in hopes of ending the malicious evil that ruled the Garden of Eden. He never wanted it to happen like this. When Peter entered the chamber, he had a plan and was willing to end his own meager existence for the small chance of success, but instead, everything changed. Four of his comrades were gone and Peter was no closer to finishing the quest. He had failed his friends, and they had paid with their souls.

With one demon gone, Uriel reasserted his might and emerged from his partially solidified form. He found the demon's combined might formidable and any misstep on the angel's part could push him right back into a losing situation. Uriel took to the air. His best defense would be moving about the chamber and striking when an opening presented itself.

Colorful energy arced through the air and turned the remaining swaths of thriving plant life into nothing more than smoldering cinders. Uriel maneuvered low, among the damaged thicket and used the structural supports of the chamber for dodging the incoming attacks. On more than one occasion, the angel tried to revive some of Hannibal's soldiers frozen in stone, but the demons where well aware of his tactics and blocked every attempt. Uriel needed help. Without an overpowering force to subdue Kea and Sitri, the fight could go on ad-infinitum. The angel turned to lock eyes with Peter standing on the plateau. Uriel said nothing, but his gaze was more than sufficient for the human to grasp its meaning.

Peter acknowledged the angel's request with a simple but forthright nod. He opened the Book of Souls and studied its inky-black pages. He still did not know how to activate the manuscript and thought back to when he delved into the circumstances surrounding the Two Trees. The images at that time were so real that Peter almost forgot he was witnessing an illusion and not the actual incident itself. In his attempt to revive Uriel, the displayed scenes immersed Peter in an experience so lifelike that the professor could feel the events happening around him. He could smell the acrid air and hear the desperation in the humans who fought by the angel's side.

Peter shook off his train of thought. The previous situations were vastly different from the current circumstance. Up until now, the Book of Souls only displayed events in a historical context. What Peter needed was a way forward, a way to navigate the present. He wanted to end the Garden of Eden today, not revisit its demise years from now. What if the knowledge he sought required a different method of reading the manuscript? No, Peter dismissed the thought. The book contained every aspect of creation, whether it was part of the past or unfolding in the present.

An idea took hold in Peter's mind: What if the pages of the Book of Souls were showing the present? The absence of images could mean that the future was not set, that choices were going unfulfilled—freewill, as it were, was still required. The manuscript worked on all of Peter's senses, not just his sight. Perhaps the Book of Souls was requesting his input—an experience of some kind?

Peter cleared his mind and concentrated on the coal-black pages of the Book of Souls. Instantly, he felt the manuscript swallow him and drag him down into its murky depths. The darkness closed in around Peter and the smells of the remnant were replaced by the unmistakable scent of rotting flesh. He gagged and fought the urge to withdraw from the experience, but he remembered what was at stake and pressed forward. He delved deeper into the nothingness and lost himself in the moment. Peter sensed the darkness getting colder; it swirled around him and chilled him to the bone. The inky vacuum was bleak and without joy. It was as if the black oblivion had consumed all the warmth in the world, leaving behind the empty husk of Creation.

Peter realized what the Book of Souls was displaying. It was not the immediate present but the future should the manuscript fall into the hands of Kea and her brethren.

Urgency swelled up in Peter as he searched for a clue—anything that would guide him to his goal. Impenetrable black surrounded him, but nothing existed within the void. Then it dawned on him: this was only one version of future events. He could *choose* to create a new destiny—an existence that was better and without fear.

Peter concentrated on the swirling nothingness around him and pushed it aside with his thoughts. He pictured grass, children playing and laughing in the sunshine. He forced himself to think about the relationship with his wife and let the good moments of his marriage come forward. Peter thought back to all the selfless acts he had witnessed in his life. No deed was too small to include in his montage. Soon, scenes of people helping others filled the space around him.

Happiness welled up in Peter. He fed off the pleasant images and took pride in his handiwork, but something was lurking within his display that did not belong. A foreign presence permeated the exposition. It was subtle at first, but gained strength in step with Peter's gushing emotions. He strained to see behind the façade of the pleasant ideality, but his vision remained restricted to its superficial surface. The mood of the imagery changed. Peter could hear whispering. A disembodied speaker uttered words and phrases in a language he did not understand. The voice spoke carefully—peacefully—as if in a kind and generous manner.

Suddenly and without warning, a bright light pierced through the medley of idyllic scenes. Peter gazed skyward, toward the source of the illumination and there, he saw a wondrous thing. A small hole of white light appeared in the black sky of the book's images. It was directly above Peter's vantage. It swirled and danced above him. There was movement, but it was too far away to see the detail behind it. For a brief moment, the spectacle reminded Peter of when he first arrived in the Garden of Eden. At that time, the light at the far end of the tunnel was cast by demons. A surge of fear ran through him, but Peter let it go. The new light was different; it cast a warm glow that filled him with joy.

"No!" Kea shrieked and grasped at her chest as if mortally wounded. She turned to look at Peter. *"What have you done?"*

The scream jerked Peter away from the deep trance cast by the Book of Souls. All around him the walls of the remnant's chamber were turning back into human souls. The people poured like blood from the stone as if from an open wound.

Kea stared at Peter with an awkward yet surprised look. She staggered around the humus and fell to one knee. Her power, once tied to the city's greatness, was weakening in step with every soul freed of her demonic spell.

Sitri broke off his engagement with Uriel and rushed to help the ailing queen to her feet.

Uriel sheathed his sword and took a position nearby. He flexed his white wings and tucked them carefully behind him. Although he tried to maintain an emotionless demeanor, Uriel let down his guard and smiled at the long-awaited outcome.

Peter marveled as the columns supporting the ceiling disintegrated into human souls. The ceiling fell in on itself, melting into individuals and throwing them in every direction. Eve and the mercenaries recovered and went to work helping the perplexed men and women reclaim their senses.

The chamber fell open to the twilight sky above. There in the sky, as it was in the pages of the Book of Souls, was the white hole. He could clearly see the light streaming into the Garden of Eden, but it was not beams of luminescence; it was a legion of angels. There were so many that Peter could not count them all

The angels flew in white waves toward the city and once there, they went to work helping those in need. Unlike Uriel, they seemed to be conversing with the humans and responding to the myriad of questions issuing forth from the confused masses. Once convinced that the luminous beings were not a threat, the humans allowed themselves to be ushered into large groups. Each angel attended to an assembly of souls independently. The divine beings outstretched their wings and produced a dazzling spectacle of power that encompassed the humans. At first, the wary souls recoiled from the display, but after several tense moments, the crowd calmed and lifted into the twilight sky. Soon, the atmosphere was aglow with soft, warm light, and huge bulbous orbs floated far overhead. One by one, the groups rose to the aperture and passed through, out of sight. In a short time, the city was gone and every soul victimized by Kea and her henchmen had been rescued.

Peter stood on the floating plateau, looking out to the unobstructed horizon in every direction. He found it strangely calming to see nothing but the demons and their human guards standing alone in the vast plain of Eden.

The Garden shook violently and sent all who remained falling to the ground. Large fissures developed in the earth and stretched haphazardly across the landscape. Chunks of soil and rock thrust upward and then fell, disappearing through holes that opened beneath them.

All around Peter, the Garden of Eden was transforming. The sky above began to brighten. The dim twilight, so prominent in the Garden before, gave way to a garish sunlight that encompassed everything in an eerie opaque hue. Below, the once solid ground rent and heaved until it disintegrated and fell away, toward the land of Hell.

Kea pushed Sitri away and stood under her own power. She threw a coy smile at Uriel. "Brother, here's to the future," she said, changing back into her demon form and taking flight.

Lilith flew around the plateau, pausing only briefly to wink at Peter before descending through the chasm.

Sitri lingered, studying the destruction and contemplating the sequence of events that led to their demise. He nodded respectfully to Uriel and took flight. The demon thrust forward and followed his queen to Hell.

Cries of shock and surprise rose through the ranks of the guards left in Eden. The men and women turned to run away from the angel but found themselves swallowed by the heaving ground beneath them. The wicked souls scrambled for handholds and screamed for help, but no one came to their aid. One by one, each individual disappeared through the ever-widening chasms created by the Garden of Eden's collapsing earth.

The cracks in the ground widened and raced to the center of the remnant. They reached Uriel's position and left him with nothing to stand on, but the angel simply beat his wings and lifted into the opaque sky.

Peter saw the ground around the floating plateau crumble into the abyss. He clutched the ancient manuscript and attempted to stay upright, but the trembling earth knocked him down. The roots of the Two Trees splintered, throwing shards of wood in every direction. The wellspring ceased producing water, causing the river to dry. Finally, the last physical remains of the Garden of Eden relented, sending him and the Two Trees tumbling into the sky toward the Avernus Sea.

Peter screamed in terror. A strong arm came from above and grasped him around the waist, halting his freefall. He glanced up to

Chapter 21

see the angel Uriel smiling down. "Thank you," Peter said breath-
lessly.

Uriel nodded in response.

Peter looked down to the sea. "What about the others—can we
save them?"

Uriel shook his head.

Tears welled in Peter's eyes as he thought about his lost friends.
They had fought selflessly in the defense of others, yet their souls
would be damned to Hell for the rest of eternity. Peter glowered in
disgust at the injustice and wiped his face dry with a free hand while
holding on tightly to the Book of Souls with the other. Reluctantly,
he turned his attention skyward and let Uriel carry him into the
heavens above.

Chapter 22

A faint noise stirred Peter from his uneasy slumber. The nature of the sound was familiar to him, but its source was hard to identify. From the position, Peter surmised that he lay on his back. He tried to turn in the direction of the sound and was met by immense pain. Every limb, so recently at his beck and call, now rebelled in great agony.

Peter concentrated on his breathing. It felt labored. He could feel the rush of air into and out of his lungs, but it was a strange sensation to process. In the Garden of Eden, Peter's body went through the motions of respiration, but he was never quite sure if the air was real or imagined. Although the rest of his body throbbed, it was surprisingly easy for him to maintain a regular breathing pattern.

The sound came back to Peter. He was certain someone was trying to speak to him. He tried to respond but found it impossible.

Peter fought hard to open his eyes. Bright light flooded his vision, but it was a different variety than that of the angels or from the skies of Eden. He closed his eyelids as a temporary barrier to give him time to adjust.

"Peter, Peter?" a woman's voice said softly from nearby.

Peter gurgled and retched trying to respond.

"That's okay," the female voice responded. "It'll be some time before you can talk again."

Peter's mind cleared somewhat. *Talk again?*

"The doctors said you are lucky to be alive."

Peter recognized his wife's voice and tried to think back to his last moments. He remembered chasing the little boy through the woods and making several unsuccessful attempts to catch him. Peter recalled the jump into midair, which turned out to be a cliff hidden behind a steep bank. Then he remembered the broken tree stump at the bottom—a jagged and splintered mass of wood that faced his falling body at almost the perfect, upward angle. Peter shuddered as he briefly relived the moment when the coarse timber tore through his flesh.

More sounds rose to the forefront of Peter's hearing. He recognized several of them: a ventilator, the slow rhythmic hum of a blood transfusion machine, and the beeping of a vital signs monitor. He opened his eyes to see his wife, Renée, sitting by his bedside.

"There you are," Renée said, uncharacteristically smiling back at him. "I knew you'd get better."

Again, Peter tried to speak, but he realized he could not due a ventilator tube running down his throat.

"Please, don't," Renée responded, placing a hand on her husband's shoulder. "I just wanted to tell you how bad I feel for treating you the way I did. I know we've had a rough marriage—" She stopped. "It's been tough for both of us, but I wanted you to know that I'll be here for you from now on, okay?"

If Peter could have vomited, he would have. He wondered if this was some kind of a trick. Perhaps, in some sick and twisted way, he was being rewarded for his final act in the Garden of Eden—he was being allowed to live again. If Peter could have screamed out in hysteria, he would have.

A nurse entered the small Intensive Care Unit and forced herself between Renée and Peter. She stood with her back to the patient and said to his wife, "He needs his rest now. We'll inform you of any change."

"Yes, of course," Renée said, standing up to gather her things. "I'll be back later, okay?"

Peter did not acknowledge his wife and simply watched her leave the room.

The nurse turned and sat down in the chair next to Peter's bed. She pulled down her sterile mask to reveal her features.

Peter gasped at the sight of Kea and fought against his restraints to rise.

Kea put a calming hand on his chest and took a long look back at Renée. "That's your wife, huh? I have half a mind to let you live."

Peter shook his head in disbelief. With the Garden of Eden destroyed, the link between Creation and Hell should have been severed. Unless Kea found a way to bridge the gulf between the realms, it was not possible for her to be in the room.

"Surprised?"

Peter nodded as best as he was able.

"The trees diminish as I speak," Kea said, "so I don't have much time."

Peter tried to alert the hospital staff, but the respirator equipment muffled his cries for help.

"No need to get excited; I'm here to congratulate you on a job well done."

Peter cocked his head.

"You destroyed the Garden, delivered the Book of Souls, and cast us all down in one fell swoop," Kea said with anger but also with an ironic amusement breaking through in her voice. "Bravo."

Peter could not tell if Kea was genuinely happy that she had been freed from her responsibilities in Eden, or if she was simply unable to do anything about her new predicament and resigned herself to the fate that awaited her.

"Lucifer is a driven and resourceful individual," Kea said. "In time, we will find a way out." She removed a liquid-filled syringe from her smock pocket and held it for Peter to see. "Your gift."

Peter struggled against his restraints, but the straps held him firmly to the bed.

Kea injected the liquid into the intravenous catheter attached to Peter's arm. "Until we meet again?"

Peter felt the substance course through his body. He was terrified at first, but then his fear turned into a calm joy as the light closed in around him and he died. Again.

www.ingramcontent.com/pod-product-compliance
Lightning Source LLC
Chambersburg PA
CBHW020905200626
46814CB00001BA/192